PRAISE FC

"[A]n intriguing and compelling tale with complex characters . . . look[ing] at the sisterhood formed in sororities that extends to those who work in, and around, them."

—*Kirkus Reviews*

"The book shines in its emphasis on the power of women having each other's backs and rooting for one another . . . A witty, wild ride and an overall gripping read with unforgettable, wholesome moments."

—*Booklist*

PRAISE FOR JEN LANCASTER

"Scathingly witty."

—*The Boston Herald*

"Witty and hilarious . . . Jen Lancaster is like that friend who always says what you're thinking—just 1,000 times funnier."

—*People*

"No matter what she's writing, it's scathingly witty and lots of fun."

—*Publishers Weekly*

"Jen Lancaster is like a modern-day, bawdy Erma Bombeck."

—Lisa Lampanelli, *New York Post*

"Hilarious."

—*InStyle*

THE ANTI-HEROES

OTHER TITLES BY JEN LANCASTER

Nonfiction

Bitter Is the New Black

Bright Lights, Big Ass

Such a Pretty Fat

Pretty in Plaid

My Fair Lazy

Jeneration X

The Tao of Martha

I Regret Nothing

Stories I'd Tell in Bars

Welcome to the United States of Anxiety

Fiction

If You Were Here

Here I Go Again

Twisted Sisters

The Best of Enemies

By the Numbers

The Gatekeepers

Housemoms

THE ANTI-HEROES

A NOVEL

JEN LANCASTER

Little
a

Published by Little A, New York

www.apub.com

Amazon, the Amazon logo, and Little A are trademarks of Amazon.com, Inc., or its affiliates.

ISBN-13: 9781662519819 (hardcover)
ISBN-13: 9781662519826 (paperback)
ISBN-13: 9781662510410 (digital)

Cover design by Sarah Horgan
Cover image: © RomanYa / Shutterstock; © serazetdinov / Shutterstock

Printed in the United States of America
First edition

*For Becca and Sarah—I can't take any credit, but I'm
so proud of who you've become*

Chapter One

Emily Nichols, PhD

How did I get here?

The question is on my heels as my best friend, Liv, and I circle the Northwestern University track many mornings, where sweat dampens my shirt from running around a giant oval. A metaphor for working hard and just continually looping back to where I started.

I ask myself this question a lot. It's an almost constant refrain, an unwelcome shadow yanking at my sleeve as I sleepwalk through life, each day some monochromatic version of the previous one. The question pulls up a seat at our breakfast bar, where I watch as Miles eats his daily dry wheat toast and single soft-boiled egg. He plates the egg in a trophy-shaped silver cup he's had since childhood. To break the shell, he'll use what was once his teething spoon to bat at the egg ever so delicately, like it's the world's most fragile piñata. *Tap. Tap, tap, tap.* Sometimes I just want to grab the egg and smash it on the counter. When the shell finally submits to his gentle pressure, Miles exhales with great relief, as though he's accomplished something monumental.

How did I get here?

This query follows me every morning, as I leave my plain vanilla condominium Miles has all but moved into, a passionless place I sometimes call "the *blando*" because it's so bland. I live in Evanston, a few miles north of Chicago's city limits. Miles convinced me I should buy a unit with views of the parking lot instead of the one overlooking Lake Michigan. Liv was my real estate agent, and in her kind way, she tried to encourage me to pick the one with the lake view; there wasn't that much of a price difference. But Miles pointed out that a northern exposure meant I'd run the air conditioner less frequently, so I opted for the eco-friendly choice.

I can't be mad at him for caring about preserving resources. I mean, part of what drew me to Miles was his quiet commitment to environmentalism. The first time I met him, he was knee deep in a trash can in front of the Hogan Biological Sciences Building, picking out all the aluminum cans, a bicycle helmet still on his head. I'm embarrassed that I assumed he was unhoused. Imagine my shock when I learned he was not only an associate dean, but one of the people who'd eventually make the decision to hire me.

I always say that morality is doing the right thing even when no one's looking, so Miles's first impression went a long way with me. I know it's shallow, but with his piercing blue eyes, angular face, and unruly mop of black hair, he's like an academic version of Matt Bomer or a two-thirds scale model of Jacob Elordi or a really beautiful Siamese cat. His looks trend more pretty than handsome, and his thick, inky lashes are longer than my own. Plus, he can rock an elbow-patch jacket and he is courteous to a fault. He even learned Spanish so he can speak with the Ecuadorian custodian who works on our office's floor. These are all fine qualities, but none of them make my pulse race now that the newness is long gone. I fear good looks and a kind heart aren't enough to sustain a relationship together, and as traditional as he is, I'm scared he'll want a deeper commitment soon.

Lately, I'm having trouble concentrating on what's right about him, instead focusing on what's wrong, and that's not fair to either of us. Yet it feels like I'm setting myself up for a lifetime of polite conversations until I die—from boredom.

After I moved into my condo, I kept the model apartment's paint, a shade of oyster gray; it seemed wasteful to change the color for change's sake. Landfills are overflowing with perfectly serviceable items because Madison Avenue convinces us that if we're not consuming, we're losing. My place is a dramatic contrast from the colorful pillow poufs and vibrant kilim rugs I favored when I was younger, when Liv and I roomed together in a dorm that was an explosion of tie-dye tapestries. A Zillow listing on acid.

If my current home were a flavor, it would be fat-free plain Greek yogurt, nothing but bleached zero-waste wood furniture and sallow paint—NPR as an aesthetic. Ditto for my life.

The ever-present question—*How did I get here?*—accompanies me as I ride my mountain bike toward campus. This bike has seen all kinds of action, with weeklong treks through hills and valleys and high-desert passes. I feel a nagging guilt about its now-mundane existence. All I do is ride it a couple of miles to work, a straight shot down the road on a paved bike lane, then home again.

There are as many blooming tulips bordering the street as there are students on the wide walkways. The coeds are giddy in the late spring sunshine as I cycle past. I'm barely a decade older than the seniors, yet I feel ancient.

I pass the tennis courts, pedaling to the *thwack!* of balls hitting the hardtop, then turn on Tech Drive, navigating through a sea of backpacks and acne as high school juniors from all over the country take guided campus tours. With my employer's 9 percent acceptance rate, they'd be wise not to fall in love with the majesty of the Northwestern University campus. Ninety-one percent are setting themselves up for heartbreak as they take selfies in front of Alice Millar Chapel.

At the Hogan Biological Sciences Building, I secure my bike, then dutifully jog up the stairs instead of using the elevator. I'm proud that I've helped lead the charge to outfit our buildings with renewable energy sources, but I still conserve where I can.

The question is tucked neatly inside my Public Thread messenger bag, made from the leftover vinyl of a discarded billboard featuring one of my first crushes, ex–Chicago Bears player Brian Urlacher.

I spot a student in front of my door, even though office hours don't start for another forty minutes. Taylor, a sophomore sorority girl with bouncy strawberry blonde ringlets, has her phone propped up on a fire extinguisher case. I chuckle, thinking, *Please break glass in case of social media emergency.*

Taylor's filming herself performing a complicated set of dance steps, yet no music plays. She mouths the words as she claps, thrusts, and shuffles in silence. I haven't seen this choreography on TikTok yet—it must be new. I cringe, knowing how Miles will re-create this, poorly, when he puts it on his Instagram Reels. He thinks people watch him because he's talented and not because his looks are that of a vampire extra from the *Twilight* movies.

How did I get here?

The question and I hang back, waiting for Taylor to finish. I'm not eager to hear whatever excuse she has for whatever classwork she hasn't done. Taylor and her ilk are why I prefer teaching advanced and grad-level environmental science classes. I want students who are committed, who remind me of me when I was their age, who understand that knowledge is power they can put into action. My environmental science majors understand the devastation of global temperature increasing even another degree; it's why they're here and passionate about conservation.

Don't get me wrong, I was thrilled when Northwestern made Environmental Impact 101 a required course for all students. I mean, I busted out a bottle of champagne. The problem is, I didn't realize the lion's share of instruction would fall on me and not a teaching assistant. My tenured colleagues have since taken over my Community Ecology and Economic Geography curricula, leaving me with the kinds of students who cheer at the possibility of an oceanfront Ohio coastline when

I talk about the potential severity of rising sea levels. I worry that I'm not breaking through to them, and I don't know how to fix it.

Taylor ends her dance with a twirl, whipping her hair around with a flourish. She throws up a peace sign and holds the pose for a beat and sticks her tongue out of the side of her mouth.

I try not to sigh audibly. I fail. Taylor spins in my direction as she collects her phone and catches my subtle eye roll.

"Sorry," I offer, but I don't mean it.

"No worries," Taylor assures me. "I'll lay the music track over the video, so that's all people will hear?" Most of Taylor's statements come out as questions due to her tendency to upspeak.

I lead Taylor into my office—a space as unimpressive as my home. The industrial beige walls are mostly unadorned, save for my degrees. There's also a framed infographic on the dangers of global warming. The large bookshelf behind my desk has personal effects on the bottom shelf, so only I can see them. I keep bamboo plants on the windowsill; they're nature's air purifiers, absorbing greenhouse gases. Still, it's kind of a cheerless space, which is more on-brand than I care to admit.

Other, more senior profs have workspaces that look over Lake Michigan. I spend my whole day trying to get a peek at the lake, between work and home. Miles is an associate dean and has a spectacular view, but he keeps his shades drawn. He recently told me, "Dark water makes me nervous." I wish I'd known that . . . sooner.

My relationship with Miles is entirely drama-free; he's absolutely literal, with no surprises. It's almost like dating an AI. Lately, I find myself fixating more on how he wouldn't have lasted *one minute* in my previous life. Not one damn minute. But that was a different time, when everything felt possible. Taylor is packing up her phone and ring light, so I close my eyes and remember. I can almost smell the briny sea.

The black water on the Southern Ocean is churning like a washing machine, against an impossibly blue sky. Our crew is off the coast of Antarctica. The water jostles the boats like they're pool toys, but I'm not afraid.

Yesterday, I saw one of the minke whales we're protecting breach over and over again, which is rare to witness. She'd rise from the water, using her flukes to propel herself, and jackknife the water on her way back down. I swear she was thanking us. When I'm arrested—again—it will have been worth it.

I want to do something. I want to get my hands dirty. The green organizations I volunteered for in Ann Arbor mostly have their people stand on street corners with petitions. But Planet BlueLove is the key to effecting real change.

We've given these poachers fair warning, having followed them for days, our vessel decked out with an enormous Planet BlueLove banner. We're definitely not in stealth mode. Plus, I'm sure they've seen us on the news. Everyone has. My poor mother—her shame and pride are really fighting it out.

We've radioed the whaling boat's captain multiple times explaining that we aren't protesting; we're enforcing international conservation law by protecting this minke whale sanctuary. They won't engage and they refuse to leave the area. The whitecaps make standing at the helm of this rigid-hulled inflatable boat an exhilarating carnival ride as I bump toward their vessel. I feel like I'm snowboarding over huge moguls and it's a total rush. I let out a victory cry; I can't help it. My endorphins are pumping like mad. The icy spray hits my raw, red cheeks like a baptism, like I'm being reborn out here, serving my purpose.

Minutes ago, divers from our ship disabled the whaler's propeller while we provided cover by flooding their decks with bottles of the foul-smelling butyric acid that comes from rotten butter. Stink bombs—childish, but so effective. We then pelted their crew with packets of cellulose powder. My throws were some of the most precise. I silently thanked Dad for making me stick it out in softball.

Using the powder was my idea. A PETA friend told me that when the powder comes into contact with chilly water, it dissolves into a slimy gel, making maneuvering on the deck virtually impossible. Once the poachers started slipping and sliding all over the place (yes, we got it on video), then I boarded the inflatable boat. Now I'm bounding across the water to hand-deliver the letter stating that the crew is whaling illegally. I hope they're ready for me.

Are they going to hit me with their water cannons? Yes, if they can get to them. Will my team's actions cause another international incident? Probably. Do I care? I do not. Because I will do it again and again until they stop. I love this work so much, I'd do it for free.

"Are you, like, stroking out? Do you smell burning toast?" Taylor asks, snapping her fingers in my face. I shake my head and quickly lick my lips, expecting the taste of salt spray instead of my beeswax lip balm.

"What can I do for you, Taylor?" She settles into the chair across from me and cracks open a single-use plastic water bottle. When I think of the resources consumed by importing water from Fiji, when we're literally steps away from a safe and abundant source of drinking water, I . . . argh. Before I can mention this fact to Taylor, she's chugged almost all of it. Posting thirst traps is thirsty business, I guess.

"My paper is late because I missed class yesterday?"

"Are you asking me or telling me?"

"I don't know?"

This happens all the time. I swear, I have heard every excuse. I had a 101 student's grandmother die five times in the course of a quarter. Five times! Even in an age of blended families, explain to me how that's mathematically possible, especially post-COVID. I didn't flunk him only because I didn't want to deal with him a second time around. Ds get degrees in my world.

"Why'd you miss, Taylor? Frat party? Emergency manicure? Bad news about Kylie Jenner?"

She gasps and clutches her chest. "Ohmigod, is Stormi okay?"

I clench my teeth. "Do I look like I keep up with the Kardashians?" I glance at my reflection in the glass door. Frumpy cardigan, messy bun, pant leg still tucked into my sock, zero makeup—just your classic schoolmarm. Definitely no longer the hot boho coed who dated the first-string lineman at Michigan. Taylor inspects her cuticles, not meeting my eye.

I press her. "Why did you miss class, Taylor?"

"I was at a demonstration?"

Wait, *what*? "Really?"

She flips a hank of curls over her shoulder. "Well, yeah. It's important to get involved."

I sit up straighter. "Totally agree. You know, I used to work with Planet BlueLove."

Taylor places the now-empty bottle on my desk and twirls it like a fidget spinner. The cap flies off, flinging beads of water everywhere. Unbelievable. In another lifetime, I'd have launched her and her bottle into next week. Now, thinking of the fallout from even raising my voice exhausts me. I can't tap into whatever used to motivate me to fight, to protect. It's like I'm as empty as her Fiji bottle.

"You were with them in the olden days?"

Olden days? "How old do you think I am?"

"Fifty?"

Fucking Gen Z.

"I'm in my early thirties," I reply.

"Okay, whatever. But, like, BlueLove . . . didn't their operatives sabotage the Kinder Morgan oil pipeline in Alberta?" Taylor asks.

So maybe she's brighter than I thought. "BlueLove could be militant." I do not admit that I was arrested more than once thanks to the Kinder Morgan pipeline. Fortunately, BlueLove had committed attorneys who kept me from serving actual time or getting a permanent mark on my record. I'd have done it anyway. I didn't care back then. I thought I was bulletproof.

Taylor eyes me up and down, clearly confused at how *I* might have been involved with such a radical group. "You, like, did their taxes or answered their phones or . . ."

I no longer look the part, but more importantly, I don't feel it. I clear my throat and brush away stray water drops from the desktop.

"It was a long time ago. Anyway, what were you protesting, Taylor? The need for gun control? Police brutality? The newest Supreme Court travesty?"

There's so much wrong in the world, it's hard to home in on just one cause. For me, it's been the environment ever since I was nine and saw my first polar bear at Brookfield Zoo. He was so majestic and regal, all beauty and power, but also so playful, swimming around and splashing as we admirers leaned over the Plexiglas partition for a closer look. He'd gotten his paws on a bucket that day and he kept sticking it on his head. I laughed and laughed and loved him so much. I wanted to bring him home with us.

Here's the thing—I was serious. I truly thought he could live with us. I'd worked it all out and the math *mathed*. As we toured the rest of the park, I started to formulate the best way to scale the enclosure walls and mentally calculated what it would cost my family to build him a new home next to our in-ground pool. We'd likely need to talk to a fish wholesaler, I reasoned.

My mom had to convince me that even if I were successful, a thousand-pound bear would not fit in our Lexus. She compromised by buying me a stuffed bear in the gift shop instead. I named him Frosty and he's still a prized possession.

A week later, my third-grade teacher taught us that polar bears were in danger because of global warming. Something stirred inside me. I remember thinking, *Not on my watch*. I was already scrappy, ready to throw down over any injustice. Preserving the planet has been my solitary goal ever since; though the way I go about it has morphed.

Generation X has been shrugging and saying, "Meh, what good will it do?" forever, but we Millennials are starting to feel that way too, now that so many of us have mortgages or children or back pain. But I see parts of that fight in Gen Z. I met Greta Thunberg at a conference last year, and I swear, I fangirled all over her. These kids hold the keys to our future, so maybe I shouldn't let my frustration—

"The Greek salad in the cafeteria?" She must notice my confusion, because she asks, "Did you, like, forget to take your Adderall today?" Then she gives my hand a light tap. "No worries. It happens to me all the time?"

I stop myself and take a breath before answering, lest I make a career-limiting statement. "Taylor, what are you talking about?"

"They're not selling Greek salads in the campus cafeteria anymore? And they're everyone's favorite, so we have to band together?"

I want to face-palm or scream into the void. During the pandemic, I read that a Japanese amusement park posted a notice about the dangers of expressing your fears aloud, due to the possibility of spraying droplets. The sign read *Please scream inside your heart.* I scream inside my heart a lot.

"Taylor, you know you can get a Greek salad almost anywhere else, so—"

She holds up a fingertip, topped with a bayonet-shaped nude-ombré nail. "The thing is, Professor Nichols—"

"Doctor."

"Okay, Professor Doctor—do you know how it feels to make a difference? Like, how it feels to have an impact?"

Do *I* know how it feels to make an impact? Seriously? I glance at an old photo at the very corner of the very bottom of my bookshelf. It's a shot of me and Jeremy.

Jeremy.

My toes curl inside my vegan canvas Danskos just thinking about him. We're giving Blue Steel faces in front of the century-old giant redwood we are protecting.

I'd just locked us into place, pushing up against his lean, hard body, the hair on his muscular calves tickling my legs and his firm chest warm and yielding. He smelled like campfire and musk. We were burning up with excitement and pride when we kissed—and a Reuters photographer captured a picture that ended up on the cover of the *New York Times* (and Mom's fridge). A BlueLove teammate took the shot I keep on my bookshelf a few minutes before the infamous Reuters pic. I'm beaming in the photo, so content with my power and place in the universe. I'm streaked in filth, leaf fragments fringing my hair, but gorgeous, like a Technicolor version of the gray person I am now. During the Oregon operation, Jeremy and I had fallen quickly, deeply, and profoundly in love. Jeremy's Aussie accent, unbridled power, and shared passion for our cause drew me in, but full disclosure, his chiseled features, flowing caramel-colored hair, and rock-hard body didn't hurt either. I used to tease him that he should be a romance novel cover model. One look at him, and I swear, it makes me forget Miles's last name. Let's just say my first impression of Jeremy was not that he needed a sandwich and a hug.

I can practically feel the heat radiating off us in the photo, like it might incinerate the wooden frame around it. The chemistry we had. Animal. Carnal. Over far too soon. Taylor asks, "Then you'll make an exception? Pretty please? Let me turn my paper in in class tomorrow?"

I sigh again. Taylor's cause is trivial at best, but it's a *cause*, and I want to encourage passion, even if it's just lunch. Plus, she had the cojones to speak with me in person. The number of parents who intervene for their legally adult children is almost shocking.

Against my better judgment, I nod and tell Taylor, "I'll make an exception." In all fairness, I have to give her credit for wanting to do the work, not just letting some chatbot write the damn thing. Maybe I'm actually getting through to her.

Taylor smiles at me. "You're way cooler than you look."

I'm annoyed for feeling flattered, but my victory is short lived as Taylor drops her bottle in the trash next to my recycling bin as she exits. "Wait, you missed, Taylor," I call after her.

"No, I didn't," she says, popping her head back into my office. "You can't recycle this kind of plastic, Professor Doctor!"

I can feel myself deflating. I can feel myself starting to spiral, burdened by the questions I can no longer answer.

How did I get here?

Why am I not like I used to be?
What can I do to get my spark back?
What am I doing with my life?
What am I doing with Miles?
When did I stop fighting?
And how can I get away?

Chapter Two

Olivia "Liv" Bennett

In and out. I can do this.

I force myself from the calm quiet of my immaculate Audi SUV, where I've been giving myself a pep talk for the past ten minutes.

It's 11:00 a.m., right after the wildly popular 10:00 a.m. spin class next door let out. Going in to the grocery store now is like entering the Thunderdome. Of entitlement. My heart palpitates as I open the car door. It dings with German efficiency, reminding me to close it after I step out.

I wend my way through rows of much larger SUVs, many with third-row seating that can accommodate half the peewee hockey team. As a proud history buff, I understand the importance of learning from the past and not repeating it. Yet this is the only time I have today. I'm in back-to-back meetings and appointments until dinner, and I promised Tommy and Tiki, so . . . here I am, history notwithstanding. I don't want to be a bad auntie. I square my shoulders as I step on the sensor that operates the sliding glass doors.

I'm in. I've crossed the Rubicon. No turning back now.

A whoosh of cold air and a mellow '70s yacht-rock soundtrack greet me, opening onto Total Foodstuffs' rows upon rows of symmetrical, organically raised produce, stacked in tidy pyramids. I need only a few items, so I grab a small basket and pull my list up on my phone.

But something's off. The Lululemon Moms are normally out in full force, fresh from JoEllen Johnstone's infamous techno spin class. Each of them with their identical buttery blonde highlights and resistance-bike-sculpted bodies, wielding their supersized carts down the aisles like essedarius gladiators riding in their war chariots. They normally whip past me and my empty basket as though I were a speed bump, but I don't see any of them today. I wonder if class was canceled. All I hear is Steely Dan, and I think, *Thank you, I will slide on down . . . to the produce section.*

Cautiously optimistic yet still guarded, I check the list on my phone. I'm cooking my specialty, chicken capellini pomodoro, practically the only thing my niece and nephew will eat other than chicken nuggets—not fingers, never fingers—and McDonald's. People assume I learned to make this when I spent a semester abroad in Florence, but the truth is, it was my favorite dish when I worked part time at the Olive Garden, fresh out of college and trying to make a go of real estate.

Let's do this.

With quick, desperate motions, I grab the first clamshell of plump, juicy cherry tomatoes that I see. After that, I swoop up some emerald-green basil, my head on a swivel, my guard up the entire time.

No trouble appears, so I begin to unclench.

This hasn't been the Battle of Antietam; it's just been a regular old Thursday.

My last midday visit was a catastrophe. This time I don't have to stand for ten minutes waiting for a pair of LuluMoms to move away from the green juice as they debate if they like pinot noir, or they *like* pinot noir. (And they weren't even in the wine aisle!) No one uses a massive Chanel flap bag to hip check me into the grapefruits, causing the whole pyramid to collapse in what seems like agonizingly slow motion.

Nobody monopolizes the bulk food aisle as they conduct an Instagram Live on which spelt to buy.

Maybe today's my lucky day?

Feeling slightly more confident, I make my way to the olive oil aisle, where . . . ah, *there they are.* Class must have let out early and they have already spread through the store. Like cancer. Three LuluMoms are blocking the entire cooking oil section with their nose-to-nose-to-nose carts. No, today is *not* my lucky day. "And then she stepped on the ball!" crows a rare redhead. The other two gaze adoringly at her, hanging on her every word. I wonder if she's their leader? She must be; she's deviating from the prescribed hair color choice.

The olive oils are the width of a cart away from me. If I could reach across their cart train, maybe? I engage my core, stretching and extending, standing on my tippy toes and . . . nope. Too far. I wait for one of the LuluMoms to notice my gymnastic attempts. They do not, so I clear my throat. "Hi, um, I'm so sorry, if I could please just—" I can hear Deandra, my older sister, shouting, "Stop apologizing for everything, Liv!" but I try to tune her out. A bit louder, I say, "If you ladies don't mind, can I quickly scooch in here and grab some—"

A second LuluMom brays with laughter. "As if we'd approve her membership! She sits in the back row at spin! Can you imagine?"

I clear my throat again. Nothing. Why am I invisible to them? My looks and figure are fine. Per my doctor, I'm healthy and fit. Also, Emily and I go to the track all the time; I can run a 7:24 mile. I even spin! I just do it from the privacy of my Peloton. I have no complaints about my appearance, especially now that influencers are painting on freckles that look like my real ones.

Given how often I'm propositioned on social media, there's an argument that I'm considered above average in looks. I mean, the men saying these things aren't all the cream of the crop. One guy asked me for a pair of used socks, but I was nice to him anyway because hope springs eternal. (I did not send the socks.) However, another creeper hired me for his Evanston two-flat listing, so it can work out sometimes.

When I was just starting out in real estate, I made the mistake of advertising on a bus bench. It was supposed to generate recognition in the community. But the number of calls I received about sitting on someone else's face convinced me my marketing dollars are better spent elsewhere.

Anyway, I competed in a few scholarship (read: beauty) pageants when I was younger and I always won Miss Congeniality, so I'm pretty much your garden-variety Hallmark movie heroine—cute, but not so cute that I'm threatening.

I'm in a bright-pink short-sleeved suit, bisected with a thin gold belt and paired with a fun silk polka dot blouse and a scarf tied around my neck, my shoes are Italian, and my bag cost an ungodly amount, and I'm guessing that's the problem: I'm dressed for my *day job* as a real estate agent and these women *do not recognize my kind.*

I try again. "Please, this will just take a second," I say, reaching toward the bottles and cans to no avail. I don't have time for this. I have some canola oil at home and that's close enough, so I move on to my next list item.

A LuluMom buzzes by me, coming from out of nowhere, clipping my ankle with her cart. I guess I didn't see her in her camo workout gear. Very effective. I yelp in pain. Then another "I'm sorry" escapes my lips even though *she* hit *me.* When Deandra yelled at me about apologizing, I told her I was sorry. My sister may have a point, as the woman didn't even break her stride to ask if I was okay.

I collect myself, limping to the pasta aisle, which is blissfully empty, and peruse the offerings. So many fine choices! Do I go with the fresh kind? (Oh, did the food in Florence spoil me. I still dream about the bistecca alla fiorentina—the trick is to leave the tenderloin sitting out at room temperature for about eight hours and then roast it over oak coals.) Or do I get the dried stuff with protein? I worry about the kids developing properly with their limited palates, so I pick the one with added vitamins. I'm reading the cooking time on the back of the colorful box when a tiny hand grabs it away from me.

"Mine!"

Startled, I glance down to see a precious little cherub parked in the seat area of a shopping cart, grasping what had been *mine*. This darling child has a deep side part and her hair is swept across her forehead, secured with a large ribbon. She's styled like a kid modeling for the front of a washing powder box in the 1920s. Her smocked gingham dress is immaculate, and her tiny, ruffled socks and Mary Janes make my ovaries hum. The Italians take their children everywhere, so I have a real appreciation for kids running errands with their mothers and not just stuck at home with nannies. Postpandemic, I'm seeing more little ones out with their parents during the day, and I am here for it.

The LuluMom escorting the child seems so horrified by what just happened that she slaps the box out of her daughter's hands in shock. The package falls and breaks open, and the thin strands spray out across the aisle. I'm impressed by exactly how much pasta that slim box held. "Winifred," the mom cries. The baby girl is a Winifred! I die! She has a twee old-lady name! I love those so much! I wonder if they call her Winnie? Or how cute would Freddie be? "Not acceptable, Winifred! What do we say?"

My gosh, the mother's going to have this feisty tot apologize to me. She's probably still got a little lisp, and it's going to come out like, *Ah sowwe.* I brace myself for the avalanche of adorable to follow. I absolutely love kids, even the worst-behaved ones like Tommy and Tiki, so I'm wholly charmed by this tiny person, especially because she's already more assertive at three than I am three decades later. I can practically feel the weight of a little girl just like that as I hold her and it makes my heart ache a little. Then Winifred crosses her chubby, dimpled arms and sticks out her bottom lip, totally noncompliant. Is it wrong that I don't want her to apologize? Maybe it's good not to say sorry as a default mode, a bad habit that could haunt her into her adult life? Plus, she's so sweet, she could steal my ATM code and I'd just stand there saying, "Get big bills, cutie pie!"

"Win," the mom prompts, hand on slim hip, impatient, enunciating every word. "What. Do. We. Say?"

"Actually, it's fine," I say, scooping up the dry pasta and putting it aside so no one slips. "She doesn't need to—"

Winifred interrupts me. "We say, 'Pisketti is da debil.'"

"Exactly." The LuluMom looks at the box I'm holding and says, "Eww, that wasn't yours, was it?"

Somehow, I feel embarrassed for even considering buying a carb, and I apologize *(That's three, damn it!)* and scurry away. Then I feel sort of sad that little Win will likely never know the fun of sitting in her high chair, feeding herself a warm bowl of SpaghettiOs, or a buttered piece of fresh bread. Oh well. Best to keep going. Surely there's some pasta in my pantry. *I've got to have better luck with the chicken, right?* I assure myself.

My best friend, Emily, tells me not to listen to my sister and that there's not a thing wrong with my being polite. Buyers and sellers want to work with folks they like, which is why I've been the brokerage's top producer for five years running. But she does worry that I let people take advantage of me, particularly my colleagues. She never mentions my family in her assessment, and I appreciate that she's too tactful to point out the obvious. No one wants to hear advice on what they can't change. Sometimes it's easier for all of us to stay stuck.

At the meat counter, I'm behind another mother-daughter combo, in matching athleisure, from their iridescent bike shorts to their flowy dolman-sleeve yoga wrap tops. My guilty pleasure is following a Utah influencer and trad wife who's all about coordinating her mommy-daughter nap dresses. I can't get enough of her content. Having a mini-me to match with is a serious #lifegoal.

I smile at the little girl, but she pays me no attention. She looks to be about six, and her expression is so very serious as she inspects the meat in the cooler. An earnest hipster butcher with a crisp white apron and labeled cuts of cow tattooed on his forearm waits on the pair. Pointing at a thick slab of marbled applewood-smoked bacon, the girl asks the butcher, "How much fresh air and sunshine did this little piggy have every day?" I am momentarily taken aback. Is . . . is this how kids are supposed to sound? I feel like Tommy and Tiki are not in the same school district as this wee Mensa member.

The LuluMom beams at her progeny. "Hortense cares deeply about animal welfare."

"I want to be a vegetarian, but bacon is too yummy," Hortense says, rubbing her little potbelly. They all laugh, and I do too. But is she not six? I'm usually pretty good at deducing ages. Why does she sound sixteen? Is it the old-lady name? Also, is that a *thing* now? Is Agatha the new Ava? And should I help Deandra get a tutor for her kids? Last week, I had to stop Tommy from microwaving a fork. He's almost thirteen.

The butcher tells her, "I'll be honest, kiddo. I don't know all the specifics of how this pig lived, but I'm curious too. We normally post our welfare ratings, so I'm not sure what the deal is here. Let me call our vendor at Sunnydale Farm and find out for you, okay?" To me, he says, "Sorry, it's going to be a few minutes."

I glance at my phone. I'm running out of time, so I have to press on. I've got to have chicken in the freezer, right? Maybe not air chilled or antibiotic-free, and maybe it had low self-esteem in comparison to the birds here, but still. At least I can get Parmesan. Even if the ingredients at home aren't the freshest, shaved Parm makes everything delish. I rush to the cheese aisle. As I try to decide which wedge to choose, I encounter yet another adorable little girl. This one is clutching a stuffed lemur. She wanders a few steps away from her LuluMom to approach me.

"Hi there," I say, giving her a big smile. "Who are you?"

"I Eunice." Eunice! My goodness, I am out of my mind with joy over these senior citizen names. If I run into a toddler Agnes or Chester today, I'm going to buy a lottery ticket. Eunice holds out her lemur. "Dis mah baby. His name Mr. Lemur."

I bend down to shake the stuffed animal's paw. "What a pretty baby, Eunice. And it's so nice to meet you, Mr. Lemur."

"Where your baby?" she asks.

"Oh, honey, I don't have a baby yet," I say. My hand flies to my midsection as though to confirm. Nope. Disappointingly flat.

"Why?"

I feel a small twinge in my chest. "Because I don't have a husband, sweetie." Not to say anyone needs to have a spouse to have a baby—no judgment here. And not because I don't want to get married. I desperately want a husband, children, a picket fence, a couple of sloppy, naughty Labradors, and an endless to-do list from the PTA. Honestly, all things being equal, I'd die to be one of the LuluMoms. I've tried so hard, but I don't know how to get there, and this feels like a huge personal failing. In my head, I understand I don't need a man to complete me, but in my heart, I can't comprehend why I perpetually put it all out there and get nothing back in return.

Eunice looks up at me with her saucer eyes, fringed in lashes to die for. "No husband? What wrong wif you, lady?"

She's got a point. I'm on all the apps, save for Grindr, which Emily explained was not meant for me. I must make it easy to be dumped, for them to trade up or move on. When guys inevitably disappear, I never confront them. That would be so off-brand. One time, I watched a guy break up with his date at Olive Garden, and the jilted girl threw a plate of fried ravioli at him, sauce and all. The tin cup holding the marinara pegged him in the eye. That would never be me.

On paper, I should be considered a catch. I graduated with honors from a fine university. I have professional success; the metrics don't lie. I'm told I'm attractive. I'm largely happy, upbeat, and positive. I'm definitely polite. But I seem to be missing the it-factor that makes anyone want to get serious with me.

I feel that familiar pang deep within my heart. "Eunice, sweetie, I'm so sorry. If I knew what was wrong with me, I'd tell you."

I stow my meager bag of groceries in the shared kitchenette fridge at the Wilmette office of Asterisk Realty. I've run in moments before I have to conduct the agency's team meeting. I work for Chase and Jase, the managing brokers. They're brothers, and they're sort of infamous in the Chicagoland Area. They're like our version of the Winklevosses. Former Ivy League athletes, tall, with Nordic good looks and a ton of family money behind them. For a while, they tried to sell a reality show about being broker brothers. But apparently, being a ridiculously attractive Realtor isn't enough of a hook for a reality show. Now they are largely absentee, save for collecting the hefty percentage all the other agents pay them. Nine times out of ten, if I need to find them and they're in the country, they're out playing pickleball.

If I were to set up my own shop, I could have a team of agents working under me and I'd get a portion of their commissions, instead of Chase and Jase getting a (huge) piece of mine. I've passed the broker's license exam, so that's in the realm of possibility. However, the idea of going out on my own doesn't seem tenable. I'm needed here. Plus, I'm gaining leadership experience managing this group of my peers. It's not like I'm compensated for my additional responsibilities, though when Emily asked me about it, I fibbed and said I was.

Our open-concept office is stylishly appointed. There's lots of exposed brick and vintage metal, dotted with provocative art. I'm no prude, but I quietly wonder if artistic nudes are the best choice for a suburban brokerage. Our desks are made from recycled airplane wings (Emily appreciates that part), and the brothers spent a mint on them. Maybe they'd have been better off with something less eye-catching instead of siphoning off so much of our commissions to pay for it all? We've had retention trouble with senior agents because of the cut the brothers take, and the new hires are increasingly younger, square-jawed men who call everyone "bruh," "bro," or "broski." Even the clients. I think it's bad business, but neither Chase nor Jase is interested in soliciting opinions.

I'm standing at the head of the wide oval table in the glassed-in conference room, about to conduct our weekly Call to Excellence. The name may be overstating our case a bit. Given who's seated at the table, it looks more like I'm running a chapter meeting at the Sigma Nu house. These boys (and I mean *boys*) are always whipping Frisbees around or taking over the conference room for their fantasy football drafts. We're in a staff meeting, but Brody and Patrick, two of the agency bros, are quietly wrapping rubber bands around an orange to see how many they can add before it explodes. Yes, *this* is the behavior people want to see from those who'll help them buy and sell the single greatest asset they'll possess in their lives. I often feel more like their mother than their manager.

My agency represents all walks of buyers and sellers, from those looking for their first studio apartment to those buying an estate on the lakefront. I have a reputation as the starter-home queen. I love helping people get into their first place, handing newbies their first set of keys. I tear up each time, I swear, so excited for them to take this next step in their lives.

I've been working to break into the luxury home market, but it's not going as planned. Every time I get my hands on a bigger listing, either Chase or Jase insists they should take it over. I've sold a ton of real estate (ten closings last month, a record!), but my name is always on smaller transactions. I yearn for those luxury listings, and not only because the commission is exponentially higher. They require more leg-work, but having the time to learn how the buyers live is crucial; that info ensures I'll find the right house for them. Many of my peers think when they show a place to a younger couple, the first thing they should talk about is the schools, but that could be a huge turnoff. Maybe the couple has been doing years of IVF and the mention is a painful reminder. Maybe they don't want a three-bedroom for future offspring, but they do want to have two home offices. When you find out who the buyers are and what they need (that's where listening comes into play), it's easy to present the perfect listing at any price point. But again, I'd be lying if I said I wouldn't prefer to invest that time and energy in a listing with a bigger commission. I want to fund my own big dreams, even if I don't know what they entail yet.

I'm at the whiteboard, reviewing opportunities and purposefully ignoring the catcalls when I bend over to pick up the dry-erase marker. Agents are supposed to generate their own leads through networking and door knocking, but when listings come in that are too small-time for the brothers, I'm in charge of assigning them to the team. "Okay, who can work Chase's open house on Tenth Street this Sunday?" I ask.

Trevor, whose desk is next to mine, raises his hand. Today he's wearing his sunglasses on the back of his head with Nantucket Reds pants, a wrinkled oxford, bloodshot eyes, and a cheese-eating grin. He looks like he just stumbled off the set of Bravo's *Southern Charm*, three Bloody Marys deep.

"Trevor!" I'm pleasantly surprised. "Are you volunteering?"

"Fuck no," he replies, leaning back in his chair so far it looks like he's lying down. "I just wanted to say that open houses suck donkey dick. They're like that scene from the *Star Wars* bar, all freaks and randoms." I wish he were wrong. A couple of the guys pantomime playing the odd horns in the bar gracing the desert world of Tatooine—a gesture I recognize only because a guy I once dated was into *Star Wars*. He eventually dumped me when I balked at wearing a metal bikini to a costume party. (It can snow in Chicago in late October, and that metal was freezing cold against my skin. I tried! I honestly did!)

Open houses can be kind of a nightmare. There's no barrier to entry for the lower-priced properties. When we're selling an upscale listing, potential buyers aren't allowed to set foot in a place if they don't first provide proof of funds or a preapproval letter from their bank or brokerage. There's too much liability if we let just anyone into a jewelry- and art-filled mansion. Plus, it's a total waste of our time to bring clients to a place worth $4 million when they're only approved for $400,000. They leave sad they can't buy it, and we end up sad we can't sell it. I totally understand the draw of seeing how the other half lives, but I'm a Realtor, not a docent. (Granted, it's a career I briefly considered, but still.)

Open houses are a free-for-all where I can't get to know anyone. I rarely sell to anyone who comes through these cattle calls, especially now that interest rates are so high and the market has softened. There are too many lookie-loos who show up for the free cheese or an opportunity to case the joint.

"Right, Trevor," I say, "but we still need people there."

"They steal all the snacks," Trevor says.

"I know. But, please, we need a person there. Chase is counting on us." I survey the room. Suddenly everyone is looking at the ground, the ceiling, the walls, the ever-constricting orange, anywhere but at me.

"I mean, *I* would do it, but I've worked the last four," I say. No one says a thing. "Jackie, what does your Sunday look like?" Jackie is the only other seasoned agent in the room, the one who keeps this office from being a total boys' club. The rest are in their midtwenties, and either their parents (largely Chase and Jase's friends) still pay their rent, or they have so many roommates, their expenses are minimal. None of them are hungry, none of them are aggressive. A lot of them had the good fortune of becoming agents during the pandemic gold rush, so they aren't yet aware of how limited their skill sets actually are. But Jackie is a true professional, always willing to step in when she can.

Jackie checks her phone, then shows me the time already blocked off on her calendar for a family commitment. "So sorry, Liv. Maddy has a tap recital. But if you need me to, I can just have Davey record it," she replies.

"Obviously, I'm not going to ask you to miss your daughter's performance."

"She's not a very good dancer," Jackie offers. "I promise you, I won't enjoy being there."

"I appreciate it, but no. Darren? How about you?"

Darren is one of Trevor's little buddies. Darren looks at his phone, which he doesn't even pretend to turn on. "Isn't that a damn thing. I got a tap recital too."

"Yeah, a *keg* tap recital," Trevor adds. Darren and Trevor fist-bump.

I take a breath and compose myself. "Anyone, please. I can't end the meeting until I have a commitment," I say. No one will meet my gaze. I know what will inevitably happen next, so it won't feel as bad if I tell myself it's my choice. I open my Google calendar and delete: *Bumble brunch with Brian!*

It kills me. Brunch dates are the best. I'm allowed to get mimosas, which help with the butterflies in my stomach. And nothing's better than brunch food; it's a personality assessment. For example, if my date opts for some sort of sweet waffle or whipped-cream-topped pancake as their main, he's not a serious person. No one can eat that much sugar first thing and accomplish anything during the day. If he does dry toast or eggs cooked without butter or oil, he's going to be literal and humorless. Not for me, thanks. From our chats, I learned that Brian is a skillet man, occasionally veering into breakfast burrito territory. He's someone who'll get protein, carbs, and veggies, the perfect blend, pairing them with a mimosa *and* a cup of coffee. That is husband material right there. The best part of a brunch date is, if it goes well, it can extend into a whole day together, into dinner and beyond. But no one volunteers to work the open house, which leaves me as the only available choice.

I tell the group, "Scratch that. Now I'll have worked the last five." I'm met with a sea of smirks and shrugs, like this is exactly what they'd hoped.

When they exit the conference room, I hear Party Marty (I did not give him this nickname) ask Darren what he's *really* doing this weekend. "Business," Darren says.

Party Marty replies, "Monkey business?"

"You know it, bruh," and then they slap their hands in an elaborate handshake before going outside to vape. As I erase the board, I hear a pop, followed by the sounds of pulp splattering the walls, the table, and the back of my skirt. I don't need to turn around to know what happened.

Brody comes rushing in with more elastic bands. He shouts, "Fuckin' A, Pat, we missed it. We gotta start over!" He heads toward the fruit bowl in the kitchenette, leaving the mess. I swab the juice, pith, and pits up with a paper towel and ask myself why I'm so anxious to have children. I don't like any of the ones I currently have.

❦

After work, I head back to my family's three-flat in Rogers Park. Ideally, I'd live in one of the charming bungalows I sell a couple of miles up the road in Wilmette and Evanston. Those neighborhoods have better schools, and it would be nice to put a tiny bit of distance between myself and my family. I want to get a dog, but my mother claims that she's allergic. This is a problem because my mom lives on the first floor of my three-family home. My sister and her kids live on the second. As for my father? He went out for a newspaper in 1997 and didn't come back . . . at least that's how my mom describes it to anyone who asks.

Actually, I remember a lot of heart-to-heart chats before he left, and how tortured he was about the potential divorce, and how worried he was about Dee and me. He even brought in our church's priest to help us with the transition. Dad was so clear that our parents' problems had nothing to do with us kids, or how much he loved us. (Also, I should mention he's alive and well in Grand Rapids, which meant I was able to swing in-state tuition at U of M.)

After he left, he became a different man, just so happy all the time, so the summers and holidays we spent there were pure bliss. I will never say it out loud, but there are days that I don't blame him for leaving. I'd love to find a guy as good as my dad is, but he sets a high bar.

I take off my shoes inside the front door because I don't want to disturb everyone as I walk up the three flights of stairs to my apartment. By "disturb," I mean "alert to my presence." I love these people with my whole heart—I would honestly die for them—but sometimes I need a minute to regroup before they burst in.

My apartment is cool and serene, with a mix of styles. There are beautiful antique Persian rugs, overstuffed sofas, and expensive knick-knacks. I've done all I can to camouflage the dated appliances and wood floors in desperate need of refinishing. I've volunteered a million times to upgrade these on my own dime, but since my sister can't afford to do the same downstairs, my mom doesn't think it's fair. I never argue, but I'm secretly delighted every time something breaks and a replacement becomes necessary. That's why the old cream-colored Frigidaire is now a stainless Sub-Zero with a clear glass door. I'm crossing my fingers that the ceramic burner Whirlpool stove goes next so I can get a decent gas range.

I set my grocery bag directly inside the Sub-Zero, grab an open bottle of Whispering Angel, and pour myself a glass. There are few ills a cup of something pink can't cure. I cue up *The Bachelor* and close my eyes, thankful for the three seconds of silence before Deandra barrels through the door like a SWAT team with a warrant.

Deandra is a good person. I feel this to my core. She's only two years older, but she practically raised me because my mom was too busy for us, between her job and her simmering resentment. When we were younger, Dee taught me things like how tampons work.

No one could make me laugh like Deandra. One time our tenant on the second floor, was um, *entertaining* a gentleman caller. We could hear the "Oh God, oh Gods" from the bedroom above as her head-board banged against the wall. Dee turned to me and said with a dead-straight face, "Sounds like Michelle has found religion," and we both died laughing.

Dee and I chose different paths. When I went off to college, she married her high school boyfriend. At twenty, she was too young to legally enjoy the cash bar at her own wedding, not that it stopped her. She had Tommy and Tiki at twenty-two and dropped out a year into her nursing program. By thirty, Dusty, her husband, started to sow the wild oats he'd never had in high school, and Dee kicked him out. He's now remarried with a new baby and a toddler, so his child support payments have become sporadic at best. Now my clever, formerly quick-witted sister with her dry sense of humor and zest for life has become brittle and bitter. Exactly like our ma.

"Aren't you gonna start dinner?" Dee demands, by way of greeting. She's still wearing her smock from Home Depot.

"I'm Door Dashing. I couldn't get everything I needed at the market," I reply.

"LuluMoms get you again?" she asks. See? She *knows* me. I give a noncommittal shrug, confirming her suspicions. "Whatever. Make sure you get chicken nuggets, not chicken fingers."

"Always," I say as I check the status of the app order. Dasher Ornaldo will be here in five minutes.

"Did you make your case for that listing on Sheridan?" she asks. I got the brokerage a contract to list a glorious Arts and Crafts–style house in a fabulous neighborhood, but Chase and Jase decided they wanted to handle it themselves, so I had to turn it over. Then the homeowners complained they weren't getting enough attention—probably because the brothers are perpetually on vacation in France—so they turned the listing over . . . to Trevor. I told Dee that I was going to fight for it. By "fight," I mean "ask politely." No dice.

"I sure did!" I fib. I know she doesn't believe me, but she doesn't badger me about it and I'm grateful.

"Any reason you're dressed like a flight attendant?" she asks, taking in my suit and scarf.

"This is Scanlan Theodore," I reply, referring to the designer. I thought it was cute?

She laughs. "Oh, yeah, Scanlan Theodore Air, out of the O'Hare hub, of course. Anyway, I need you to babysit tonight."

Brian from Bumble and I had rescheduled our brunch for a quick drink later tonight. He really does seem promising. Jackie went to school with him and she says there are zero red flags. He's smart, he's nice, just an all-around golden retriever of a man. "I wish I could help you, but I have plans. What about Ma? She can't do it? She's always home."

"Dragon pox." Dee raises a single eyebrow. Just another cool thing she can do and I cannot.

"I'm sorry?"

"She claims she has dragon pox."

"Is that a thing?" I ask. I can't keep up with all the new diseases. I thought it was *monkey* pox.

"Only if she enrolled at Hogwarts without telling us." Seeing my confusion, she clarifies, "It's from *Harry Potter*. Ma watched it with Tiki last week."

Since Dad left, Mom has struggled with one fictional malady after another, despite being in peak health. Her hypochondria is another member of the family at this point, ever present. The only thing that seems to work is humoring her, some may call it enabling. On the plus side, this makes Christmas shopping easy. She was thrilled at the glucose monitor I gave her last year, despite her not being diabetic.

Dee says, "Listen, I wouldn't ask if I weren't desperate. I picked up an extra shift because the dentist says Tommy's gonna need braces. I mean, look at his front teeth. He could eat an ear of corn through a picket fence." She's not wrong.

Resigned, I comply. "Okay. Lemme just cancel my thing." I text Brian, changing our plans yet again. This is the fourth time in a week. I won't be surprised when I don't hear back from him.

"You're a peach," Dee says. She shouts toward the front door. "Hey, animals, get up here. I'm going back to work!"

Tiki and Tommy explode into my apartment, each of them carrying a plastic to-go bag from the Door Dasher. Tiki parkours over the back of my couch, piledriving into me, and Tommy swoops down and grabs the remote, flipping through the channels at breakneck speed. I grab my wine glass to keep it from spilling onto my phone. No response from Brian. Three dots appear, but then they disappear. I know that in situations like this, no answer is the answer.

"I mean it. You're a peach, sis," Dee tells me, stealing a sip of my wine.

Tiki starts tearing through the bags like a raccoon in a dumpster. She pulls out her meal and pops open the Styrofoam lid, fixing me with an accusatory glare. "Tell me these are not chicken *fingers*."

Shoot. "Oh, no, Tiki, I'm so sorry, I swear the menu said nuggets," I say. "Do you want me to make my pomodoro, only with spaghetti noodles? I'll have to defrost some chicken, but I bought a nice block of Parm I can grate."

Tiki eyes me. "You don't have the powdery kind in a can?"

"I don't."

Tiki curls her lip. Fortunately, she does not share her fraternal twin's overbite. "Pass."

Any good real estate agent always has a pivot. "I can get you nuggets from a different place."

She snorts. "Yeah, you will." Well, that's settled. I quickly type in a McDonald's DoorDash.

Tommy's still whipping through the channels. "You still got the parental controls on this thing?" he asks.

"Yep, a real peach," Dee repeats as she beats a hasty retreat, and I feel jealous that she gets to leave, even though being surrounded by kids is the dream. Just . . . not *these* kids.

I gaze at my half-empty glass of Whispering Angel. From behind me, I hear an enormous crash, and all I can think is, *Please let them have broken the stove.*

Chapter Three

EMILY

I'm nostalgic, and I find myself scrolling through a file of photos from my time with Jeremy and Planet BlueLove, a lifetime ago. I feel like the shots should be sepia and cracked, but they were taken on a digital camera and uploaded to the cloud, so they're absolutely pristine.

The first shot is of my old team after the Oregon assignment, before some of us left for Brazil. We'd been kayaking through the Class V rapids on the Deschutes River. We're wet and beaten up, but you'd never know it from our expressions—just sheer joy.

I enlarge the photo, trying to see what's so different about me between then and now. Other than finally giving in to societal pressure to shave my legs (Liv was quietly thrilled), not much has changed, at least on the outside. So how is it that I look so altered? I remember one of the best days of my life.

I got it! I finally got the call I've been waiting for. This is it. This is the big dance. My chance to effect some major environmental change in the place most desperate for it. I'm so elated that I feel weak in the knees.

We were still in bed when the call came in, since we're three hours behind the New York central office for BlueLove. The minute the phone rang, I threw on a robe. I felt like I should be at least partially dressed to accept the greatest opportunity of my life.

"You got it? Beauty!" Jeremy exclaims. He's still on the hotel bed, clad only in a crisp white sheet. "When do you leave?"

"Next month," I say, my mind already racing with everything I'll have to prepare before then.

"I'll miss you," he says, pulling me close.

"Why?" I ask, wedging in beside him. "You'll be with me. I'm choosing my own team. I choose you."

He seems hesitant. "I'm not sure that's the best idea, love."

"Not the best idea?" I'm incredulous. "It's everything we've worked for. I mean, yes, I can do it without you, but I don't want to. I want you there. You're the best there is. I need you. BlueLove needs you."

"And I want to be with you, it's just . . ." Why is he hesitating? I thought he'd be ecstatic. We're being called up to the pros, playing first string. It doesn't get bigger or better than this for what we do.

Maybe we've moved too fast, going so far as throwing the L word around of late. "Listen, J, this thing between us, it doesn't have to be serious. We can stay exactly what we are to each other right now. Nothing has to be formal. We just make the decision to be together, and if one of us wakes up one day and decides that it no longer works, then we'll still have had what we had. And it was real and true in the moment."

He scoops me up and wraps me in his powerful arms. "If I go, and I'm not saying I will, I need you to promise me something."

"Anything."

He squeezes me tight, almost as though he's afraid I'll slip away from him. "When you think of me someday, always remember this moment. You and I are real and this love is true, no matter what else happens."

And then we celebrate.

Then, I come across a selfie of Jeremy and me in Brazil, before . . . the thing that happened. We'd been rappelling down a waterfall, against a backdrop that may as well have been the Garden of Eden, exploding with lush tropical vegetation and birds in brilliant hues of blue, yellow, and orange. They'd looked like something Willy Wonka might have created. Oh, to be there again.

The two days of travel via planes, trains, boats, and buses to get deep into the Amazon basin feel worth it when I finally see what I'm sworn to protect.

The biodiversity of the rain forest manifests in an explosion of sounds and colors; it hosts 10 percent of all flora and fauna known to humankind. My eyes trail up tree trunks many stories tall. I see snatches of golden sunlight and patches of cerulean sky.

The leaves form a mosaic of millions of little pieces that appear to be lit from within. It takes my breath away. Being here is like standing under miles of the finest stained glass. This is sacred ground, the church that nature built. Even though I'm agnostic, it's impossible not to feel the hand of God here.

In my halting Portuguese, I ask Augusto, one of our guides, if he ever takes any of this for granted, ever gets used to it. His weathered face is wreathed in a smile as he answers, "Nunca."

Never.

Days later, I tell Jeremy, "I want to stay here forever. How will I go back to normal life after this?" We're lying on the smooth, slick rocks adjacent to the pounding waterfall, sunbathing between rounds of skinny-dipping.

"Why go back?" he says. "You'll never have an ordinary life; you'd shrivel up and die. The idea of someone like you with, what, a time card to punch? Working for a multinational corporation? It's hilarious."

"Ooh, maybe I'd have a condominium full of cats. Maybe I'd have a crossword puzzle addiction."

He laughs.

I keep scrolling. Here's a bunch of BlueLovers on the steep face of the still largely unknown Milho Verde. I look so *alive* in every picture. There's a shot from when I was free-climbing and lost my grip. I crashed about fifteen feet into some brush, emerging with a small gash on my head, soaking my bandana and shirt collar in blood. There are actual sticks in my hair and my forearms and legs are absolutely shredded, yet I appear to be having the time of my life.

Now I don't even drink a glass of wine without taking an Advil.

"What happened to me?" I ask aloud.

There's a knock at the door. It's Miles returning from his morning bike ride. Though he has his own key, and most of his stuff—including his ridiculous egg cup and even more ridiculous bike—resides in my place, he insists on acting like a guest.

"Don't make me get up, Miles," I call, hesitant to end my journey down memory lane.

I hear his key in the lock, then Miles pokes his helmeted head in the doorway and says, "Knock, knock!" He's in head-to-toe spandex and covered in protective padding, more suited for a running back than for an associate dean on a casual spin down a tree-lined bike path. It's not his best look. "Mind if I come in?" He stays over four nights a week, and he just left here for his ride an hour ago; it's not like his being back is a surprise.

"Stop asking, Miles. Just come in." He wheels in his recumbent bike with a massive orange flag on the back. I snap my laptop shut. "Good ride this morning?" I ask.

He nods enthusiastically. "I felt the burn!" I know it's weird, but I am overcome with the irrational desire to pants him and stuff him in a gym locker. I realize this is not a healthy feeling, nor does he deserve my ire. He's done nothing wrong but be his lovely, sweet, sane self.

"Nothing like a slow workout to really get the blood pumping," I deadpan as he undoes his chin strap.

"I concur!" he replies. When he doesn't pick up on my sarcasm— which is my love language—I feel like the meanest person in the world. I hate it. Why can't he just *banter* a little bit? I watch as he fills his ever-present stainless water bottle from my filtered tap and takes a couple of delicate sips. He'd be as likely to buy a bottled water as he would to fly to Mars. I used to appreciate that about him, but now, like the egg cup, its presence annoys me.

He must be feeling refreshed, because out of nowhere, he announces, "I'm about to kiss you all over" and approaches me.

Well, *this* is an interesting turn of events. It's not even the weekend! I close my eyes and tilt up my chin and . . . I feel him sweep up my Devon rex cat, Chairman Meow, from his perch on my shoulder. Miles hugs the cat tightly, planting a series of dry pecks all over his pointy face and abnormally large ears.

At least the Chairman enjoys his affection.

The Chairman hops out of his arms and returns to my shoulder, nudging my cheek with his face, a sweet reminder that he loves me too. Meow got me through some lonely times when I first moved back to Chicago and didn't know anyone but Liv. I adopted him because he was the oddest-looking cat at the rescue, his giant head out of proportion with his slender body. People would pass his cage, beelining directly for either the fat and fluffy cats or the tiny kittens. No one wanted the one that looked like an alien life-form who'd just crash-landed at Roswell.

Miles places his helmet in the basket on the back of his bike. While the storage area is large enough that he could take Chairman Meow on rides, this is where I draw the line. I cannot imagine voluntarily having Saturday sex with someone who takes cats for bike rides. It's a slippery slope from there to pushing a cat around in a screened-in stroller.

"Guess what?" he asks. "No, don't guess. I'm too excited. Something special for the Great Helmsman!" He rips the plastic off a package he must have picked up at his place two blocks away, revealing first a man-sized argyle sweater vest and then one in a cat size, plus two pairs of horn-rimmed glasses and two pipes. "It's for our Instagram. We're celebrating our academic realness."

What I initially thought was a one-off joke has morphed into a phenomenon. #MilesandMeow has become an internet sensation. I thought the business with Chairman Meow was funny, especially because Miles was so serious about it. The internet was built on cat pictures, and while Miles might not be my normal type, he really owns the dorky-sexy look. He's super photogenic. Plus, he thought having an online presence would make him more relatable to his students, make them more comfortable with him, like he was one of them. Of course,

Meow was a willing participant because nothing makes him happier than being made the center of attention. (I feel like he'd have thrived in ancient Egypt.) But instead of posting a couple of Instagrams and losing interest like a normal person, Miles ramped up their joint social media, adding music and learning to edit video. He brought in a stylist *for the cat.*

That's when it stopped being cute to me.

Once the university brass found out about his account, I felt relieved, like, *Whew, enough of that.* But turns out, they love it, especially when Miles and the Chairman demonstrate scientific principles in their videos. The one where they're both in Einstein wigs and lab coats has a billion views. With a *b.* He got a plaque from YouTube and a huge check that he signed over to the cat rescue group where I found him. The school credits #MilesandMeow for an uptick in our department's enrollment, and Meow seems to love being dressed up, so the account isn't going anywhere. Argh.

"Did you have to pay for those?" I ask, gesturing toward the costumes. I don't know what's worse: his forking over hard-earned USD for such things or being so well known in the cat costume space that he may have realistically received them gratis.

"Of course not. A sponsor sent them." He gives the sweater a closer inspection, rubbing it against his cheek. "Ooh, it's cashmere!"

Free is worse.

I glance longingly at my closed laptop. I need the me from those pictures to be sitting on this couch. The cool girl. The fun one. The brave one. How do I find her again?

I want the kind of purpose and empowerment I used to feel. I tried antidepressants, but they did nothing but give me dry mouth and constipation. Miles and I both need a big refresh, something that gets our blood pumping in a way that recumbent biking definitely cannot or doing the Dougie with the cat cannot. Is it possible for us to get to that place together?

That's when I realize the answer is *right in front of my face*. I may have a way. I need to find that girl in Brazil again. And if Miles did it with me, we'd add that element of danger and excitement that I've so missed. Maybe this is what *we* need.

"Hey, Miles? What would you think if I went back to Planet BlueLove? Not to work, just to volunteer?" Before he can answer, I quickly add, "And not just me, you too. They can always use people with our skills—especially someone with your knowledge and passion."

He glances up from his academic cosplay. "What do I think?" I can practically see the wheels of his brain churning, weighing out all the possibilities. Miles really does have good raw material for Planet BlueLove: a scientific background, a logical approach to problems, unparalleled risk assessment. The BlueLove way could help harness what he knows and turn him into—

"I think that we're too old for ecoterrorism."

"No, seriously," I say.

Miles looks puzzled. "I'm always serious. You used to be so reckless before you cut ties with that group. Honestly, I worried the university wouldn't hire you because of your past, but fortunately, everyone voted with me. Anyway, might I use the bathroom to freshen up?"

Like that, I feel my energy leach out. "Just say you're showering, Miles."

I open my laptop when I hear him collect his shower caddy (why, God, why?) and carry it into the bathroom. I seek out my favorite shot of Jeremy as Meow purrs in my ear. It's almost sunset, and we've just built a fire on the shoreline. His whole face is lit in the pink and gold hues of the magic hour, and he's staring into the camera like he's seeing the very depths of my soul. I run a fingertip over the small scar on his chin, from the time that he crashed his motorcycle and—

The screaming rips me from my memory, and Meow scatters at the noise. I rush into the bathroom, where I find Miles naked but wrapped in a towel. Miles looks great in clothes, like they're made just for him. But pale and wet, I can't help but compare him to a plucked Cornish game hen. He shaves everywhere, believing it makes him more aerodynamic. Apparently, speed is important on noncompetitive bike paths.

Miles is cowering on the tub's lip, pointing at something in the corner. I spot the object of his abject terror.

A spider.

Just a regular old house spider, smaller than a dime. It's definitely not one of the dinner-plate-sized goliath birdeaters I ran across in the rain forest. Despite the name, they rarely eat birds, mostly snakes. Imagining Miles witnessing a spider eating a snake gives me a perverse stab of joy, but I keep this to myself and instead try to sound patient. "Again, Miles? They're harmless." I gently sweep it out of the corner and into my palm, planning to deposit the tiny guy in one of the planter boxes on my balcony.

This moment feels like a Bizarro World photo negative of Jeremy.

I remember running my hand over Jeremy's solid bare chest and arms. *"How'd you get this one?" I asked, pointing to a jagged line on his forearm.*

"Bar fight in Pamplona."

"Did you start the fight?"

He laughed. "Nah, but I finished it, didn't I." He lifted his hair by his ear, showing a two-inch-long raised strip of white skin. "Caught a bottle right here that night as well. Didn't stop me from running with the bulls the next day. That's where I got this." He revealed a crescent-shaped mark on his left shoulder.

"Were you gored?" I asked.

His laugh was the best sound in the world. "Yeah . . . by a fence post when I stumbled. I may have been overserved the night prior."

From the corner of my eye, I noticed movement by the tent opening. Then I spotted a small scorpion making its way up Jeremy's calf.

"Reckon it's looking for a threesome?" Jeremy calmly asked.

"Not on my watch." I quickly grabbed the scorpion at the tip of its tail and flicked it out of the tent. Then I returned my attention to Jeremy. "Two's all we need."

As for Miles, I can understand his paranoia. He was bitten by a brown recluse on a Boy Scout trip and he never got over it. I hold the spider up on my flattened palm so Miles can get a better look. "See? He's totally chill. This is the kind of beneficial spider that—" That somehow flies out of my hand and directly into Miles's thick hair. He shrieks, stumbles, and brings the whole shower curtain with him.

🦋

A couple of EMTs deem Miles to be fine, as there's not a scrape, bump, or bruise on him, but Miles takes the day off anyway. He's cocooned himself in quilts and wrapped his head in ice secured by an ACE bandage and a roll of gauze. He looks like he fought in the Battle of the Somme; though, between his shower curtain parachute and the tub pillow and mat he moved into my bathroom (don't ask), his fall was nicely broken.

"You didn't even hit your head," I say, setting him up with herbal tea, chicken soup, and a sleeve of crackers. He also requested that I place bottles of ibuprofen, Tylenol, Tums, and an antidiarrheal within arm's reach. I stack one of my many *New York Times* crossword puzzle books next to him, as well as a pencil, the TV remote, his phone, and his iPad. I should feel sorry for him, but all I can think is, *I can't keep doing this for the rest of my life. Something has to change.*

Miles wraps his arms around his legs and begins to moan and rock. Concerned, I ask, "What just happened? Are you in pain? The guys said you were unscathed."

"I'm having psychosomatic pain over what could have happened. It's like Camp While-A-Way all over again. The potential danger is just too much for me."

I grit my teeth. As if he's ever been in real danger.

Jeremy's voice is rough and hoarse as he strains to whisper in my ear. "I reckon they'll spare you, but you have to go." He's pleading with me as the guerillas frog-march us away from the campfire. But that doesn't make sense. *He's not our leader; I am. I'm the target of value. I'm the American. I'm the better bargaining chip.*

"*I won't leave you.*"

"*Be serious, love. It's our only chance.*"

The underbrush pulls at my clothes and my skin as they force us down the path, but I barely feel it. I remember what I said to him the night he braided a vine and placed it on my ring finger. "Whither though goest, I will go." It wasn't an engagement so much as a promise of more to come.

I've mentally prepared for this. Hostile actions have always been a possibility with the work we do. We're trying to stop deforestation, and billions of dollars are potentially on the line, between the value of the natural resources and the criminal enterprises that operate out of here. Getting between someone and their money involves risk.

BlueLove trained us on what to do if we're taken. Unless there's an extraordinarily strong chance of escape, the protocol is to submit, obey, and try to establish a rapport. If the taken gain their kidnappers' respect, they're less likely to be injured.

I don't know specifically who's got us; it could be anyone from drug and arms traffickers to illegal hunters to emissaries of those who profit from deforestation, like the chocolate companies that destroy orangutan habitats to harvest palm oil. These men could be anyone. Most outside groups haven't gotten in this deep. Usually, the violence here is aimed toward Indigenous people, guardians like the Uru-Eu-Wau-Wau.

I guess we just got lucky.

"*You have to try to escape,*" *Jeremy says. We bump along the trail in the dark, surrounded on all sides by captors in ex-Soviet camo gear, faces concealed, carrying heavy-duty weaponry and equipped with night vision apparatus.*

"*Even now, it's cute that you think you're in charge,*" *I reply.*

Though his wrists are bound, Jeremy's able to pass me the small switchblade he keeps in his sock. "*Here's what's going to happen. Cut your hands free. When we get to the fork in the brush, I'm going to create a distraction. I'll stumble and you will run. You will run and run and you will not look back.*"

"No, we're in this together."

"Emily, no." When I look in his eyes, I see fear. This fear throws me off my axis; it sends me reeling, scrambles my judgment. He implores, "Promise me you'll run. Promise me you'll run and you'll never come back here. I've never asked you for anything, but I'm asking you for this. Promise me you're done here."

I don't say anything.

We're almost to the fork.

Decision time.

I go against my gut. "I'll run, but only because I'm faster than you and I can find help."

When we get to the fork, Jeremy stumbles and plows into the men on our right flank. While the men swarm him, I break free and run, even though every atom of my being tells me to stay and fight. Under a blanket of stars on a moonless night, I run for hours until I reach a village with a satellite phone fifteen kilometers away.

I never stop regretting this action.

"It doesn't hurt, per se, but it's the potential for pain that gets me," Miles says, snapping me out of my memory.

I bite my tongue. It's not just me. Even Chairman Meow has had enough of him today. He's currently lounging on top of the fridge, watching the nonsense from a distance. I am vaguely concerned that Miles will try to wrap gauze around his head for an impromptu twins selfie. I'm trying to figure out how best to respond to this foolishness when my phone pings. It's a text from Liv:

meet me for coffee? now? please??

Miles rocks and keens, racked with his imaginary aches. Meow's tail twitches, and he shoots me a look that telegraphs, *Go ahead, I got you, girl.* I glance back and forth from Miles to Meow to my phone:

on my way

Chapter Four

Liv

I wait for Emily by the front of Community Brew and Chew, an indie coffee spot midway between her home and university office.

Emily rushes down the sidewalk, her bag flapping against her hip. "You okay?" she asks, concerned because it's rare I send a 911 text. "What happened?"

"Oh, shoot, I'm sorry, was I too cryptic? No emergency. I just wanted to have a conversation that didn't involve my tatas," I reply.

"No problem, I was happy to leave. Wait till you hear why." She pauses, looking me up and down. "Although I will need more explanation about the tatas business first."

Emily and I were touch and go before we became best friends. We'd emailed a few times over the summer when we found out the housing department placed us together at Michigan, thinking it was so great that we were both from the Chicago area. Like, how different could we be?

On our first day, I have to admit that she scared me. She was loud and bold and didn't care what anyone thought of her. That made her wildly popular. My very first impression of Emily was that she was a badass. I could hear one of the girls on our floor fighting with her boyfriend as I approached our shared room with my cart full of suitcases. Before I could even introduce myself, Emily took off like a shot down the hall and strong-armed that guy to the elevator, telling him not to come back until he could control himself. And he was at least a foot taller than her! She was instantly everyone's hero.

As the trimester progressed, Emily went out every night, yet still managed to ace all her classes. To this day, I don't know how she did it. When Emily wasn't cheering her face off in the Big House, she was organizing campus protests and sit-ins. She had so much passion and energy that everyone started calling her Action Emily. She was always doing something to push the envelope. I knew she was destined for big things. What I appreciated is that she could look at me, her polar opposite, and see all I had to offer too. She made it her mission for me to believe in myself like she believed in me. If Emily took a person in, it was like the sun shining directly on them. Everything in her orbit flourished.

I missed her so much when we graduated and she went off to travel the world. She was never quite the same when she got back. She's no longer who she used to be, but in many ways, I wonder if it's a bit of a relief. I wonder how anyone could sparkle as brightly as she did for that long.

It's always quiet here in the shop, perfect for conversations, largely because their in-house roasted, sustainably sourced, ethically farmed, GMO-free coffee product is sort of awful. It's hard to make coffee equally bland, bitter, and acrid, but they manage. That there are a handful of other patrons here today is surprising.

"So, what's up with your boobs?" she asks.

"I bought this new shirt. I hesitated this morning after I put it on because I realized it's a tiny bit lower cut than the stuff I normally wear. But it was so cute with its little daisy print and the ruffled sleeves."

"Mmm hmm. Nothing says pornographic like a floral Ann Taylor blouse," Emily adds. Her humor is a lot drier now, but she can still make me crack up.

"LOFT, actually," I say.

"Same difference."

"Anyway, the problem is, it gaps a little in front, which you can only see if you're taller, or you're standing over me while I'm seated. I made the mistake of trusting my coworkers to conduct themselves like adults. All morning long, they've been passing by my desk, trying to drop office supplies in my cleavage. It turned into a game." I purse my lips. "They're calling it Tittyball."

"Jesus." Emily clamps her hand over her mouth. "This is outrageous, but a small part of me wants to laugh at the sheer audacity. How does the game work?"

I'm prepared for this question because they wrote the rules on the dry-erase board in front of me, like I was a willing and enthusiastic participant. "Points vary depending on what office supply they use, like, a wadded Post-it is two points. I actually have a paper clip wedged in there right now—five points—but I refused to pull it out for them to verify, so now Trevor's mad at me for being a 'poor sport.'"

"What made them think this was okay?" Emily assesses me with a gimlet eye. "May I assume you didn't put one of them in a choke hold and say, 'This is not fucking acceptable,' but instead you tried to peace keep in a situation where you were the victim?"

"Ah, I see you've met me." The guys I work with aren't evil; they're young and immature and no one's ever demanded their respect, including me. Especially me. I just want to get them on the right track before they pull this with someone who has an actual spine and they experience real consequences.

"Although it's not like I'd have put anyone in a choke hold either. Not lately," Emily says, wistfully.

"Spring break, senior year to be exact," I remind her, remembering what little I can of that wild trip down to Daytona.

Emily laughs. "What can I say? I warned those frat guys not to touch the loggerhead turtle. They should have listened to me."

"It's been a while since I bailed you out of jail, huh?" I say, nudging her shoulder with mine. I don't want to admit how afraid I always was for her when she was with BlueLove. Secretly, I'm glad she came home and went to grad school. I doubt she'd have seen thirty otherwise.

"Too long. Don't worry, though, you'll always be my one phone call."

My favorite barista is working. B-Money wears his hair in twists and he has swagger to spare. He does a cool dance spin when he sees me, thrusts his chin up, then says, "'Sup, queen? How you livin'?"

"Hey, B-Money, nice to see you!" I reply with a big smile. Give him a word and I swear he can rhyme it with anything, not just the most obvious choice. He's working on something about how the expression of transgression leads to dispossession and succession.

"B-Money?" Emily says. "Hold on. Shit. Why have I been calling you Blake for the past year?"

He shrugs. "Maybe because it's on my name tag?"

"His shift manager won't recognize his MC name," I explain. "But it's a respect thing. I mean, would you call Jay-Z *Shawn*?"

"If it were on his name tag, yes," Emily says. B-Money and I exchange a *look*. She doesn't get it yet, but that's okay. We'll get her there.

Emily notices our eye contact and says, "Wait, how am I the bad guy for reading a name tag?"

"What's your poison?" B-Money asks. As sour and pungent as the house blend is, that may not be the best question.

"Chamomile tea," Emily replies.

"Since when?" B-Money asks.

"You're Ms. Americano! I never see you without a proper coffee," I add.

"Miles has me on an herbal tea kick. He says that coffee feels 'too confrontational,'" Emily says with a sigh.

I've seen her date a number of men since our first year, and I have no idea how she ended up with Miles. Don't get me wrong, he has a lot going for him. He's honorable and kind. He's successful in his field. Lots of women would swoon over his almost androgynous, pretty-boy looks.

I've never met anyone as smart as he is. Sometimes I'll text him when I get stuck on the daily Wordle and he always nails it, and he's so happy to have been of help. Plus, he's devoted to the same causes as Emily. He'd never lie to her, never cheat on her, but he'll never excite her. Therein lies the problem. There's nothing mysterious about him, no enigma. Emily's always been drawn to men who challenge her, who don't let her call all the shots. She thrives on that push and pull. Without it, she seems lost and bored.

"How about you, Queen?" B-Money asks.

"Whatever you'd like to make," I reply. "I trust you."

"One large confrontation, coming up. Leave room for cream today?" he asks.

"Always, thanks so much!" I whip out my credit card before Emily can get to her wallet. "These are on me. Don't argue."

We sit while B-Money preps our drinks. There's usually something interesting and local posted on the bulletin board, whether it's a place to volunteer or an open spot in a community garden. The board is where Emily found the rescue's adoption ad for Chairman Meow. I was so happy she brought him home. He was the first thing I saw that genuinely made her smile, after everything.

There's a man in the corner I recognize, humming to himself as he types. He has such a nice aura that I'd love to talk to him, but he strikes me as both shy and busy, so I don't bother him. He's sitting one table away from a LuluMom I've bumped into before. She was one of the women who liked pinot noir but didn't *like* pinot noir. She's serving her child quartered grapes while she sips a green juice. (The juices here are also vile.) In the other corner, there's the older, impeccably dressed man who practically camps out here, and he is grumbling at his phone.

Emily fills me in on the spider incident. I don't want to pressure her, but I have to inquire. "I thought you were going to break up with him after the Incident."

We talked about the Incident *a lot* after it happened.

The gist of it is, Miles recently came home with what was clearly a women's pocketbook. He proudly told Emily, "The salesperson called it a satchel." She replied, "Yet, Tory Burch calls it a purse." She argued with him, but he was resolute. Even after she'd proved that it had been part of Tory's 2023 spring women's handbag collection, he thought it was too useful to give up. Emily said she didn't mind what he carried, but between the handbag and his social media, she worried people would mock him. However, his social media comments are super positive—everyone loves his account and he's popular with his students. Emily claimed that she was trying to save him from himself, but I suspect she was just embarrassed by how happily he embraces being uncool.

"I was going to do a lot of things," Emily replies. Her self-loathing is almost palpable. Action Emily wouldn't recognize this person.

I shift, and the paper clip stabs me in the ribs under my right breast. "Ouch." I reach into my shirt and pluck it out. "Five points for me." I hear someone gasp, but before I can look around, my phone pings. I glance at my texts and whisper, "Dang it."

"Such offensive language from a proper lady." Emily motions toward my phone. "What was that about?"

"The other agents found out I'm here. They just texted me their drink orders."

Emily smacks her hand on the table and it startles us both. "Olivia Louise Bennett. You are their *supervisor*. Stop taking orders from that overgrown pack of beer-funneling Peter Pans, literally and figuratively."

"I know." I sigh. "And I would, but I'm already here, so . . ."

"I thought you said you were going to make a stand."

I nod, ashamed. I was going to do a lot of things too.

B-Money delivers our drinks, plus a couple of chocolate-covered cement biscotti, and we sip in silence, content to observe the rhythms of the shop. A well-built guy comes in and posts a new notice on the bulletin board. Now, *he* looks like Emily's type. In college, we'd joke that no neck was thick enough for her. The big guy and the LuluMom chat for a bit, but his back is to us the whole time. Emily practically stares a hole through him. There's no way she can be happy with mild Miles. Just zero chance.

I catch Emily's eye and we smile at each other. The nice thing about an old friend is there's no need to constantly fill the silence with words, as I so often do. Sometimes just sitting with Emily is the balm that soothes my soul.

B-Money busses an empty plate from the happy-as-a-clam guy, whom he calls Vishnu. Vishnu's just so jovial, relishing whatever it is he's doing on his computer. I love seeing folks delighting in going about their lives when they think no one's watching; you learn so much about them.

When the LuluMom takes a phone call, B-Money reaches into a basket by the counter and pulls out a pack of crayons and a blank place mat. He brings them to the little girl with the grapes, and she claps her hands appreciatively. "Here you go, Ms. Hazel. Maybe you can draw me something," he says. (Ahh, her name is Hazel! Just like my great-aunt!)

I watch as B-Money brings a refill to the man who's flummoxed by his phone. "Hold up, you struggling again, my man? Lemme see what the problem is, Michael," he says, setting down the pot.

A young guy, likely a Northwestern student, enters. He's wearing a backpack and surgical mask. B-Money nods at him. "'Sup, bro, I'll get your order in a second."

The guy shrugs, looking up at the menu board. "It's Gucci."

"Let's see what you did." Michael hands B-Money his phone. I can't help but admire Michael's immaculate manicure, with his smooth nail beds and moisturized cuticles. Presenting your best self isn't vain; it's a shortcut to demonstrate your professionalism.

Selling real estate is a detail-oriented business, where a single missing check mark can mean the difference of thousands of dollars. Dirty fingernails, for example, speak to a level of carelessness. While you can be great at real estate *and* sloppy, perception really is half the battle. I'm friends with an agent in another office who now owns two cars, one for transporting her kids and one for clients. She lost a buyer when he sat on a Go-Gurt tube and ruined his pants. That's when she bought the second car.

"It's broken," Michael says.

"I promise you it's not," B-Money replies. B-Money taps the screen and hands the phone back to Michael. "You just had to X out of the app. See? All better." To the new customer, he says, "Okay, my man, what'll it be?"

"How do you think he knows everyone's name?" Emily asks.

"Probably because most of us are regulars. Plus, he writes our names on the cups," I reply. "There are so few patrons, it's probably not hard to remember us all."

"But he didn't ask me," she says.

"You serve the same people all the time, you learn who they are. See? Mine says *Ms. Olivia*. And he drew a crown on it." It's really cute.

Emily turns her cup around. She tightens her lips into a thin line. "Mine says *Liv's Sarcastic Friend*."

"Show me the lie," I say, but before Emily can dole out one of her snappy retorts, everything goes utterly and completely off the rails when the guy in the mask pulls out a gun.

Chapter Five

EMILY

Life can change immediately; that's something we often forget. If we dwelled on it, none of us would get out of bed in the morning.

The robber yanks a rubber horse head over his face and surgical mask, the kind we've all been wearing for a few years. We're used to seeing masks in this postpandemic world, so it didn't trigger my spidey sense like maybe it should have.

The robber fires one shot into the ceiling. Bits of plaster rain down, layering our table with a fine coating of grit and larger chunks. Brew and Chew is in an older building with a tin ceiling, and suddenly my mind goes to the dangers of inhaling asbestos, like *that's* our biggest problem.

Everyone is screaming. The highest-pitched keening doesn't come from Liv or that mom, or even the little girl. Its origin is the man who was so happily working at his laptop moments earlier.

Correction.

Everyone's screaming except for *me*. I'm not doing anything. I don't jump. I don't fly into action. I'm not throwing elbows or high kicks. I just freeze. I'm sitting here like the softest of targets with no means of defense, as the memory of the worst day of my life comes careering back. It's Brazil 2.0, except now I'm just frozen.

I'm more angry than afraid, watching the others scatter and try to conceal themselves, as my mind flashes back to that moment, running from Jeremy into the night. I gave up almost everything I loved as an insurance policy that I would never again be endangered, leaving Brazil and BlueLove for grad school.

What was it all for?

Why did I turn down the volume so far on my big life, only for it to hover in the hands of a guy in a jackass mask robbing the till at a third-rate café?

The other customers look around, all of us silently willing each other to act. Won't someone do . . . something? Is this who I've become? Is this who *we* are? We see danger and we just sit here, maybe recording video on our phones if we're feeling bold? Shouldn't we rise to the occasion? Shouldn't we be the heroes who grimly agree, "Let's roll," as we rush the cockpit, sacrificing ourselves, steadfast in our decision to not let the terrorists win? Aren't we better than this?

When did I become the anti-hero?

How did I get older but not wiser?

Vishnu, who was so happy a few minutes ago, cradles his head in his hands. "This is what I deserve—I lied. I called in sick so I could take this beautiful day to work on my novel. I am so sorry, universe! I am so sorry, everyone!"

The robber turns his attention to the Indian man, bemused. "You couldn't take a personal day?"

"My boss is a difficult man and he will not allow it."

The robber snorts from behind his mask. "You need a new job."

This is surreal.

The robber waves his weapon toward B-Money and says, "You. Cash. Now." Tears stream fast and free down B-Money's face as he complies. It's mean, but I can't help but think, *So much for your street cred, Blake.* Like I have any room to talk. So much for mine.

"There's only twenty-three dollars in here," B-Money says. "Unless you want a few rolls of quarters?"

I need to do something. What's stopping me? Why am I so inert? I spot the LuluMom quietly positioning her little girl behind her as she folds her stroller into something akin to a weapon, or at least a block-ade. That small action spurs me on, gives me a confidence boost. If this lady is ready to fight, I should be too. Diving in headfirst and asking questions later was once second nature to me. I mean, I've taunted a grown man driving a big yellow bulldozer straight at me.

That was *me*. *I* was the "not on my watch" person. I was willing to stare down a bulldozer, not even to save human lives; I was doing it for some scrubby pine trees. These are *people* in this café, with hopes and dreams. There's *a child* in here. *Liv* is in here. What good am I if I can't act when it really counts? When did I deem it okay for my watch to end?

I muster my courage. I ball my fists and rise in my seat, ready to take back the hero's cape. The robber whips around at the sound of my chair scraping the floor and aims at me, and I remember the echo of a single shot that rang out through the Brazilian night as I ran away. I'm briefly sucked under with the grief of that moment and my knees buckle. I can't do it. My spirit is willing, but my body remembers and it won't let me.

The robber shouts, "The rest of you, fast! I want wallets, computers, jewelry, phones. Now!"

All of us comply as quickly as we can, piling him up with electronics and wallets. Michael, the nattily dressed man, must be carrying at least $1,000 in cash, and his bills and credit cards spill out like clowns exiting a Volkswagen. The robber fumbles with his treasure, dropping twenties and Liv's prize cameo necklace because he's having trouble seeing through the eyeholes of the rubber mask.

Liv volunteers, "Excuse me, would it be easier if you use this mesh farmers' market tote I keep in my—"

I pinch her, hissing, "The fuck, Liv? Stop being helpful!"

Quietly, she whispers back, "Helping may get him out of here quicker." She grabs hold of my hand and grips it tightly. I grip hers right back. She's not wrong. Compliance is actually the better strategy. Vishnu and B-Money have already humanized themselves. They're doing what BlueLove taught me to do in the same kind of circumstance.

Michael has complied by giving over his wallet, but he's reticent to hand over his phone. The robber barks, "I said phones too!"

"But I don't know how to save to the cloud!" Michael wails. "I'll lose all my contacts!"

This throws the gunman off his game. "Wait, you mean you can't—ugh." While he tries wrestling the phone out of Michael's surprisingly viselike grip, the LuluMom stealthily pulls a jumbo forty-ounce steel Stanley handled tumbler from her bag. With the grace and strength of a panther, she springs up and clocks him in the face.

I don't know if it's the force of the blow or the element of surprise, but it's enough for the guy to drop his gun. The weapon skitters across the floor to Vishnu, where he promptly pulls his legs up on his chair as though it were a rabid rodent and not the key to getting us out of here alive. The robber lunges for it, but his mask's askew and he's having trouble finding it on the floor.

The mom grabs the stroller's handles and wields it like a bat, catching him across the face, bashing in the mask's muzzle. She slams him again and again in rapid succession. The sounds of contact are ghastly, the crack of metal on flesh and bone. The robber stumbles around blindly, trips over a chair, then collapses briefly into a heap.

No one makes a move to get a hold of the guy, so he's able to collect himself, but he seems almost too hurt to proceed. He'd be so easy to neutralize and restrain right now. Yet he staggers out the door and into a getaway car idling in the bright sunlight right at the curb, as no one else steps up. None of us even gets the plate number. Of course we don't. We just sit in silence, waiting for someone to tell us it's okay.

It is not okay.

Finally, Michael breaks the ice. "I can save to the cloud," he protests. "I was keeping my phone so I could take his picture for the police!" He pronounces the last word as "*po*-lease." There are hints of the South in his accent.

Vishnu chimes in, "And I was going to turn his gun on him as soon as it cooled down."

"Cooled down?" Liv asks, still shaken but also confused.

"Yes. Don't they get very hot when you shoot them?" he replies. Liv shrugs.

B-Money tries to regain his street cred. "And I was gonna toss scalding coffee at him, but I didn't get a chance to brew any."

The LuluMom assesses us one by one, balancing her little girl on her hip. I can feel the disappointment in her fellow patrons radiating from her, but her ire can't possibly burn as fiery as it does inside me.

She shakes her head, sadly disgusted with us. "You all were going to do a lot of things."

Chapter Six

Liv

"Well, I keep a gratitude journal, and I review it every night before I go to sleep. Today's entry will be all about perspective. What happened here has given me a healthy dose of much-needed perspective," I explain.

One of the first responders offered us Mylar blankets. Most of us have wrapped ourselves in them, despite the pleasant temps. The layer of protection feels comforting, even though we look like we all just failed at running a marathon.

"From your perspective, what happened?" Detective Gemelli is nicely appointed in a plaid sport coat, a starched oxford, and chinos. His curly salt-and-pepper hair is well groomed, and he has tiny white lines around his eyes from where he must have spent time squinting (or smiling) in the sun. He pulls a small notepad and a stubby pencil out of his blazer pocket—so old school—but of course the historian in me likes this detail.

I tell him, "My perspective is that I've been afraid of all the wrong things. I've been so scared, to disappoint my family, to come across as rude when I go places like the grocery store, that I allowed myself to be pushed around. And I've been so afraid at work, too anxious about making waves to assert myself. But today has been a gift. I've been shown what I actually should fear in this world. And, of course, I have to appreciate that no one's hurt. In a way, it's like I've snatched victory from the jaws of defeat, like when John Paul Jones—you probably know him best as the father of the American Navy—captured the *Serapis* during the Battle of Flamborough Head. But only metaphorically."

Detective Gemelli glances up from his pad. "Ohhh-kaaaay, so would you describe the alleged perp's build as medium or—"

I didn't want what happened today, but I *needed* it. This was a blessing in disguise. "Are you familiar with the Tudor home on Green Bay designed by Harvey L. Page? It was built right at the turn of the nineteenth century."

The detective makes a note. "Is that where you think the perp went?"

"No, no, I have loved that house my entire life. The pitched roof? The gables? The half-timbering? To die for. Anyway, that house is why I developed an interest in selling real estate, because it meant I could go to historical properties like that every day. And guess what? I worked my tail off, and I finally got the chance to list that place. You see, I've been sending the owner little things here and there for almost a decade, trying to cultivate a relationship. Like two years ago when I found an antique book that described some of the home's original details. So I included a note saying, 'I ran across this about your house and I thought you'd find it fascinating.' And guess what?"

The detective rubs the bridge of his nose. "I'm guessing it has nothing to do with the attempted robbery?"

"No, and I'm really sorry, but I have to get this out because it feels like an epiphany," I say.

A cute paramedic with spiky hair and the name *Washington* embroidered on his uniform approaches. "Is she okay?" he asks, gesturing toward me with his chin.

"Stick around a minute, Washington. She might be in shock," Gemelli replies.

The day I got that listing was the best day of my life, so I naturally recall every detail. "The homeowner called while I was in the Bloomingdale's fitting room. I was standing there half in and half out of a swimsuit because I was going to Miami for the weekend. It was a Miraclesuit, and those can be difficult to pull on because the Lycra's so minimizing. A lot of times you have to size up, but I didn't know that. Anyway, the phone rang and I *always* answer the phone, even if I think it's a telemarketer, because you never know. Success is built on showing up, right? The suit had an asymmetrical single shoulder strap, which I was iffy about because of tan—"

The detective closes his notebook and I take that as my cue to move it along. "It was the lady who owned my dream listing. *She* called *me*. She said she and her husband were thinking about selling because the winters were just getting so hard and they have grandkids in Arizona, and . . . I can see by your expression that part's not important. I'm sorry, it's been quite the morning."

"I bet the Arizona part's important to her grandkids," Washington offers.

"You know what? You're right, thank you. It really is all about the clients for me," I reply. "Anyway, I forgot about my trip to Miami, and instead I went to the appointment over the weekend. When I got to the home, I was feeling confident because I knew everything there was to know about both the house and the neighborhood."

"What school district?" Washington asks.

"Dewey."

Washington nods with approval. "Nice. Fully renovated?"

"Better," I gush. "Complete restoration, all the original fittings, including the leaded glass. Just fabulous." I glance at the detective and quickly press on. "Short of it is, I nailed the appointment. While I was there, I asked the owner, 'How many agents have you met with?' and she tells me, 'Three so far, but I tell you what, I know I don't need to meet the fourth.'"

Washington raises his hand, poised to give me a high five. "And you got the listing?"

"I did." We smack our palms with a resounding clap, and the noise makes Vishnu yelp. "Whoops, sorry!" I say. He nods, wrapping the Mylar tighter around his shoulders.

I continue. "And I thought, *Finally, I'm getting a big listing; all that time selling condos and bungalows has paid off.* I'd tried so hard to get a foothold in the luxury market, but I'd lacked the confidence, and this was my calling card, my way in."

Mr. Washington cheers, but I have to stop him. "Let's not celebrate too hard. You don't know what happened next. I got the listing because I knew my stuff, and I was on cloud nine, just so ecstatic. Then I got back to the office and told everyone, and Jase, he's one of the brokers—"

"That the big Viking douchebag on all the billboards?" Washington asks.

"One of them, yes. He just muscled his way in on the listing. He said I wasn't ready to handle such a big sale on my own."

"Is that a usual thing?" Washington asks.

"Unfortunately, yes. So, I managed the staging and I created all the marketing material and I was there for every showing. I mean, I was the one who came up with the Gatsby-themed broker's open house. It was featured in *North Shore* magazine! It was me who negotiated the deal, getting the seller multiple offers at a price well over asking. It was all best-case scenario, and I proved that I could do it all myself. Yet Jase insisted on splitting the commission because it's his name on the brokerage. Somehow, on the listing I'd cultivated for years, he convinced me that he should get 75 percent of the commission, so I got only 25 percent when it closed. And everyone congratulated *him* for *his* hard work."

"That's outrageous," Detective Gemelli says, now firmly on my team.

"Exactly," I say. "And *that's* the perspective I've gained. I treated the thing with Jase like it was life and death because I'd never actually been in a life-and-death situation before. But today, ta-da! *Perspective.* I feel like going forward, I could be less afraid to claim what's mine." I swear I am going to march back into my office and demand to take the lead on that Arts and Crafts–style house on Sheridan.

"You know what?" Gemelli says. "I'm glad something good came out of this."

"Thank you," I reply. "It means a lot to me that you said that. Also, I just remembered that the robber was wearing suede Golden Goose sneakers, if that helps."

"Nice taste. I'll make a note of it," he says.

A heavyset uniformed officer with a bushy mustache and real "Da Bears" vibe gestures to Gemelli. His badge says *R. Bonaparte.* "You talk to Darby yet?" That must be the LuluMom's name. "You've gotta hear her tell the story; she took that guy all the way downtown. Boom, baby!"

We join the rest of the group seated at one of the long community tables by the front window. Officer Bonaparte waves a meaty paw at Darby and says, "This witness says she took him on entirely alone. But surely one of youse guys helped."

B-Money, Michael, and Vishnu are all in various stages of distress, despondency, and dispassion. But no one seems more bummed than Emily. Action Emily would have had him hog-tied in two shakes, and then we'd all have gone out for body shots to celebrate. I guess I'm not surprised that she froze, but I hope she finds a way to forgive herself.

Bonaparte raises an eyebrow and none can meet his gaze. Darby is completely composed, so much so that she's actually retouching her lipstick. The pale plum-colored gloss really suits her complexion. As Officer Bonaparte bags the busted Stanley mug, he looks at Darby with admiration. "What the hell are they teaching you ladies in Zumba these days?"

Darby lets out a musical laugh and says, "Zumba? Please. I didn't learn any of that at the gym. Absolutely not. I've been training with Zeus at Fearless Inc."

"What's a Zeus?" Michael asks.

"What's a Fearless Inc.?" Gemelli adds.

Darby laughs again, showing off her square white teeth. She definitely grew up in a household with fluoridated water. "Only the best coaching program ever! Zeus showed me how to improve every aspect of my life, my physical, mental, and spiritual acuity. He taught me to channel my fear and turn it into action. You should talk to him; he was here with me earlier; he may have seen something on his way out. I mean, you should talk to him regardless because he is ah-*may*-zing. He took me from a regular old stay-at-home mom to someone who can kick ass on demand."

Huh. Fearless Inc. actually sounds interesting. There are a million places trying to sell this kind of real estate coaching, but those programs always struck me as silly and not genuine. But this one may actually have some value.

"It's like she turned into Wonder Woman without even changing into a superhero costume," Vishnu adds. "I was so grateful. We are all so grateful. Here," he says to B-Money. "Let us show them what she did. You have to have seen it to believe it."

Vishnu mimes hitting B-Money with a cup. B-Money does an exaggerated stagger around the room. Then Vishnu pretends to beat him with the stroller, first the windup and then the massive bat. B-Money crumples to the floor and convulses, pretending to die. Even the reenactment is kind of amazing, only reinforcing my new perspective that today should be a turning point for me.

"Kick ass on demand? Mission accomplished, I'd say," says Bonaparte.

"It was very impressive," Vishnu adds, returning to his seat. "Meanwhile, I may need to buy new pants."

"I can give you the name of my guy," Michael offers. "Yours look like they came from Costco."

"That is my favorite store!" Vishnu exclaims. "They gave me a very fair deal on snow tires."

Michael grimaces. "Pro tip. Don't buy your trousers in the same place you purchase your automotive supplies."

Vishnu nods dutifully. "I will make note of that, thank you."

"Let's circle back to the incident," Bonaparte says.

Darby tucks a few loose strands of honey-colored hair into her high pony. Her daughter is on her lap, chewing on a slice of the shop's grain-free banana bread. Spoiler alert: it's dreadful.

"Once I had Hazel here, I knew I had to protect her at any cost. I never want to be a 'victim,'" she says, making air quotes with elegant, tapered fingers accented with the popular square-tip glazed-donut mani. "Standing around after the fact, wrapped in a shiny safety blanket like a baked potato. No thank you."

"Don't nobody want to feel like a victim," Bonaparte agrees.

As Darby and Bonaparte speak, Emily shucks off her Mylar blanket, growing agitated. Out of nowhere, she says, "I protected a pod of minke whales from poachers in the Southern Ocean."

Bonaparte blinks at Emily, unsure what to do with this non sequitur. The whole table is quiet. (It's a little cringey.) Finally, B-Money says, "Poached whale sounds delicious. Served up with a side of baked potato? Damn, son, crime makes me hungry."

"No!" Emily snaps. "The point was keeping them alive."

No one says anything, and the only sounds are the hiss of the espresso machine and the quiet droning of the other uniformed officer's radio as he dusts for fingerprints. "We were off the coast of Antarctica," Emily adds. Her cheeks are flushed, her pupils dilated. I haven't seen her this agitated since Michigan lost to Notre Dame in 2012. For the rest of the fall, out of nowhere she'd shout, "Fucking turnovers!" because she couldn't let the game go.

Bonaparte blinks.

"It was very cold." Emily's aggravation is growing. I'm not sure what she's trying to get at, but I admit it's nice seeing her passionate. Before Brazil, she was a force to be reckoned with, but she hasn't had that spark in years. Honestly, I'd have been surprised if she had turned into Action Emily. It's like that part of her is dead and gone.

Now, I've heard that officers will often remain quiet while interrogating a criminal (I'm true crime podcast obsessed, thank you) because the guilty will sometimes be so uncomfortable, they'll fill the silence with what amounts to an admission. But what does Emily have to admit? Regardless, words keep coming out of her mouth. Emily clenches her jaw. "We weren't even wearing wetsuits."

Is this a "fucking turnover" moment, I wonder?

There's another pregnant pause before Bonaparte returns his attention to Darby. "Anyway, how'd you hear about this Zeus fella?"

Darby flicks her wrist toward the bulletin board. "A flyer a lot like that one. I found it at Total Foodstuffs about a year ago." Of course, Total Foodstuffs. The Fearless Inc. flyer has little *Contact Us* strips with the phone number at the bottom. "I almost didn't because who doesn't use QR codes these days? But something made me tear one off and here I am, a crime fighter, a hero. Does anything feel better than saving the day?"

Emily's hands are balled into fists, her knuckles white. In a low, vaguely menacing voice, she says, "They sprayed me with water cannons."

Yes. Yes, it is a "fucking turnover" moment. Uh oh.

"The whales?" Darby asks.

"No! The fishermen. But I soldiered on for a just cause," Emily replies. "I know a little bit about being a hero too."

"Guess it's a shame the perp had a gun and not a harpoon. Maybe then you coulda helped," Bonaparte offers. He's trying to be nice, trying to include her, but I know her well enough to immediately recognize that was the wrong thing for him to say.

Emily glowers at the officer.

Washington comes over and does a double take when he sees Emily. "Hey, I met you earlier today with the shower fall. You have had a day, haven't you? Lady, I don't know how to say this, but I think you might be kind of a shit magnet, like trouble follows you."

Emily gives him a half smile. "That is one of the nicest things anyone's said to me in a long time."

See? *Perspective.*

🦋

When I get back to the office, the place has devolved. I shouldn't have left the boys without adult supervision. I don't know why they're here and not out on appointments, or hustling for listings.

Trevor and the other agents are tossing around a Nerf football, which hits me square in the solar plexus, but I'm so deep in thought that I barely register it and the ball falls to my feet.

Today has been so eye opening in so many ways. I feel that we were spared somehow and that I can't let the opportunity go to waste. Like this was my sign that I need to make some changes. I'm not sure how it should look, but I am sure that I need to alter my path. First things first, I feel ready to fight for my Arts and Crafts listing right now.

"Where are Chase and Jase?" I ask, looking at their darkened offices. I want to take advantage of this adrenaline rush and reclaim what's mine while I have the guts.

"Spain," Jackie replies.

Damn. I may not have the courage if I have to wait for them to return. Should I call? Or email? Or would it be better to do on Teams? What about Zoom? If they could see the determined look on my face right now—

"Yo, boss lady?" Trevor says.

I snap out of my fog. "I'm sorry, yes?"

Trevor points to the Nerf. "Little help?"

I paste on a smile, because I always want to appear professional, and I pick up the ball. But Trevor must notice that something is amiss because he approaches me, sitting down on the corner of my desk. "You okay?"

I'm quick to dismiss his concerns. "Yes, of course."

"Really?" he presses. "'Cause you look like ass."

I find myself telling him all about the robbery, and I'm pleased to note that he listens intently. There may just be hope for him yet. I explain, "Ultimately, everyone's fine, but it was scary."

"Dude, that sucks."

I'm encouraged by his rare flash of empathy. If he can develop that, really home in on his people skills, he may have a future as an agent after all. "Thank you, Trevor. It did suck." He tentatively places a palm on my shoulder, awkwardly attempting to comfort me. You know what? It feels good to be seen, to be heard, to be—

He says, "So I guess the robber stole our drinks?"

That's it.

That's my moment of Zen.

That's when I tuck the Nerf into my tote bag and march out of the office. On the street, I stuff the ball into the nearest garbage can before driving back to Brew and Chew. When I enter, I pass the few members of law enforcement still milling around and head directly to the bulletin board to stare at the flyer for Fearless Inc.

Are you tired of being afraid?

Do phobias prevent you from living your best life?

Does your inability to say no make you miserable?

Is your fear of success keeping you stuck?

Then call Zeus at Fearless Inc. and learn to master every aspect of your life!

You know what, Zeus? I'm ready. It's time.

I tear off a strip, and it takes me a moment to realize that while the bottom of the paper was full just a few hours ago, now half of them are already gone.

Chapter Seven

Emily

Staring out my window, I focus on the faculty lounge. Someone appears to be having a late lunch; it looks like tuna salad. I don't have the wherewithal to fret about it being dolphin-safe. I'm too mad at myself for my performance at the Brew and Chew. The old me never would have frozen up. Darby called me a baked potato, and that's what I feel like. Jacketed in a beat-up papery shell, full of uselessness and empty carbohydrates.

There's a knock at my door, and before I can say anything, Taylor and her clone, Hailee, let themselves in. "Please, come on in, door's open," I say. My sarcasm doesn't register.

"Hey, Professor Doctor?" Taylor asks. *Argh. How is this my life?* "I told Hailee you were cool with late submissions?"

I eye Hailee, who is chewing gum with an open mouth and nary a thought in her head. "Were you also at the protest?"

"Huh?" Hailee asks. She's in my 8:00 a.m. class, and every time we meet, I'm surprised at how much makeup she manages to apply before class. I literally rolled out of bed as an undergrad, some days not even changing out of my pajama bottoms. What time does she get up to paint all those contoured lines and angles on her face, let alone whatever she does to make her lashes long enough to touch her eyebrows?

There's a degree of commitment I should appreciate here, misguided though it is.

"The salads?" Taylor prompts her.

"What, ick, no. I was in line at Sephora. Fenty's new Gloss Bomb lip gloss dropped," Hailee says. She puckers her overinflated lips. I'm concerned if she bumps into a plate glass wall, she'll suction herself to it. "Check it out, I'm wearing Fu$$y. Do you love? I love, no cap. It's giving clean-girl energy."

I must appear confused because Taylor clarifies. "She's hyping up for hot-girl summer."

I feel a wave of weariness wash over me, threatening to pull me under. "You do understand that I can't accept that excuse for a number of reasons? This paper is one-quarter of your grade. If I have to fail you, you'll need to get ready for hot-girl summer *school*."

Hailee's response is to work her gum more aggressively and slow-blink at her counterpart. Taylor informs me, "Professor Doctor, I'm not sure if you know? But the university code of conduct says that if you make an exception for me, you have to make one for everyone?"

Another wave hits me. I have just been bested—by freaking *Taylor*. I have a doctorate and $68,000 in student loan debt, and I have been bested by a fool who fights for feta. In unison, Hailee and Taylor drop their papers on my desk and both call out, "Byeee!"

They're not even out of earshot when I hurl their papers at the door in impotent rage.

I can't go on like this.

I need a change.

❧

B-Money is behind the counter when I enter today. I guess I thought that after yesterday, he might have quit. There's a casually but expensively dressed woman seated at the counter. Her blonde pageboy is preppy and ageless, and her white shirt is so starched, it could be considered a weapon. At first glance, I think it's Martha Stewart. As bizarre as the past twenty-four hours have been, why wouldn't Martha be hanging out in Evanston?

B-Money seems genuinely happy to see me. I guess now that we've been through a trauma together, we're bonded. "Yo, Liv's friend. This is Bitsy, my moms."

"I'm sure this lady has a name, Blake. Perhaps you'd like to use it?" Bitsy asks, but it isn't a question. Though her face is kind and smiley, I detect a steel spine. What she posed as a question telegraphed like a command. My suspicion is confirmed when we shake hands; her grip causes me to gasp.

B-Money immediately snaps into a different mode altogether. "Hello, Emily, how may I help you? May I serve you another chamomile tea?"

I'm wondering if B-Money called his mom because the incident yesterday scared him so badly. Despite being well into middle age, this woman looks like she could kick ass on demand. Calling her in to be his muscle probably wasn't a bad choice.

"Espresso, please. Make it a quad."

He gives me a wry grin. "You feeling confrontational?"

"Yes, I am."

"True dat." He glances over at Bitsy, who is watching him intently. I suspect that this lady doesn't need Zeus to train her to be a badass; it just comes naturally. She radiates power and confidence. "I mean, yes, given yesterday's circumstances, I support you in that endeavor."

As he fires up the espresso machine, I find the flyer on the bulletin board and tear off one of the few remaining strips. I've been searching for something for a while.

Maybe Fearless Inc. is what I've needed.

Liv and I idle in front of a warehouse with its blacked-out windows. The GPS directed us to this sketchy neighborhood on the city's near west side.

"We're here," I announce.

Miles was terrified when I mentioned I was driving into the city. He asked me three separate times to text him when I got here, and he's already checked in twice. I should appreciate his concern, but I'm largely just annoyed. Also, Chicago has some problems, just like any other large city. But to hear Miles talk about my town like it's completely lawless grates. He's from St. Louis, the city with *the highest violent crime rate in the country*.

Someone recently created a line of merchandise with the slogan "Shut the fuck up about Chicago," and I am tempted to purchase a shirt to wear around Miles. Granted, as I ease my dusty old Prius into a parking space, I am concerned about being abducted and sold into sex slavery, but I am shutting the fuck up about Chicago because it's probably fine.

We approach a half-open metal garage door on the loading dock. "Should we?" Liv asks. She sounds anxious. I can't say I don't feel the same, but I want to come across as brave for her. It's like how you look to the flight attendants on a choppy flight. If they're fine, thumbing through their phones or chatting with their coworkers, it's a sign that all is okay. But if they're panicking, clasp your knees and find religion.

I want to give Liv some flight attendant energy, a flash of the old Action Emily. "What's the worst that could happen?" I reply, hiding my anxiety. Besides, the way the clouds are gathered, it's about to start raining, so we're better off indoors. "Do the math. I've already been confronted at gunpoint multiple times in my life, almost run over by three bulldozers, shot with a half dozen water cannons, and chased by poachers, and once I was on a plane that briefly lost pressure and was too small to have oxygen masks. Also, there was the time I found that eyelash viper in my sleeping bag. Statistically, you're probably safe with me. Let's do this."

I don't want to say that I'm unkillable, because that tempts fate, but I have narrowly avoided disaster with more frequency than most. Besides, I have to press on. The prospect of changing my life for the better is too powerful to ignore. I want Action Emily back, and if I have to make some sacrifices, so be it. Liv seems to relax after my pep talk.

We make our way down a dark hallway toward murmuring voices as Liv grasps my sleeve. We enter the fluorescent-lit, hangar-like room. I survey the surroundings, taking in everything and seeking out emergency exits (old habit). There's a boxing ring in the middle of the room, and lots of free weights. Metal folding chairs are arranged around the ring. A few of the seats are occupied by people I recognize. Everyone involved in the café robbery is here, save for the lady with the little kid.

"I see we've gathered the whole sack of baked potatoes," I say as I choose an empty seat closest to the boxing ring. And exit door.

B-Money offers me a fist bump and I return the gesture. "Hey, Liv's friend," he says.

"Hey, Bitsy's son," I reply. We've definitely bonded.

"My moms sent these for you." He hands me a gorgeous hand-woven basket covered in a checked napkin.

"What? Wow, that's so nice. What are they?" I ask, peeking under the cloth. When I peel back the parchment paper, I spy rows of perfectly symmetrical little squares, topped with a mirror-smooth chocolate glaze that's so shiny I can practically see my reflection. The scent of coffee and cocoa is overwhelming and intoxicating. I normally avoid chocolate because so few companies use ethical or sustainable practices, but I'm not sure I'll be able to resist these.

"Triple espresso brownies. Moms said we'd all be better off if we were more confrontational." Then he holds up a finger like he remembers something important. "She also said to tell you the chocolate company's profits benefit Dian Fossey's gorillas, and the coffee is shade grown and supports Indigenous farmers."

"How did she know I'd love this?" I ask.

He shrugs. "You guys talk. I eavesdrop," he replies.

I really am pleased about the chocolate. If a civilian saw the damage even one multinational conglomerate has done to the rain forest, they would never touch mainstream chocolate again. Last year, we lost something like eleven soccer pitches of primary rain forest *per minute*. And without these crucial natural resources, we're never going to limit global warming to preindustrial levels. That his mom cared enough—knows enough—is touching.

Delighted to be relieved of baked-goods guilt, I tear off a small bite and suddenly feel like I've been punched in the tastebuds with a bag full of espresso beans. I mean this in the best possible way. "Holy shit, please tell her thank you and that this is the most delicious thing I've ever tried. You should get your mom to supply the café with these."

"Negatory. I don't want people comin' in for fresh brews or tasty chews getting in my business. I'd never have time to work on my music."

"Fair point." I look around the room, and Vishnu does a two-handed wave like a little kid, the eagerness just spilling out of him. Michael seems less enthusiastic as he shoots his cuffs and adjusts his pocket square.

"So," Liv says, "who's ready to master their life?" Liv immediately starts her nervous talking thing, trying to be everyone's favorite cheerleader. Occasionally her prattle can fall into restating-the-obvious territory, but that's who she is. We should all be so lucky if our biggest fault is being incredibly friendly.

Our first couple weeks of college, I thought she was going to drive me to distraction with her constant stream of sunshiny chatter. She's a morning person and she was up at 6:30 a.m. every day—even weekends. She tried to be quiet, but the second she saw me move, she assumed I was awake and ready to converse, despite having rolled back into our dorm room a couple of hours earlier.

I'll never admit this to her, but I actually talked to our resident advisor about changing rooms. I didn't think I could deal with her constant babbling. As an only child, I was used to quiet and privacy, and the transition to sharing everything (with a smile) was disconcerting.

My RA was a lot better at figuring out people than I was. She helped me understand that chitchat was how Liv was trying to adjust to her new life, and I'd be better off if I leaned into it rather than fought against it. Eventually, Liv and I got into a groove, and I learned to appreciate her ability to talk to anyone about anything, to look on the bright side. The two of us were yin and yang in those days, balancing each other perfectly. Together, we were unstoppable, especially as I'd get us into trouble and she'd ease us out of it. She's the only reason I wasn't kicked out of the dorm after that incident with our neighbor's barn-dance date who didn't consider "no" a complete sentence. We were the best team.

Liv's ability to make sure everyone feels comfortable and included is a gift, and I need to make sure I remind her of that.

"Who's ready to be fearless?" Liv adds, and I give her my biggest smile and an enthusiastic nod.

Vishnu immediately raises his hand, just full-on pick-me energy. He beams at Liv, and when she smiles back, he blushes a deep purple. I realize that I may not be the only person in this room who needs to change the way they interface with the world.

Michael checks his watch. "It is now 7:04 p.m. Apparently, promptness is not a Fearless Inc. virtue."

B-Money looks at his phone. "I got 6:59, bro."

Michael taps the face of what is surely an expensive timepiece. "This is a precision Swiss watch."

"That runs precisely five minutes fast," B-Money replies.

From the dark perimeter of the vast room, a man emerges from a smoky corner, timed precisely to a clap of thunder and lightning flashes. Everyone gasps.

As the haze around the man clears, we get a better look. He appears to have been minted in the John Cena/Jason Momoa/the Rock factory. Liv squeaks and quickly pinches my arm. I swat away her hand. She has no need to point out his obvious lats or baked-ham-sized thighs or the thickness of his neck; I am well aware. I'm glad I'm not standing, because a specimen like this leaves me weak in the knees. I grew up staring at the framed Monsters of the Midway poster my dad had in his office from when the Bears won the Super Bowl. When I was growing up, even though I'd eventually learn we shouldn't judge based on appearances, that's what I thought men were supposed to look like. That predilection stuck. I've been a Bears fan—and big-guy fan—ever since. Give me a Kelce-brothers type every day, and twice on Sunday.

In a deeply timbred voice, the man says, "Tolstoy said that happy families are all alike, yet each unhappy family is unhappy in its own way."

The Greek god man pauses to step fully out of the shadows. He commands the room with his silence and strikes a power pose, which he holds for an uncomfortable length of time. There's another well-timed flash of lightning as some inexplicable wind howls.

It's weird. And annoying. And a little bit hot.

Vishnu immediately raises his hand, and the man nods, permission to speak granted. "Shall I take notes?" Vishnu asks.

"At Fearless Inc. we say that the strong are all alike and the weak are each weak in their own ways."

"I'm going to take notes," Vishnu confirms to no one in particular, whipping out a small tablet and a stylus.

I look around at all the rapt faces and have to wonder what in the fresh Tony Robbins hell is this nonsense. The only thing missing is AC/DC's "Thunderstruck" playing in the background while this man poses and flexes for another thirty seconds.

The Adonis man finally says, "Let's address your physical weakness first. Everyone, grab some boxing gloves and—"

I interrupt, "Um, hi, are you planning on introducing yourself or is this all part of your little act? I'll go first. I'm Dr. Emily Nichols, the academic kind, not the physician kind."

I try to ignore how Liv keeps poking me in the thigh, like every one of my senses isn't already aware of his being.

"Ah! I *am* the physician kind!" Vishnu blurts. "Dr. Vishnu Rai, at your service!"

I say, "See, that's how it works. You say your name and we tell you ours."

Thor, god of Thunder The guy approaches and levels his gaze at me. Are . . . are his eyes topaz? I thought that color only existed in romance novels. After another inexcusably long pause, he says, "I'm Zeus."

Oh, wait, *this* is Zeus. This is who Darby was going on about.

"Zeus what?" They have to be colored contacts, right? No one looks like this in real life. The last time I saw eyes this color, I was face to face with a tiger cub I'd helped rescue in Myanmar. Liv pinches me again.

"Zeus It's-Not-Important."

Wait, what? No. Not acceptable. "Seriously?"

"I'm always serious." He delivers this line with a glint in his gemstone eye, almost as though he knows this is something Miles says that makes me redline.

Vishnu scribbles furiously during our exchange.

Zeus says, "You've come to Fearless Inc. because I know what's wrong in your life and I'll make it right."

I'm not buying it. How would he know what my problem is? I didn't even fill out a form or anything. My entire social media is just retweets of environmental infographics, so there's not much about who I am as a person, what I love, desire, or want, other than fewer carbon emissions. (I don't even post shots of Meow; I leave that to Miles.) Besides, I'm not sure *I* know the answers to those questions anymore. When I was completing tenure paperwork, I had the hardest time stating my goals. It's incredibly difficult to look forward when all you want is in the past.

Under her breath, Liv whispers, "Miles *who*?" but I ignore her.

"Just like that?" I say. "How can you know how to help us when you've never even met us? It's not possible, unless you're some kind of roadside psychic who specializes in cold reads."

"It's probably all part of the job, right?" Liv offers, trying to defuse my newfound—or maybe refound—aggression.

Zeus appraises us, and I try my hardest not to let him win me over, but his physical presence makes it difficult. I mean, does he have an auburn man bun? Check. Angular jawline? Check. A scar on his right cheek with an otherwise flawless face character? Check. Does he appear to have been chiseled out of a single slab of marble? One hundred percent check. Not that it matters, right?

Regardless, here? Today? I am too old and too jaded to simply fall for a handsome and perfect physical specimen snake oil salesman. You know what? I'm already over this Fearless business. I'm not sure what this guy is after with all the cheap stagecraft, but I don't buy it. And that makes me angry, because I need change, not amateur dramatics.

Zeus says, "You mean, how can I help Liv learn to self-advocate?" Liv's entire expression changes, and I can see that she's already Team Zeus one line into all of this. She lets out an audible gasp. Damn it, Liv. "Or Vishnu gain confidence in his talent?" Vishnu flushes purple again, but this time he's also nodding. "Find direction for rudderless B-Money?"

"Yo, I think he's been talking to my moms," B-Money whispers to me.

"Make Michael comfortable with technology?" Michael uncrosses his arms and legs, leaning forward in his seat.

I'm not convinced.

"Or tap into the courage that once defined you, Emily?"

I let that marinate for a long beat. Finally, I reply, "Boxing gloves are where, now?"

Chapter Eight

Liv

"Damn, you pack a wallop, girl," B-Money says, rubbing his jawline. "You might have some repressed rage and shit." We're in our third week of training, and I'm really coming to enjoy our sessions. Mostly we've just boxed, which feels more and more cathartic.

"I'm so sorry," I tell him. "I promise you it wasn't intentional."

"Listen, if this is what we gotta do, I'm here for it. We're Gucci," he tells me.

I still feel terrible about how hard I hit him. I didn't know I had it in me either, yet a bit of me feels proud about it. Like I have a secret power I'm just discovering each week. When we started to spar with each other a few weeks ago, I thought it would be more like when I took that cardio boxing class, you know, making the motions, swiping at air. Whoosh, whoosh, duck, weave. I never imagined my fist connecting with anything.

Given how exhausted I am tonight, I wasn't expecting much from my own performance. Deandra had to work an overnight to do inventory, and at the last minute, my mother couldn't be with Tommy and Tiki, due to menstrual cramps. Given her hysterectomy twenty years ago, it's physically impossible, but I think dragon pox is too.

So the kids came up to my place last night, and in the few moments they weren't full-contact, MMA-style fighting (Tiki's a biter, that's new), they were tearing through my place. I lost two vases, an end table, and my favorite antique bowl, all within the first half hour. Tiki left tooth-marks in my leather handbag. I'd be okay if a dog chewed it, because they don't know any better. But a seventh grader should.

I try to accommodate my niece and nephew; I try to give them what they want, because I have the resources. Unfortunately, from watching the other women in our home, they've learned that what adults say or do for them doesn't matter, so they have no respect for me or my rules and don't appreciate any of my sacrifices.

I should be tough, but I can't help but feel sorry for them. Deandra's always working, and their useless father (Dee's words), Dusty, is too busy with his new life to bother. It must be hard for the twins when their dad has no time for them and Dee's perpetually in a foul mood for having to do all the caretaking.

I'm lucky that my dad was diligent in keeping up with us after the divorce and I never felt like he left *us*. I had a front-row seat to my parents' marital problems (largely stemming from my mom's unhinged behavior), so I understood why Dad had to get out. Honestly, summers and vacations at his house were a treat. Eventually, when he married my stepmother, Judy, she became the mother figure I always longed for. Judy took care of me instead of me having to caretake her. She did everything to make me feel welcome, from embroidering my name on the pillows in my room to recording all my favorite shows. I used to feel terrible about having a nice time in Michigan, so I'd lie to my mom and say we'd had no fun at all. If I'm at all well-adjusted, it's because of Dad and Judy. When I get married, I'm hoping they'll walk me down the aisle together.

I wish that the divorce had been a wake-up call for my mom, but it only increased her perpetual victimhood. She never did (or does) accept blame for her actions. Her narcissism opened the door to her hypochondria. She's been spiraling for years, and my only defense is to comply.

Anyway, I did what you're never supposed to—I negotiated with the terrorists. To get them to sleep, Tommy demanded I buy him a Nintendo Switch Lite. That was easy and cost less than $200. Done. For Tiki, I had to obsessively refresh Ticketmaster until 4:00 a.m. There were rumors of a secret drop for a Taylor Swift show at Soldier Field. The drop never happened, and now I'm tasked with procuring tickets from a reseller. They start at $1,700. Each.

I know all too well how this story ends.

After a night like that, I just thought I'd sit in the background today, and I was surprised how quickly I got into the boxing part of this evening's session. When we first started, I'd throw weak little jabs. Zeus would stand next to me, encouraging me to let go of what was bothering me. The more I thought about my daily life, the harder I hit. I was all, *Really, Jase? A seventy-five/twenty-five split?* Wham! *No, Dee, I'd be happy to cancel the dinner reservations it took me two months to get so I can babysit for your terrors.* Bam! *Sure, Trevor, help yourself to the pricey champagne I bought as a closing gift for my clients!* Slam! *You feel dehydrated, and instead of just drinking a Gatorade like a normal person so I can go to my scholarship pageant, I have to take you to the ER again, Ma? Sure thing!* Ka-bam!

I guess there is something primal about putting on the gloves and getting out all the aggression, even though I'm afraid I may have hurt B-Money tonight. After a particularly solid right hook, I swear I saw little cartoon birds circling his head.

Zeus's training approach has been different for each of us. When sparring with B-Money, he withholds his swing every time B-Money spits a rhyming bar. For Vishnu, he's the very model of gentle encouragement, getting into the physiology behind where to hit. He explained that you don't have to be powerful so much as smart. Vishnu loves the scientific aspect. Vishnu—we've learned—works for his parents' radiology practice. Turns out, that day in the Brew and Chew, he'd been trying to write a romance novel. How sweet is that?

With Emily, Zeus makes a point of mansplaining the exercise to her and then watches with a smirk as she swings away at a punching bag. Emily has no trouble tapping into her anger, and it's honestly nice to see.

Michael is a successful ad exec, and his longtime assistant just retired. He has no idea how to do anything technological, so he's feeling a bit like a dinosaur. There was a whole incident where his new phone accidentally captured an unfortunate photo (read: dick pic) while he was in the bathroom, which he somehow sent to everyone in his contacts list. Had he not owned the agency, he'd have been fired. As is, he lost a ton of clients and doesn't want to show his face (or anything else) at this year's Clio Awards. For every swing he agrees to take—made particularly difficult by his wardrobe choices—Zeus talks him through something technical. Tonight, it's about uploading Uber to his phone. I have to give Zeus credit. He's right about the weak being weak in different ways.

We're back in the folding chairs, waiting to begin the second part of tonight's training. Zeus just toweled off, and don't think I didn't notice Emily biting her bottom lip. She believes she's so discreet, but I know her tells. She's done nothing but complain about him now for weeks. She never obsesses when she doesn't care.

Zeus returns. His back is ramrod straight, and he's holding his hands behind his back, which causes his biceps to ripple. A bead of sweat rolls down Emily's temple, and I'm pretty sure it's not from the sparring; she finished her turn thirty minutes ago. "You've been taking the first steps in a long journey."

We all beam like kids on the nice list on Christmas morning, emboldened by our individual performances. "Now, tell me what you each fear."

See you later, smiles.

Zeus says, "You can't conquer your fears if you can't name them."

Vishnu's hand shoots in the air. "Me! I will name them! I am afraid of change. And new things. I am afraid when I can't prepare myself for what is next."

B-Money looks at him. "But that's life, bro."

Vishnu nods enthusiastically. "Yes, you are correct. I am afraid of life."

"That was a really brave share, Vishnu," I tell him, folding him into a side hug. He gasps but lets me pull him close.

"Hey, Dr. Creeper, did you just smell her hair?" Michael asks. He's sort of bitchy, but somehow it adds to his charm, like we could sit on a porch with cocktails and canapes and gossip.

"It was not intentional! I am sorry! My face was there and I had to breathe," Vishnu protests. "I couldn't *not* notice the wildflower and citrus of the shampoo."

"Sweetie, you're fine," I tell him, and he grins. When I release him from the hug, he leans against me for a moment.

"I am willing to share more," he offers. Emily says Vishnu has a crush on me, but I'm not sure that's possible. I think he's too shy to like anyone.

"Liv, how about you?" Zeus asks. "What do you fear? What keeps you awake at night?"

I consider his question. Whoa, there's so much I fear that I'm not even sure how to articulate it all. But if I condense it down, I'd say mostly I'm afraid of disappointing the people in my life, of being any sort of burden or trouble. That's pretty universal, right? Don't we all want to be pleasers to some degree?

I was always a good kid, but I didn't consciously try to be the shiniest, happiest person until my parents split. I didn't want to be yet another one of my mom's problems. I earned straight As and I never stepped out of line. Dee went the other way. When I was in the library or at majorette practice or volunteering at the senior center, she was smoking behind the gym, dating guys who drove panel vans, and skipping school. One time she came home drunk with a tattoo across her lower back. (She had the word "Jailbait" made into an orca whale after her kids were born.) Dee craved the attention, negative as it may have been, so she sucked up all of what Mom had to give.

I can't help wondering if Zeus wants me to say all of this, or maybe he wants me to tell him something more specific, more actionable, something that could be cured by cognitive behavioral therapy? I'm so afraid of not giving him the answer he wants that I can feel my heart palpitate, so I blurt out the easiest phobia I can articulate. "I have a real fear of enclosed spaces. I'm super claustrophobic. Whenever I have a stress dream, it's always about me being stuck in a confined area." Dee once locked me in her closet and then forgot about me. Between the dust and the dark and the pungent tang of her gym uniform, I was not okay.

Zeus nods and seems satisfied with my answer. Relief relaxes my shoulder muscles. Emily coughs the word "bullshit" into her hand, and I can't meet her eye. Okay, maybe claustrophobia isn't my *biggest* fear, but it is up there. I give her a tiny pinch and she laughs at me.

"What about you, Michael?" Zeus asks.

Michael shoots his cuffs again, which I'm picking up as one of his tells. "Other than technology? Honey, I'm afraid to get dirty. I mean, look at this suit. It's Brunello Cucinelli."

"Yo, that sounds delicious," B-Money says. He's not wrong.

"Why do you wear suits to our training sessions?" Emily asks.

Michael is puzzled. "Why wouldn't I?"

"Are you mysophobic?" Zeus asks.

"Of course not, why would I be afraid of chickens?" Michael says, brushing imaginary dust off his lap.

"That's not what that means," Emily whispers to me. I shrug, making a mental note to look it up later.

"Then how about you, Blake?" Zeus asks.

"Well, you're getting into it right there," B-Money says. "When I hear the name Blake, I'm triggered about how much I'm disappointing my dad, and that scares the living shit outta me."

"He doesn't support your music?" I ask. "Has he heard you? You're really talented."

"Truth bomb? I'm afraid to perform in front of a crowd, so he's never had the chance. That's one problem. The bigger problem is, he wants me to go into the family business, but I can't. I don't mess with bugs," he replies.

"Are you afraid of spiders too?" Emily asks.

"Not the ones around here," he says. "They're all pretty harmless and small."

"Exactly!" Emily crows. Everyone's puzzled by her outburst but me. Miles spent days after his shower fall with ice packs and ACE bandages around his head, even wearing them on campus. Emily was mortified.

"What's your family business?" I ask.

B-Money looks oddly sheepish. "My dad's an exterminator." That strikes me as an honorable job. It sounds like he's an entrepreneur. No one gets rich working for someone else, which is a thought I should stick a pin in because Chase and Jase are doing my financial future no favors. They still haven't given me the chance to talk to them about the Sheridan Arts and Crafts, and every day they blow me off, I get a little bit angrier. It's been three weeks! I set a goal to get this straightened out by the end of the week . . . or else.

(I have no idea what I mean by "or else," but I like thinking it.)

Emily peers at B-Money more closely. Something seems to dawn on her. Her eyes grow huge and color rushes to her cheeks. For a second, she looks like my old college roommate again, only thankfully without that unfortunate foray into locs. "No. *No.* Hold the phone. Is your dad *the Exterminator?*"

"Did y'all not hear him just say that?" asks Michael, perturbed. His natural state seems to be cranky, sort of like an old cat.

B-Money responds with an embarrassed shrug, and Emily literally flies out of her seat, like she got hit with a lightning bolt or someone dumped scalding hot coffee on her lap. "Oh, my God. *Oh, my God.* Do you know what this means? Oh, my God! Your dad is the Exterminator! Your father is one of my idols!"

"Did you have a terrible infestation?" Vishnu asks, profoundly confused.

Emily is more excited than I've seen . . . possibly ever. Definitely more than when we beat the Hokies in the Sugar Bowl. More than when she got plastic straws banned in the campus frats. She's literally hopping up and down, absolutely jubilant. "Ahh! I knew your face looked familiar, but meeting your mom threw me off. You guys! His dad is Harris 'the Exterminator' Robinson!"

"Okay," says Michael, dismissive, completely bored with conversations that aren't about him.

"No, you people don't understand! Holy shit! The Exterminator was one of the 1985 Chicago Bears Super Bowl champions! He was a Monster of the Midway! *Your* dad was on a poster in *my* dad's office my whole life! Do you have any clue how many times I've watched him do his piece of 'The Super Bowl Shuffle'? Ah-mazing! Picture it—this total Mack truck of a man trying to clap along with the beat, dancing super awkwardly." Emily clutches her heart. "Wait, does he still have the mullet?" Suddenly her response makes sense. Before her parents retired to Florida, they held season tickets. Emily can go on and on about how only true fans understand the grit it requires when you're huddled in the Soldier Field stands, swaddled in layers of wool and down, trying to drink a beer with mittens and hand warmers, as an icy January wind whips off the lake. No, thank you.

B-Money laughs. "Nah, the Jheri curl was long gone before my time. Thank my moms for that."

Much to everyone's surprise, including her own, Emily begins to rap. "'My name is Harris, but they call me the Exterminator. To all the players on the field, I'm surely gonna terminate ya.'"

B-Money backs her up by beatboxing into his cupped palm.

"'My horoscope says that I'm a Sagittarius. But if you wanna see stars, I'mma grab my Stradivarius.' Then do you know what happens?

He pulls a motherfucking *flying violin* out of the air and the dance music stops and then he plays a dirge as haunting as anything. He's an incredible violinist. Just amazing."

"What in the hell does this have to do with his fear of bugs?" Michael huffs.

I put the pieces together for him. "B-Money's dad was a famous football player in Chicago and now he owns a pest control company. I'm sure you've seen it advertised. They're nationwide."

In unison, B-Money and Emily say his dad's line from the cheesy commercials: "'Then I turned my Exterminator fame into Exterminator infamy.'"

"I have no idea what is going on," Vishnu says, leaning in close, excited nonetheless, like a dog hearing his owners celebrate.

I whisper to him, "What's going on is Emily just found her motivation to keep coming back here." Until now, she's been so iffy about the whole thing.

"Okay! Does that mean you will also be here?" he asks.

"Of course!"

"Then me too." He gives me a cute smile before blushing once again. If this sweet guy can get past his shyness, he's going to make some woman very happy.

When Emily and B-Money start quoting the rest of the ad, Zeus asserts himself. "Emily, when you're finished with your dramatic reenactment, you can tell us what fills you with dread. What keeps you awake at night?"

Emily, her cheeks in high color, considers the question. She shudders and says, "Clowns. I fear clowns."

"What?" I say. She's not afraid of clowns, I know this for a fact. The movie *It* bored her. She's never even been afraid of John Wayne Gacy, and no clown could be scarier than him. We listened to a podcast about him on a road trip a few years ago, and I had to sleep with our hotel room light on that night, while she went down in about thirty seconds.

What's her angle? Before I can say anything else, she pokes my thigh and gives me a pointed look.

"Who doesn't fear clowns? So many people in one tiny car is just unnatural," Vishnu says.

Zeus claps his hands with a mighty boom. It's so loud, Vishnu jumps. "That's it for today. This week, monitor your reactions. Challenge yourself. Consider what bothers you and address it differently. Be back here next Tuesday, same time." Zeus heads back to where his office must be.

"*I'll* be on time," Michael announces to no one in particular. The fact that we've yet to start on time is driving Michael to distraction. I think Zeus does it on purpose.

Emily must still be high on the news about B-Money's dad because she's bold enough to yell after Zeus. "Stop! You can't go yet. You've got to tell us what frightens *you*. This—whatever this is—should be a two-way process. Fair's fair."

Zeus stops and appraises her. "Good point." He doesn't hesitate. "I guess I fear that Taylor Swift will never produce an album more sonically cohesive than *1989*."

"Be serious!" Emily says.

He shrugs. "I'm always serious. I have two great loves in my life: exotic birds and Taylor Swift's music. That's everything you need to know. They are my reasons for existing. Everything in my world goes back to my passion for these two things." He opens a door and exits. Seconds later, we hear the opening bars to "Clean."

B-Money mutters, "My man's a Swiftie. Did *not* see that coming."

I'm still invigorated when I arrive at the office in the morning. Even though I was exhausted, I was too keyed up to sleep, so I stayed in bed later than usual and didn't have time to do my whole healthy smoothie and oatmeal routine.

Feeling saucy, I stopped at the Brew and Chew for a (lousy) latte and a cruller. This doesn't sound noteworthy, but this is the first time I've ever brought food just for myself to the office. I've lived by the "Did you bring enough for the whole class?" rule ever since elementary school. Until today. Now I'm challenging myself to take a slightly different path.

I'm just opening up my laptop when Trevor saunters up. "Hey! You brought doughnuts again!"

Before he can grab it off my napkin, I reply, "No. I brought doughnut. Singular. Just for me." Then I take a bite.

The cruller tastes like glue and cardboard, but the look on Trevor's face is absolutely scrumptious.

Chapter Nine

EMILY

I reread the description one more time to make sure this is the best choice. Per the back of the Benjamin Moore paint swatch: *Hummingbird Green is vibrant, buzzing with energy and confidence.* We have a winner. I'm sold on those keywords alone.

I'm not quite Action Emily, but I do feel different today, like I've taken a step or two back toward her. I'd never have guessed that mixing up my routine or punching things really hard could be just what the doctor ordered, could knock something loose inside me, yet here we are.

I'm tired of gray walls; they make me feel gray. I'm ready to add some color back into my life, and Hummingbird Green is just the ticket. What the description doesn't mention is that it's the color of the Brazilian canopy of jungle leaves at midday, when the sun is filtering down through them, but that's probably only a selling point to me.

The thought of recapturing a tiny bit of the feeling I had when I first entered the rain forest is too profound to ignore. I can't help but think of Jeremy that day by the waterfall. Maybe it's dangerous to paint the walls a color that brings me back to an old love, rather than to my current one, but I sort of don't care.

I texted Liv about my plans earlier and she texted back an endless string of hearts and an I love that for you!!!

"Hi, I want this one," I tell the young paint store clerk. She's a cool girl with pierced eyebrows and a purple streak in her bangs. She sets down her thick Sarah J. Maas fantasy paperback and takes the paint swatch from me.

"Ooh, solid choice—lots of dimension," she replies. "This color reminds me of dragon scales."

I'm taking this as a compliment.

We're in the week before spring finals, so I have time to paint the living room—I'm using the same final exam as last year. A lot of professors change their exams from quarter to quarter, but since my students aren't serious about this class, it doesn't matter, anyway. If the students go into their fraternity test banks and study the answers from the last exam, maybe they'll absorb something. Maybe they'll just pass and move on. I don't care.

As the paint shakes in the giant mixing contraption, I gather what else I'll need: drop cloths, tape, paint rollers, really, everything. I haven't done a single improvement to my place in the two years I've lived there. I plan to tackle the walls later, as soon as I finish office hours, and I'm actually kind of excited. I'll get a big iced coffee, maybe listen to a jam band, make it a party. Miles hates Dave Matthews so I stopped listening to him. Today calls for a little *Under the Table and Dreaming*, I think.

I anticipate my office hours being busy. The kids who skipped all quarter will approach me with Hail Marys to try to pass the class. I'm guessing I'll have at least ten dead grandmas, six ugly breakups, four cases of strep, three work-based dilemmas, two car troubles, and one wild card.

Truth? I look forward to the wild card. The wild card excuse for missing class could be anything from an alien abduction to a blistering case of gonorrhea. That kid I actually believed; if you could choose any lie—and I have heard them all—it wouldn't be that. His attendance had been good prior to his ill-fated spring break trip to Matamoros. He shared more details than I cared to hear. There was some crying as well, ugly crying, necessitating a handkerchief. My advice to him was to (a) take a strong antibiotic, stat, and (b) never again accept a double-dog dare from the buddy everyone called Garbage Mouth. Fun fact: I have yet to fail a single student who's hit me with the wild card. Sometimes their fabulism is the only thing that gets me through the quarter.

When I'm back in my office, my door flies open and Taylor launches in, uninvited. She's all panic, no disco. She's in such a state that she's not even filming herself. "I thought we were dope?" she demands. She waves her term paper at me.

"Dope in what respect?" I ask.

"You said I could turn in my paper late, and then you failed me anyway? I don't get Fs?"

Hoo-boy, that paper was a hot mess. She really should have tried to pass off AI as her own work. She put a lot of effort into demonstrating that not a single thing I've taught this quarter sank in. If possible, she lost knowledge. "Except in this case, you do. I didn't fail you for a late paper, Taylor. I gave you your exception and I didn't penalize you. You or anyone else, for that matter. No, I failed you because you demonstrated zero understanding of the importance of recycling—your chosen topic."

She knots her impeccably sculpted brows. "I disagree?"

I say, "I'm feeling magnanimous today, so I'll make you a deal, Taylor. If you can talk me through some of the concepts, I'm willing to reconsider the grade. Maybe you're better at tests than essays. Does that sound fair to you?"

"I don't know, but okay?"

"Great. Let's do this. So, tell me, what is slurry?" I'm referring to the soupy mixture of insoluble particles, like lime or mud or concrete, often generated on construction sites. It's crucial to test slurry before disposal because pollutants in the mixture can cause higher pH levels and they're often toxic. Improper slurry disposal is dangerous because it can lead to flooding and erode metal. That said, slurry can also contain valuable nutrients that help mitigate ammonia emissions in agriculture. I actually saw how farmers used slurry in Ireland once, which resulted in a long weekend with a ginger named Seamus. This was in pre-Jeremy time. He had a neck the size of a corned beef. It was a glorious three days.

Thinking about Seamus reminds me that I had a pretty exciting life before Jeremy and it's possible I could have one after. (How wrong is it that Miles isn't even in the mix of my thinking?)

If Taylor can touch on any facet of slurry—hell, if she even mentions drinking a Guinness—I'll chalk it up to poor wordsmithery and let it go. She can have her D.

Taylor appears hopeful. "Slurry sounds icy and delicious?"

I am trying to give this to her, I really am, but she has to show me something, anything. "Nope. How about this—what is photodegradable?" This is an easy one. It means capable of decomposing when exposed to light, particularly sunlight. If she just takes the prefix "photo," which means light, and pairs it with "degradable," which means . . . degradable, she's got this. Also, the infographic about this is two feet to her left. She doesn't need to think, she just needs to turn her head and read aloud. I cut my eyes toward it, trying to give her a fat clue.

Taylor chews on one of her pointy nails while trying to come up with her answer. "When you're tagged in a bad Insta?"

"Strike two." In good conscience, I can't pass her if she doesn't demonstrate a kernel of understanding. But I also want her out of my hair next quarter, so I pitch her the lowest, slowest ball I can think of, even though that's totally against my nature. "What does it mean to *go green?*" If she doesn't understand that I'm referring to being environmentally conscious, then abandon all hope ye who enter here.

She screws up her forehead, really trying to work this one through. I can almost picture the little hamster running in the Habitrail of her brain. "Something about St. Paddy's Day?"

Heavy sigh. A first grader could answer this question. "Taylor, you didn't earn an F. You earned an F minus. You literally didn't grasp a single thing I taught you," I say.

"Isn't that more a reflection of your efforts than of mine?" she says with a pout.

Okay, that smarts and maybe requires some self-reflection, but today is not the day. "Your failure is my final answer, Taylor. I suggest you study hard for the final if you want to pass the class."

"But I disagree? And I'd have to retake the class over summer school because I've already got my fall coursework set?"

I shrug. "Again, your destiny is within your hands, not mine. Hit the books. Maybe see if your sorority house keeps a copy of the exam on file and use that as a study guide." I am trying to throw her a bone, truly.

She changes her tactic from righteous indignation to pleading. "But I didn't use AI to write it?"

"Too bad. AI actually knows what it means to recycle," I reply. "Here, I'm going to type 'go green' into Bard AI. It says: '*Go green* is a phrase that means to make lifestyle changes that are more environmentally friendly. It can also refer to products or services that are considered environmentally friendly.' Honestly, Taylor, that's the answer I wanted. I can't simplify it more, and trust me, I wish I could."

Taylor scowls and crosses her arms. "Then why don't I go talk to the associate dean about how unfair you are?"

Ah, I see we've moved on to threats. I came back from Brazil fearful of a lot that never previously scared me, but a ditzy, entitled nineteen-year-old isn't one of them. "Then I'll tell you where to find his office. He's down the hall and to the left. His name is Miles. By the way, don't stick your tongue in his ear; he'll get vertigo."

Taylor lets out a frustrated yip before turning on her heel and stomping off. I chuckle. *If only she'd told me she had gonorrhea.*

"Byeee!" I call.

Probably not necessary—or terribly mature—but damn, that felt good.

"How's *that* for taking a different approach to what bothers me, Mr. Zeus It's-Not-Important?"

Wait, what if I *do* need to know?

I think it's time for a Google search. You can find everyone on the internet if you try hard enough. Fact.

Chapter Ten

Liv

I've outdone myself; everything here feels perfect. The hardwood's gleaming, the surfaces sparkle, and the staging is on-point. This place looks like it stepped straight out of Pinterest.

When I landed this listing two months ago, the owners wanted to put the home up for sale as is. They'd seen how hot the market had been and assumed the ride hadn't ended. Had it been circa 2020 to 2022, they'd have been right to list without the tweaks—people were so desperate to leave the city that they were willing to put in the sweat equity themselves for a taste of the suburbs.

At the height of the pandemic, people snapped up homes sight unseen, with bidding wars that went many thousands of dollars over asking price. You could have set a cardboard box on a weed-choked lot and people would have lined up with their printed-out Zillow listings to tour it. But that was before interest rates went up. Unfortunately, people aren't buying as much now, because they're not anxious to sell and lose their 3 percent rate. So the market has stagnated and upgrades and staging are now essential.

I knew that if these owners let me guide them, we could get this house up to speed and list at a far higher asking price. I convinced them to refinish the floors, paint over their mauve walls in a color that honors the home's history, and update the brass fixtures. It's made all the difference. Persuading them to put their vintage collectibles in storage was the coup de grâce. Now the place feels fresh and modern instead of like the haunted doll museum it was.

There were a lot of dolls.

Like, *a lot*.

I'm such a sucker for a Craftsman-style home. If I'm out and I see a Craftsman I love, I will literally go to the door and try to talk to the homeowner. Armed with an extensive knowledge of neighborhood comps and true enthusiasm, you'd be surprised at how many people will talk to you. Half my listings are this style.

I love the simplicity of this gracious abode. There's something approachable and friendly about its low-pitched triangular roof. Inside, the exposed beams and rafters give everything a warm and inviting feel, and the large windows flood the home with light. (I'm practically writing the MLS listing again!) But this is a home where kids and dogs would happily roam, stylish yet functional and comfortable. The covered front porch is welcoming, with rocking chairs and hanging ferns. I just want to sit out there with a glass of lemonade and chat up all the neighbors. This seems like the kind of neighborhood where the block party would be lit, and no one would try to sneak relish into the egg salad.

I'm hosting an open house, which is not the most effective use of my time, but the sellers wanted it and I couldn't say no. Trevor wasn't wrong about the kind of clientele who frequent these. My serious buyers will make appointments to see the listing when they can take their time and tour the space in private. The majority of the people who show up on Sundays are just looking for snacks after church and they don't have a Costco membership. If I'm very lucky, I get some nosy neighbors. I love when they show up—I can give them my card and see if they have any friends looking to move into the neighborhood. And sometimes when they see how much I'm listing Bobby and Suzy's house for, they want in on the action! But largely, the Open House sign adorned with all the balloons is like a homing signal for the bored, hungry, and weird.

Ever since the robbery, I've been worrying more about my safety when I'm at these things alone. I have pepper spray and emergency settings on my phone activated. I hope that's enough, at least until I get better at all the self-defense moves Zeus promises to teach us.

I pull a beautiful cheese platter from the fridge. It's displayed on a marble cutting board and adorned with all the fixings—seeded crackers, a briny olive assortment, sweet fig jam, and salty Marcona almonds. I place it next to the bottles of water with my picture and contact info on them. You'd be surprised how much business I've gotten because of these, and they cost less than sixty cents apiece! They're the best marketing dollars I've ever spent. I arrange for my waters to be handed out where people are hot and thirsty, like at the finish line of a 5K, at the lakefront, and in dog parks. (I learned this from my real estate TikTok idol, Glennda Baker.) One lady held on to a bottle for almost a year because she knew she wanted me to help her sell when she was ready. She'd gone running and forgotten her CamelBak and said my water felt like a lifesaver.

I arrange the MLS printouts next to a guest book and the cheese on the kitchen island. I fan out napkins and my business cards, then carefully realign a hanging picture by the front door, which suddenly flies open. In rushes a haggard-looking family, the parents in matching Mountain Dew tank tops and four children in various stages of disrepair, all with dirty hands. A mangy dog trails behind them on a rope leash. It snarls at me as it passes.

"Hi, welcome, I'm Liv, thanks for coming!" As jumpy as I've been since the attempted robbery, I'm prepared for *this* kind of chaos. It's as inevitable as the tides. I'll still do my song and dance because I never want to make assumptions based on appearances. I mean, Balenciaga had a runway look made from trash bags last year; you just never know.

The mother barely even glances at me as she breezes past, saying, "Chet, I'm gonna see if there's a medicine cabinet here." The children swarm the cheese platter, and the father pulls a Busch Light from the pocket of his cargo shorts.

Okay, *sometimes* you know.

Chet, the dad, sidles up to me. I tell him, "So glad you're here. This place is a gem, freshly updated, so I'd love for you to see—"

The father leers at my chest. "I already like what I see."

I put one hand on my pepper spray and wrap my blazer more tightly around me. I give him an anxious smile, pretending to be oblivious. Sometimes perverts need two-car garages too. And he's arrived with a minivan full of children.

"The school district here is one of the top ranked in the state. I bet a dad like you—"

He snorts and moves closer. The smell of cigarettes and regret wafts my way. "They ain't mine."

My self-protective instincts kick in, and I begin to herd him toward the front door. I'd rather be outside in full view of every dog walker and family playing hoops than alone inside while the wife looks for Oxy. (*Of course* I have the homeowners stash every valuable, med, or pocket-sized treasure before an open house; it's not my first rodeo.) "Why don't we check out the front porch?" I suggest.

I'm pointing out the features of the flowering magnolia tree on the front lawn as an earsplitting whistle stops me cold.

"Kids!" the mother screams. "Time to hit the next buffet."

The (not) dad winks, takes a card from my hand, and sticks it down the front of his pants. I try not to visibly shudder. The family clatters out the door, causing a framed picture to fall.

I don't even need to look to know the cheese platter is decimated, save for a single olive.

But the steaming pile of dog turds by the gas fireplace is a new one, I'll give them that.

❦

"How'd it go?" Deandra asks me. She has a rare afternoon off, so she's sitting on our front stoop with a Diet Coke, enjoying the sun. Years ago, my dad enclosed the back porches for more storage. Later, my mom paved the backyard for additional parking, so the stoop is the only outdoor area that we've got.

"You want the numbers?" I ask. "Six cheese plates, three indecent proposals, two damaged family heirlooms, and one pile of runny dog shit. Also, zero legitimate leads."

"Yikes, sorry." In the afternoon sunlight, I can see the webbing beneath Dee's eyes and fresh threads of gray in her hair. She looks worn out. It doesn't seem fair that with everything we have in common, her life went so much differently than mine.

The best thing I can do is suffer with her. So I add, "Today was rougher than usual. A couple of senior citizens came in—two older ladies, maybe in their seventies. I knew they were there for the snacks. And I truly didn't care; they're probably on fixed incomes and can't afford little luxuries like nice Gouda, you know? But they come in and go, 'Does this place use gas or electric?' And I say, 'The furnace and stove are gas.' One of them—the leader—tells me she thinks that I'm wrong and I should probably go to the basement and check. I show them the spec sheet, and the second one gives me the stink eye, really insisting I go to the basement."

"Did they just want privacy to steal the cheese?"

"What do you think?"

Dee takes a pull on her soda and then offers me a sip. I oblige. It's warm and flat, exactly the way she likes it. When we were kids, she'd open sodas hours before she planned to drink them, just for this reason.

"I think you probably went to the basement anyway and came back to find they'd wiped you out of forty-seven dollars' worth of Trader Joe's cheese."

I laugh. "It was fifty-six dollars. There were some dried cherries on that platter. You know, some things aren't worth the fight." Although maybe I could stand to develop a little more fight. I'll bring this up with Zeus.

We sit in companionable silence and watch a hipster try to negotiate with his stubborn pug flat-dogging on the sidewalk. Even with the day I've had, sitting on our stoop, I can't help but think of the grassy green lawn of the Craftsman I showed today. The lilacs out front are in bloom and buds are already formed on the peony bushes that line the house. There's a bluestone paver patio and the cutest wooden pergola that would be darling strung with solar lights. The yard is fenced—which might have been nice for that family's dog—and the lot is deep in the back. It's ideal for swing sets and tree forts. Like the Velveteen Rabbit, it's waiting for love to become real.

"He skipped his alimony payment again this month."

Her ex, Dusty, is useless. "Shit, Dee, I'm sorry. How can I help?"

"I have to pick up extra shifts. Can you keep an eye on the monsters, and maybe deal with her?" She gestures with her chin to our mom's apartment.

"What's the malady of the day?" I ask.

"Zika."

"Wasn't Zika like five years ago? And only in the tropics?" I ask. Our mother is getting worse and we both know it. "What are we going to do about her?"

Dee shrugs. "We? *We* are not doing anything. She charges me $600 a month in rent. I'm going to humor her as much as I can because any other three-bedroom around here would be more like $2,500 and I just can't. If I could get that promotion to management, I bet I could. But right now, I've got to smile and nod and keep on enabling. But you? You don't have to be here."

I gesture toward the broken piece of sidewalk in front of our building. "What, and leave all this?"

Dee grips my shoulder. "Liv, I'm serious. I know you worry about me, about us. But you can't let me hold you back. Trust me, if I could escape this place, I would in a minute, and I would leave your skinny ass in the dust. That you can and you won't? I don't get it."

When we were kids, Dee was a demon on her ten-speed. She could ride fast as the wind. As motherly as she was, as much as she took care of me, when we'd get to a straightaway on the lakefront or on Dad's quiet Michigan street, she would pedal like she was being chased by the hounds of hell, leaving me in the dust no matter how much I yelled for her to slow down. So, if she says she would extricate herself if she could? I believe her.

I brush away her hand. "Dee, it's fine, I mean it. I'm not going anywhere."

Yet for the first time that I can remember, I honestly start to consider: *How much better would I feel if I did?*

I picture myself living in today's open house, imagining it to be all mine. I'd decorate it the way I wanted. I wouldn't have to answer to anyone or be subject to the constant stream of their opinions. I'd have privacy. I'd have my own fat pug . . . or two, one black and one fawn, and I'd name them Romeo and Juliet. If someone came in and broke my stuff, it would be a crime and not just an inconvenience.

I suspect I would feel pretty damn good.

Chapter Eleven

Emily

Miles has been sitting across the dinner table making huffing noises every few minutes, as though challenging me to ask what's wrong. He hasn't been eating his farro grain bowl so much as he's been moving the components around. I know he wants me to engage, which is why I've only been mentioning how nicely roasted the broccoli is, how perfectly seasoned the chickpeas are, and how tangy the lemon-tahini dressing is. Now that the living area has that fresh coat of Hummingbird Green, everything tastes fresher, more vibrant.

I spent every free second of my office hours searching for information on Zeus, but he's an internet ghost. I was salty that he wouldn't tell us his last name, so I decided I'd find it out myself. I've vetted more than one creep for Liv this way. While my sleuthing skills are top notch (and research is part of my job), it's like Zeus has invented himself out of whole cloth. But weirdly, instead of making me drop the class and insist Liv do the same, all I felt was energized, and excited about the can of paint that was calling my name. So I made short work of the painting because it gave me a nice break from all my sleuthing.

Finally, Miles sets down his napkin. Meow is perched between us on the table, looking back and forth as though watching a tennis match. I'm pretty sure Miles is pissed, but making him mad is like angering a baby bunny—even at their worst moment, they're entirely harmless, to the point that their ire is kind of adorable. "I just thought you could have talked to me before you painted this place such a garish color of green. My mother will hate this," Miles says. He sniffs disdainfully.

Oh, did I not mention that Miles is a mama's boy?

The pop of color has put me in such high spirits that I can't help but toy with him. "I'm curious, are you suggesting that I get permission from you—or your mom—about the color I paint the walls in my home, the home I bought with my own money, where I pay the entire mortgage?"

I say this with the utmost sweetness. He's smart enough to realize the pile of patriarchy he's almost stepped in. If he says anything else, he'd have to turn in his rather extensive collection of *Male Feminist* T-shirts. He changes the subject, but not before he gives the walls one more withering look. "Um, yes, anyway, I spoke with one of your students today. She was very upset with you."

"Taylor, right?" I nod conspiratorially, leaning in close as though sharing the hottest tea. "Did you tell her it sucks to suck?"

He gasps. "I absolutely did not! I would never! I just wish you would consider the counterpoint that she raised about your actions."

"And what was that?" I stab a broccoli spear and stuff the whole thing in my mouth. So crisp and caramelized! The red pepper flakes really give it some zing.

"That the way you failed her, and then humiliated her in your office, made her feel bad—like she isn't capable of succeeding."

I hold up my pointer finger, which still has bits of Hummingbird Green on the nail bed. I make him wait for me to chew and swallow the large bite. "Yet failing her made me feel great, so you can see my dilemma."

Miles scans the room as though searching for evidence. His gaze lands on my giant iced latte cup. "Have you been drinking coffee?"

I smile and reply, "By the bucketful."

❧

We're full of excited chatter as we gather in the warehouse, waiting for our next session to begin. I don't know if we're supposed to call it training or coaching, but whatever it is, it's making me feel things that have been long buried. Given everyone else's enthusiasm—even Michael, who doesn't seem to register that emotion easily—it's had a similar effect on the rest of the crew. It's been less than a month, but everything already feels different.

I lean into the group and say quietly, "Not only could I not find his last name, I couldn't find him at all. No Yelp reviews, no Facebook. He doesn't even tweet."

"I have no idea what that means," Michael says.

"Who exists in this decade without a digital footprint? Even Chairman Meow's on social media," I say.

"Chairman who now?" Michael asks.

"Her cat," Liv says.

Michael reacts as though I suggested he wear polyester. "Don't give me that face, Michael. It wasn't my idea," I say. "I love the cat with my whole heart, but I have nothing to do with the account."

"Hold up, Chairman Meow with all the matching outfits? With the eyes that take up half his head? And those ears? He's your cat? Whoa! I love that lil guy," B-Money says. "The duet that Sia did with him was off the chain! But who's the pale dude with him in all the pictures?"

"That's Miles. He's my . . . associate dean," I say. Technically, this is true. Liv raises her eyebrows. "And boyfriend."

B-Money looks like he just bit into a lemon. "Bruh. *Bruh.* He's spending too much time getting pretty with that cat. You can do better. He's giving 'I keep my dead mother in a rocking chair' energy."

I don't reply. When Miles said he had to go home last night because the walls were "too loud and I can't sleep," the only thing I felt was relief as I snuggled with the Chairman, happy to have him all to myself. I have to end things with Miles. I'm not happy and I can't imagine that I make him happy. It's like we're a couple by default, staying together for the sake of Chairman Meow, and my apathy has kept me from action. I've chosen security over satisfaction.

The worst part is, it was all my own doing.

I'm grading my first round of exams as an official assistant professor when Miles comes by with more new-hire paperwork. Before he enters my open door, he says "Knock, knock" instead of just barging in, and I appreciate the gesture. It's oddly formal and old fashioned, but not unappealing. Of course, I thought he was cute when I saw him digging in the trash that day, and we got along nicely during my rounds of interviews, but I didn't think too much of it then. I suspect he pushed hard to have the school hire me, as he kept sending me suggestions on formatting my research and how to address upcoming questions. I hadn't had anyone on my team for a while, and it felt good to be the object of his attention.

We chat briefly about how I'm settling in, and I assume he'll leave after the conversation reaches its natural end, but he's sort of poking around in my office, looking at my personal effects.

"Might I ask the name of this handsome gentleman?"

A weird question, but Jeremy had that movie-star it-factor that—

"Those enormous ears!" Jeremy's ears were totally normal, not too big or small or cauliflower-like from boxing or anything. "Those blue eyes!" Jeremy's eyes were dark as coal, deep and mysterious, containing hidden truths.

That's when I notice Miles is holding the shot of my new cat, not my old flame. "The seal point coloring! That wavy coat!" He lands in the wooden chair across from my desk, half swooning.

As Miles starts telling me about all the cats he's loved from afar due to his allergies, I find myself disarmed by his lack of guile. There's no part of him that's trying to be cool or tough or to impress me in any way.

"He's a Devon rex," I say. "Did you know they're hypoallergenic?"

When he lets out a gasp, I realize that this man has something, something interesting and refreshing. He would never be taken at gunpoint from me by Brazilian guerillas. He'd be as safe—and as exciting—as a pair of training wheels. But when you're trying to ride a bike again, sometimes training wheels are exactly what you need.

So, when I suggest he stop by my house to meet the Chairman, he says yes.

If I hadn't made the first move, we'd have never gotten together. I have no one to blame but myself.

When I told Zeus I was afraid of clowns, I had a particular image in mind. I was picturing Miles out on his bike, in his biking outfit, pedaling past a jewelry store, being inspired by a display of engagement rings.

I'd say I don't fear clowns so much as I fear a clown hopping off his recumbent bike to buy me a diamond ring. Making our situation permanent terrifies me.

Liv glances at her phone. "Hmm. It's getting a little late. I wonder where Zeus is."

"Are you sure your phone is correct?" Michael asks. "My watch says 6:55."

"You've got the wrong time again, my man. I think you need a new watch," B-Money suggests.

We sit in silence for a couple more minutes. "I mean, he's late every week, why would tonight be different?" B-Money muses.

"You know, I can Uber now," Michael announces out of nowhere. "Of course, Chairman Meow probably can too."

We continue to wait, each braced for whatever dramatic entrance Zeus has planned. But the longer we wait, the more we begin to doubt our purpose.

"Zeus has given me the confidence to make progress on my novel!" Vishnu says. "Before, I just had an outline, but now I have real words on the page!"

"That's wonderful, Vishnu!" Liv says. "How much have you written?"

He deflates a bit. "Title page, dedication, and half a chapter."

"Zeus has been helpful AF. Last week, I didn't have a plan. Like, I didn't even know how to find open mics. But this week, I suddenly have a plan to . . . google how to find an open mic," B-Money says.

Liv admits, "I brought only my coffee to work this week instead of enough for everyone, and it was so empowering. But later, I bought pizza for the whole office because I felt guilty."

After being so snotty to Miles, I felt bad and bought him and Chairman Meow matching American flag outfits for the Fourth of July, complete with straw boaters. I hate myself for this.

There's some grumbling about how long we should stick it out, and if maybe we shouldn't all call it a night. All the faces that had been so animated when we arrived now look disappointed and defeated, and I'm hit with an epiphany that does not feel good.

"Wait, what are we saying? Are we all saying that maybe we didn't make as much progress as we'd initially hoped? For me, I want this. I need change. I need to fight for us, all of us, like I couldn't do in the coffee shop. What if we're all so afraid of being challenged that we're trying to find bogus reasons to quit?" I ask.

"That doesn't sound like us," Vishnu says.

"Doesn't it?" B-Money replies.

As the minutes tick past, our seeds of doubt root further. Michael looks at his watch. "It's 7:22. Even if my timepiece is slow, he's late. Unacceptably late."

Liv begins worrying her hands. "I can't buy pizzas every day."

I admit, "I don't actually fear clowns."

"Is it really so important that we become fearless?" Vishnu asks.

Silently, we reach a consensus that whatever is going on with Zeus, he's not showing up tonight, so we begin to file out. To stop our momentum now feels like a huge missed opportunity. Like if we walk out this door, the odds are we're not going to walk back in. Liv will get busy doing something for someone. Michael won't know how to schedule an appointment on his calendar to remind him to come back. B-Money will get distracted, and Vishnu will crawl back into his shell. Everything inside me is shouting that we should stay, stay, stay.

I take one final look at the door where Zeus exited last week and think, *We are never ever getting back together.*

In the parking lot, it becomes clear that we're reluctant to part, even though we're gathered in a borderline terrifying area. "We'll definitely all see each other at the Brew and Chew, right? We should make plans to meet up," Liv says.

"I would like that very much," Vishnu replies.

"If I do a rap battle, would you guys come?" B-Money asks.

"I would like that somewhat less, but yes, I would still come and have a smile on my face to support you," Vishnu says. He and B-Money fist-bump. Theirs would be an unlikely friendship, a comedic buddy picture I'd pay to see.

We hear glass breaking in the distance, and screaming follows.

"We need to clear out of here," I say. "Now." As we each dig for our respective keys, a panel van screeches up, and I hold out hope that it's Zeus, profoundly sorry for being so late.

The doors to the van fly open and two people in clown masks hop out, brandishing weapons. What is happening? The taller one yells, "Get in!"

Ever the rule follower, Liv grabs Vishnu and they enter the van, while B-Money tries to hide behind them.

I want to tell everyone to stop, to not comply. You're never supposed to go to a second location. It's almost always more dangerous. Does no one else listen to the murder podcasts Liv has forced on me? They're so prescriptive! We need to stand our ground. We need to fight. We have to muster our resources—there are more of us than them. Liv could blast them with her pepper spray. Vishnu could go for one of their weak spots, like their eyes or nose. He could apply pressure to whatever artery would knock them out. I could throw elbows and high kicks, like the old days. We outnumber them.

We can do this.

We can take them.

We cannot be led into the unknown.

But I don't say any of this, because I'm frozen. Again.

The taller clown brandishes his gun, and that gets almost everyone moving, except for Michael. They shove me in the back of the van, but I can still hear Michael outside protesting. "Be careful—this suit is a linen blend!"

The second, smaller clown is female and just as scary. "Do you want me to put a bullet hole in it?"

"Back seat okay?" Michael asks.

After we're all herded into the van, the two clowns collect purses and phones. Fat tears roll down B-Money's face and he cries, "Not again!"

Chapter Twelve

Liv

The walls are closing in on me. My heart is racing and my palms are drenched in sweat. My chest is so tight that I have to take little sips of air or else I feel like I'm choking. My skin feels electric, and I just want to slap at it to make the zapping stop. I'm trying my hardest not to panic, but the walls are definitely closing in, and I am starting to have a full-on panic attack.

What if I die here? Who's going to help Deandra with her kids? Who's going to bring my mom to all her doctor's appointments? Who's going to take over my listing on that Craftsman? Not Trevor. Please don't let it be Trevor. It can't be Trevor. He'll sell it to someone who'll raze it and fill every square foot of the lot with a McMansion.

"Should we try the door again? We should try it again," I suggest. I need air. I need air. I need *air*.

Emily grabs my arms and stares into my eyes. "Livvy, do your Pilates breathing, okay? In through the nose, hold for four counts, then out using your diaphragm." She helped me through my first panic attack during our third week as roommates. She'd taken the top bunk and I was on the bottom. Her comforter had fallen over in the night and turned my bunk into a cave, and I completely lost it. I thought I'd been buried alive. She sat with me and made me concentrate on my breaths until my pulse stopped racing, and then we swapped bunks for the rest of the year so it couldn't happen again. "You're okay. You've got this."

Our captors have taken us to a dank, dark, foul-smelling basement. There's a thick wooden door and a single, small window, far too high to reach. Condensation leaches from the brick walls. There's a lumpy mattress and one dirty sheet. It's all so small. Like a coffin. Like a Volkswagen, slowly submerging in a lake, its pocket of oxygen ever shrinking. Like a closet filled with my sister's dirty gym clothes. My breath turns shallow and gasping again.

"Breathe, Liv. Breathe," she tells me. She throws an arm around me, knowing not to hold me too close. Her scent is familiar—Tom's of Maine toothpaste, Dr. Bronner's peppermint soap, and neroli oil—and it comforts me.

I get the feeling we're not the first to have been taken here. What does this mean? Why are we here? What the hell is this place? And who are these people? The scariest part of all is the plastic bucket in the corner. I shudder to imagine its purpose.

This place is every one of my fears come to life.

B-Money throws himself against the door, bouncing off and onto the floor. He clutches his arm and tries to shake it off. "Way too solid." He picks himself up and gives his twists a shake. "Are there silverfish down here? Ugh, all those lil legs give me the squigs. What if something laid its eggs in my ear just now when I was on the floor?" He bats at his face.

Vishnu is huddled in the corner opposite the bucket, arms wrapped around his knees, rocking slightly. "'Become fearless,' they said. 'It will be fun,' they said. 'You will create material for your book,' they said."

"I don't recall saying any of that," Michael says, furiously running a miniature lint brush over himself. "This suit is summer weight and exceptionally special. My dry cleaner will never get all the limestone dust off it. This is my fault for daring to wear linen to class. But it's just been so hot lately!"

"Yeah, it's called climate change," Emily says. "I can tell you all about it." Then she mutters something under her breath about not dressing like Idris Elba on the red carpet when he comes to class, but Michael doesn't hear her.

"Eh, I feel like climate change is something Al Gore made up," Michael replies.

"Yo, Mikey, why are you worried about your fit when we're in some straight-up *Silence of the Lambs* shit? Those guys are gonna make suits outta our skin. Tell me you don't see a bottle of lotion in that bucket, please, God," says B-Money.

I will die before I voluntarily look in that bucket.

Emily gets up from where she's been sitting beside me. She paces, and I can see her wheels turning. I'm glad someone's trying to come up with a plan because all my brain is saying is, *Get me out get me out get me out.*

"Everyone take a breath and let's talk about this. Let's be logical and rational. How do you think we got here?" Emily says. Her voice is confident and commanding, and I want to cling to it like a life preserver. A sandbar of calm in an ocean of panic. She was frozen up in the van, but being thrown in here must have broken something loose; she is settling into Action Emily mode now and I'm here for it. I haven't seen her this animated since that homecoming weekend senior year when she promised to flash her boobs for every hundred empty beer cans the frat boys picked up for recycling. She collected more than two hundred pounds of aluminum that day. (And a whole bunch of phone numbers.)

"I am pretty sure it was those people in the van," Vishnu offers.

"I mean, metaphorically. Why us? Why here? Now? Is this related to the coffee shop robbery? Did the guy find out who we are and capture us in some weird form of revenge? But what did we do wrong? We literally did nothing." She asks questions too quickly for us to answer. Action Emily is a sight to behold, and it's making me feel slightly less claustrophobic. Four (very tight) walls cannot contain Action Emily. I need this. I need her to be strong.

She muses, more to herself than to us, "But how would he have known who we were and that we'd be together? Wouldn't he go after the lady who hit him? We were bystanders. We literally stood by. We weren't even on the news. Or is that the key? It doesn't make sense. The pieces don't fit."

Emily paces back and forth across the dirt floor as she tries to find something to connect the two seemingly unconnected crimes. "Or, and I hate this option, are the ultraconservative news sites actually right, and Chicago has become so lawless that senseless acts of violence are the norm and this is now just business as usual? I can't believe that. Not in my town. Chicago is full of *Chicagoans*, and we will always emerge victorious, I'm sure of it. Think about it. Gino's. Giordano's. Lou Malnati's. The Bears' '85 season. Bulls, back to back to back. Cubs winning the World Series. Okay, it took a hundred and eight years, but we did it."

"Yeah, shut the fuck up about Chicago," B-Money says.

"It's not like we're in St. Louis," Michael adds with a snort.

Emily points to him. "I like your energy. But put a pin in the part about Al Gore. We're not done there. Right now, we're going to worry about the closest alligator to the boat." Action Emily claps her hands. The color in her cheeks is high and her eyes are shining. "Okay, years ago, I was rock climbing with a bunch of newbies. We were looking up a cliff face that was so high and flat, just so straight. My team said, 'No way, we can't,' and I did not accept that answer. I told them, 'You are strong, you are brave, and I believe in you. And if you fall, I'll catch you.'"

"What's your point?" Michael asks. He pulls a tube of lip balm out of his breast pocket and smooths it on, then he pulls out an even smaller vial and dots some liquid under his eyes. He notices we're gawping at him. "If my face gets dehydrated, it's game over."

B-Money slaps it out of his hand. "If we don't come up with a plan, it's game over! Now's not the time for self-care! At least not the cosmetic kind." Anxiously optimistic, he adds, "But also, Emily, *do* you have a plan?"

"Yes. I can get us out of here," she replies. She is decisive. She is relentless. She is the Emily of old, organizing the big U of M Earth Day serve-a-thon. It's about time she showed up. Regular Emily who complains about Miles and her disconnected students and dresses like a septuagenarian librarian has vanished. We're getting the superhero version, and if I weren't about to pee my pants—nope, not considering the bucket—I'd be cheering her on.

"What does that look like?" B-Money asks. "We're just gonna take on these people with guns? After a few boxing classes? Cool story, bro. We're gonna die."

Emily power poses with one hand on her hip and the other pointing skyward. "No. We're going out that window."

"It's like thirteen feet up," B-Money says.

"Absolutely inaccessible," Vishnu adds. "We cannot get on shoulders and then on shoulders. We are not circus performers."

"Maybe you aren't." With the dexterity of a mountain goat, Emily fits her foot and her fingers into the tiny cracks between the bricks and scales the wall, and I just want to applaud; it's like the Cans for Cans drive all over again. I feel like the vise grip around my heart loosens just a tad.

"What if it's locked?" Vishnu asks.

"No one locks a window from the outside," B-Money says.

"Captors do," Vishnu says and starts hugging his knees again.

"Climbing a wall is great for her, but no one else here is Spider-Man. How are we supposed to get up there?" Michael asks. "I am old and slow and weak."

"It's stuck, but I think I can get it." Emily works on the pane, rocking it back with one hand while she grips the sill with the other. All that biking and running must be working, because from here, her calf muscles are like twisted steel. (Am I allowed to be secretly happy she finally shaves, or is that the patriarchy making me think that?) She works the frame back and forth, and . . . it opens! "Liv, start ripping the sheet into a few wide strips. We need to reinforce it with a bunch of knots we can use as footholds. Who can tie a good knot?"

She climbs back down the wall and lands on the floor in a plume of dust.

B-Money raises his hand. "I sail a thirty-six-foot masthead sloop, so I can tie anything." We all gape at him—it's not what any of us expected—but hey, I'll take it. "What, I can't be a skipper *and* an MC?"

I try to follow Emily's lead, channeling my fear into action. I rip while B-Money ties, and quicker than I would have imagined, we've fashioned ourselves a crude, cursory rope. We yank on it and the braids and ties seem to be working.

Emily then tries to maneuver up the wall again, this time with the rope looped around her shoulders. Some of the brickwork crumbled on her first climb, so it appears to be tougher going this time. Halfway up, she begins to slip, but B-Money and Michael catch her before she hits the ground.

"Oof, you're heavier than you look," Michael says.

"Never say that to a woman!" Vishnu says. "Even I know that!"

Emily squirms around in their grip, positioning herself to climb again. "This is quite a view," Michael says.

She whips around. "If I'd known we were being abducted, I'd have worn looser pants." She continues her ascent, slower this time, each footfall causing more of the limestone brick to crumble. When she reaches the window, she says, "I'm going to pop outside and make sure the coast is clear. Then I'll brace my feet against the wall as a counter-balance, and you guys climb up."

After a few heart-pounding seconds, Emily pops her head back in. "We're clear." She tosses down the rope but it only reaches two-thirds of the way.

Vishnu cries, "It's too short! We need more length!"

Without hesitating, I pull off my Lululemon Define zip-front because the fabric is both strong and stretchy. I know I've been anti-Lulu because of the grocery store, but after watching Darby move so freely that day, I figured she was onto something. And their leggings are like butter! Vishnu begins to hyperventilate. I understand; I'm feeling the same way.

"My man, have you never seen a sports bra before?" B-Money asks as Emily leans in the window, giving us a few extra feet. B-Money reaches up on his toes to tie the jacket to the end of the rope. "Wait, are you one of those forty-year-old virgins?"

"I am thirty-six."

"That means yes," Michael says, sotto voce, but we all hear him. Vishnu looks like he wants to die.

I tell him, "Vishnu, your personal business is none of our business, but if that's the case, I think it's very sweet, because it must mean you're saving yourself for your great love."

"Yep. That's why," he confirms.

B-Money holds up the end of the rope. "Not long enough. We need more fabric. Gimme your jacket, Michael."

"Hard pass. It's Thom Browne."

I begin hyperventilating. We can't have come so close to give up now.

"Do you want to give up your jacket and get out, or do you want to be buried in it?" B-Money asks. Michael weighs his options, conflicted, so B-Money swats him on the back of the head. "Rhetorical statement, motherfucker!" Michael swats back at him, and a good old-fashioned Three Stooges–style slap fight breaks out. This is surreal. Clearly, neither one of them absorbed anything from the boxing lesson.

I look to Vishnu for help and he reluctantly interjects. "Stop it, both of you. They will hear us!" Michael finally pitches the jacket at B-Money after removing his grooming products. B-Money gleefully shreds it, then ties on the extra pieces. It's finally long enough, thank goodness!

"Okay, ladies first," B-Money says. Michael goes to grab the end, then notices all of our expressions. Holding our ad hoc rope, I position my legs on the bottom knot, supporting myself with my arms.

"Use your leg strength, not your arms. Propel yourself up with your quads," Emily instructs. "And please hurry. I hear voices!"

Every time I bump the wall, the brick crumbles, creating little poofs of dust. But I would so much rather breathe basement dust than remain in this tiny room for another second. I try to tap into what Alex, one of my favorite Peloton instructors, always says: "Breathe in confidence. Exhale doubt." I take a deep breath and I dig in. I breathe in confidence and exhale dust. After a coughing fit, I get into a groove. Pull. Breathe. Pull. Breathe. Muscles I didn't know I had burn, and my hands ache from my grip.

"You've got this, Liv," Emily promises, and I believe her.

When I get to the window, Emily grips my calf and helps pull me out. I take giant gulps of air, finally able to fill my lungs. Once I feel like I'm no longer drowning, we throw down the rope and I try to get my bearings.

"Where do you think we are?" Emily asks.

I try to piece together the clues. "Well, given the drive to get here, the depth of the basement, and the style of the brickwork, we've got to be somewhere on the South Side. In the 1850s, the streets in places like Bridgeport were raised to accommodate sewer pipes and drains, and roads were built on top of them. Prior to that, wastewater would just flow into the street and people died from waterborne illnesses. That's why there are houses down here with these weird moats around them."

Emily gives me a quick grin. "You never cease to surprise me, kiddo. Now, help me get a grip on this."

There's a great deal of cursing from inside the building, but shortly after, Michael's head pops up and we pull him out. It's a tight squeeze, and the window appears to be giving birth to the world's most dapper baby. "Those bricks scraped up the bottom of my loafers. I'm going to have to get them rewelted," he tells us. We toss the rope back while Michael rubs at his shoes with his pocket square.

From the basement, we hear B-Money say, "Hey, small problem."

I pop my head in and see Vishnu struggling to climb the rope. His feet are slipping off the knots and he keeps losing his grip. "You guys, hurry, please," I say.

Emily adds, "It's clear up here, but I don't know for how long."

"I cannot do it," he says, defeat etched all over his face.

"You can do it!" I tell him. "Your mind is your strongest muscle." (It's another Peloton instructor quote, and I'm trying to inspire so I go with the experts.)

"You are you, and that's your superpower," B-Money adds, which is a quote from a different instructor. He must spin too. B-Money grabs Vishnu squarely by the shoulders and says, "Here's what you're gonna do. You are gonna need to picture yourself as the hero in a spy novel, okay? I need you to be James Bond right now."

"Ian Fleming is one of my favorite authors outside of the romance genre," Vishnu admits.

"All right, then you know this story. If you're James Bond, as soon as you climb this rope your hot new girlfriend is gonna be waiting for you and you'll be James *Bone*. You got it, my man? Do this! You gotta do this!" B-Money tells him while clapping him on the back. That must have been the shot in the arm Vishnu needed because he begins to propel himself up.

"You're doing it!" B-Money cheers.

"Yes, I am! I am doing it!" Vishnu replies. Slowly, surely, with his feet slipping all over, but never lessening his grip, he inches up the rope. The poor guy is sweating and shaking by the time he reaches the window, so Emily and I wrap our arms around him and get him the rest of the way out. "Thank you to everyone for your kind assistance. B-Money, I will definitely attend your rap battle now," Vishnu promises.

We toss the rope down for one last pass. B-Money is light and lithe, so he makes short work of the rope and . . . he's out! We're all out! The five of us—even Michael—group hug, clinging to each other in our victory and relief. We made it!

Then Vishnu asks, "Wait, so what do we do next?"

Chapter Thirteen

Emily

Muscle memory means that you are able to reproduce certain physical actions without thinking because your body remembers; the movement is etched deep in your subconscious. Muscle memory is why on that TikTok, the elderly ballerina with Alzheimer's could still do all the arm movements from *Swan Lake* when the music played. Our bodies remember. Essentially, muscle memory is a neural pathway in the brain that allows you to perform or compete, even in high-stress situations. Muscle memory is how we're able to ride a bike or type on a keyboard without having to talk ourselves through the steps each time.

Action Emily's muscle memory took hold and helped us get through this. Whatever used to work for me made its grand reappearance, and not a minute too soon.

When we landed in the back of that van, I felt lost, depleted, like I was out of juice. An empty husk. I couldn't muster what I needed to get it together, to get us out of it. For some reason, I thought about the first time Jeremy and I went climbing, something he was new to and I'd been doing my whole life. My dad and I had been climbing Starved Rock basically since I could stand. Even though I was small in the beginning, I was never afraid, because my dad always told me how much he believed in me. Soon climbing became as natural as breathing.

The cliff face is absolutely flat, high and smooth and straight. I've done this a million times; I could do this in my sleep. But Jeremy, big, tough, fearless Jeremy, is looking up at the wall of rock like it just dumped him right before prom. He's defeated, and it's not at all like him.

"Love, not sure I can do this," he tells me.

"Of course you can," I say. "You have the strength and dexterity. You're certainly brave enough, plus you've got those catlike reflexes. You're going to be a natural."

"It's really high and flat."

I take his rough, calloused hand in mine. "I believe in you; you just need to believe in yourself." Then I wrap my arm around him and pinch his butt. "Besides, if you fall, I'll catch you."

He laughs. "Seriously?"

I shrug and deadpan, "I'm always serious."

Then he takes a tentative grip on the first rock and begins his ascent.

I'd forgotten some of the specifics of our relationship dynamic. I recall deferring to him in times of stress or danger, but *we were equals*. There were times he saved me, but just as many when I was the hero, like when our kayak tipped and his jacket got stuck on submerged branches. When I run through the mental carousel of our lives together, I remember that *I* was strong, that I was Action Emily. I needed to remind myself of all that I had achieved on my own, long before I met him.

I've always had it in me, which means *I still do*. And after a prolonged absence, Action Emily returned to the scene of the crime, and just in time.

Muscle memory.

While I'm incredibly excited at this development, I may also throw up. Those guys could find us any second now, and I can't imagine our treatment will improve after a successful escape. "We have to run. Right now. Far from here," I tell everyone once we stop hugging.

"To where?" B-Money asks. "Where the hell are we?"

Michael looks puzzled. "Aren't you from . . . around here?"

"Yikes. That is definitely a microaggression. Not okay, Michael," Liv says.

"Yeah, I live in Winnetka, ya racist," B-Money says. He's from one of the toniest towns on Chicago's North Shore.

"Yes, yes, apologies all around, and we'll have teachable moments later, but right now, we need to be running!" Vishnu exclaims, practically shoving us.

We take off down the street, passing empty lots and abandoned properties, running through wan pools of light cast by the streetlights. Our feet pound out a rhythm on the bricked alley, and we have to be careful not to stumble on the uneven surface. If one of us falls, it's likely the end.

We pass tagged garages and bleak lots choked with weeds. We hurtle past yards where vicious dogs lunge at us, separated only by shoddy chain-link fencing.

After about four blocks at a full sprint, the men are legitimately exhausted. B-Money whips out an inhaler and takes a long drag. "I need a second," he wheezes.

"May anyone get a hit off of that?" Vishnu asks, sucking wind. B-Money hands it over and Vishnu takes a greedy inhale.

"These shoes were not made for running," Michael says, quietly seething. He reaches down to retie his shoe and adjust his pant legs.

I mutter, "Gym clothes, motherfucker," but Michael pretends he doesn't hear me.

"What are we going to do?" Liv directs her question to me, as I'm apparently in charge of the operation. I like the feeling; it's like reconnecting with a long-lost friend. "These guys are spent. Not sure how much more running they have in them. Do we knock on doors to ask for help? Do we find someplace to hide?"

"That seems like a good way for something bad to happen," B-Money replies.

"Are there police patrolling?" Vishnu asks. "Perhaps we could flag someone down?"

"No idea," I reply, racking my brain for an alternative.

"Wait, why don't we call an Uber?" Michael suggests.

"They have our phones! We cannot!" Vishnu replies.

"Mine's still in my sock," Michael says. That information stops us in our tracks. He fishes under his pant leg and retrieves it. "What? It's a fitted suit. I can't ruin the lines with a bulky phone in my pocket."

I'm trying to keep the rage out of my voice. "You had a phone with you this entire time?" I ask. Given the look on Michael's face, I am unsuccessful at this endeavor.

"My bad."

"I swear to God, I will kill you if these evil clowns don't first," B-Money says, cuffing Michael on the back of his head. Michael swats back and another slap fight ensues.

Liv breaks them up and demands, "Uber! Now!"

Dire though the situation seems, I'm proud of the way Liv handled that. "Really assertive, Liv. Well done."

She beams. "You think?"

"Totally. So proud." I wrap her up in a hug, and Vishnu tries to slide in like it's a DM.

"That means a lot to me, coming from you, because—"

Michael interrupts. "Okay, Jesus, literally our savior, is coming in one minute. He's driving a Suburban."

"Weird," muses B-Money. "I always pictured Jesus coming back in a chariot or whatnot."

We hear someone shout, "There they are!" A man and a woman are about a block away and closing in fast! We run into the street, hoping to intercept Jesus before these devils take us again.

"Faster, everyone!" I shout. "Come on, move!" The captors quickly close the distance. They're close enough that we can hear their ragged breath. But before they can reach us, a black Suburban skids between our groups and I throw open the door. "In! Now!"

We scramble in. B-Money is still clinging to the doorframe as we drive away, and Vishnu and Liv pull him into safety.

Liv is full-on hyperventilating now. "Ohmigod, ohmigod, ohmigod!"

I hold her face in my hands. "Slow breaths, Livvy. Slow it down, you've got this. Inhale, one-two-three, pause, one-two-three, then exhale, one-two-three. Come on. You can do it." Her breathing slows and the panic begins to leave her eyes.

"Praise Jesus," Michael says. Not sure if he's referring to the son of God or the guy driving, but at this moment, they're indistinguishable. In the back two rows of the cool, calm car, we catch our collective breath.

As our panting quiets, I can hear the strains of Taylor Swift's "Out of the Woods" coming from the speakers.

"Hi, excuse me? I just want to say thank you so much! You saved our lives. We're definitely giving you five stars, but I'd also like to write a letter to your supervisor. You were really something!" Liv says.

Yep. She's okay.

The driver nods.

She says, "To confirm I'm saying it right, can you tell us, is your name pronounced Jesus, like the Lord, or Hay-soose, like the Spanish pronunciation?"

He says, "It's Hay-soose. But you can call me Zeus."

I would know that voice anywhere. One by one, it dawns on the rest of the group exactly who's driving our getaway car. WTF?

"But how?" Vishnu asks.

"That's a twist I did not see coming," says B-Money.

"Hay-soose?" Michael asks. "But it's spelled Jesus, like the one on the cross with the abs."

"You are so not woke," Vishnu replies.

Michael is still confused. "Can someone please tell me what in the hell is going on here?"

Zeus looks at us in the rearview mirror. "That was your first test. You passed. Congratulations. Your training officially begins now. Welcome to Fearless Inc."

❦

"So, it was a scam," Miles says. We're sitting in bed, and he's thumbing through a copy of the *Atlantic* while I pet my lapful of the Chairman. I don't even know why he decided to stay; I didn't invite or encourage him, and usually he'd ask my permission. I wonder how eager he'll be to camp out here if I paint the walls the brilliant navy of Oregon's midnight sky. As poorly as he reacted to the green, blue might just cause him to blow a gasket.

"No, you're not getting it. This was more like an initiation, like the Sea Baptism when you cross the equator for the first time and the shellbacks initiate the pollywogs." I'm referring to an age-old seafaring tradition, a celebratory hazing where experienced sailors absolutely torment those on their virgin crossing. It can involve eggs and head shaving—it's a whole *thing*.

"Not one word of that makes sense."

"It was a challenge, Miles. He wanted to confront us with all our fears and then see how we reacted, both individually and as a group," I explain, giving the Chairman the head scritches he loves so much.

"Since when are you afraid of clowns?" he asks.

"It's been a while coming," I reply tersely.

Zeus was surprisingly chatty after he picked us up, although I imagine he had to be, lest we press charges. Apparently, he does something like this with every class. He tailors the exercise to the group since each class has different strengths and fears. For example, he knew about my history as a rock climber, so he factored that into our scenario. He knew what an accomplished sailor B-Money is, so he made sure we had (almost) enough material to fashion a rope.

I was mad at first—furious, actually—but that gave way to grudging admiration. He'd thought through every scenario, really digging into what makes us *us*. Ultimately, he got me to tap into what's been dormant inside, and that's exactly what I needed. I feel like I've been asleep for so long, and something about this experience is making me wake up, finally. It's exciting to me, and likely frightening to Miles, hence his attitude.

"Anyway, it sounds like a scam." Miles's tone is dismissive, and I'm aggravated that he's not grasping how important this is to me. Instead, he's kind of shining me on while he skims the articles' titles and bolded phrases; he thinks it's a close enough approximation of reading the whole thing. Every time he wants to turn a page, he licks his finger first. It's a tiny gesture, but the fury it engenders in me is huge. "If I were you, I'd be a lot more worried about your tenure interview. I'm worried that it's not a sure thing, so maybe it would be better if instead of rope climbing, I helped prep you?"

I don't know if his offer is more sweet or more infuriating. Judging from how my blood pressure just spiked, I'm going with infuriating. I *should* care about my upcoming tenure review, but I don't. Tenure means permanence, and I don't want to be stuck teaching these intro classes to nonscience majors. Maybe not getting tenure would be a blessing. However, I do not raise this point, because Miles would want to debate me on why it's so important and then we'd never get to sleep.

I am exhausted, but it's the good kind of exhaustion, the deep-down delicious kind of weary you feel after running a race or facing off against illegal whalers. The adrenaline dump today was real, and there is no greater high than that.

"The *New Yorker* had an article about something like this not long ago," Miles says. "The group leader was a total mountebank."

I sigh and toy with Meow's tail. "Just say 'con artist,' Miles."

He asks, "May I?" and leans over to kiss Meow on the head, and then me on the cheek. Then he digs his night guard out of the nightstand. He says, "All I'm saying is, you're a scientist, and I know you won't proceed without empirical evidence. Good night." He switches off his light, adjusts his mouthpiece, and lies flat on his back with his arms crossed over his chest, like King Tut in his sarcophagus. It's creepy.

Leave it to Miles. I swear, it's like he revels in being a wet blanket, a buzzkill. One time, I took him to Bears Fan Fest out at the convention center. I was so excited to meet some of my favorite players, and I was having the best conversation with a young QB who'd recently become a spokesperson for a new sports drink. It was a big deal. An endorsement like that could take care of his family for life.

Instead of just shaking the player's hand, Miles had to drone on and on about how companies like the one he was representing spread myths about hydration. I know he was being sincere and genuinely trying to help, but he literally ignored every sign I tried to give him to stop. The whole thing was mortifying.

Later, I looked into what he'd said about sports drinks, and he wasn't wrong. Somehow, that made me even madder.

I had planned on going to sleep, but now that tiny seed of doubt that Miles planted is irritating me, so I start googling to see if I can find out anything else about Zeus and Fearless Inc.

Chapter Fourteen

Liv

The Not-So-Fearless Five, as we're calling ourselves, have started a group chat. Thus far, Michael hasn't responded to our ongoing message chain, but we're pretty sure he's read the texts. That in itself is progress.

As I wait for my clients to arrive, I dash off a quick message to the group:

This training works! It's working!

B-Money immediately replies with a string of emojis I can't quite interpret, and Vishnu sends a big red heart.

Emily writes:

Woo-hoo!

I know it's working, because yesterday I mustered up the courage to march into Jase's office and tell him it's not fair that he and Chase pawn every low-budget buyer and seller off on me. They know that I have my broker's license and that I could start my own agency. I don't need them.

Whatever I said (honestly, I was kind of in an adrenaline fog after our big night being semikidnapped) must have gotten through to Jase, because not only did I finally convince them to give me back my Arts and Crafts–style listing on Sheridan, I'm now waiting to meet some clients with a seven-figure budget! A potential million-dollar-plus sale! No one knows the area like me, so I'm supremely confident that I can find the perfect place for them. I have a whole day of appointments set up based on the parameters that Jase collected. Obviously, I'll ask my own questions, but I guess they were insistent on seeing houses immediately, as time is a factor.

First we're viewing this show-stopping, freshly rehabbed two-story brick Georgian listing on Oak Street. It's in the most gorgeous neighborhood. This is the kind of place a really sweet sitcom could be based. I bet everyone here has borrowed a cup of sugar from their neighbors, and I promise you some of these homes hand out full-sized candy bars at Halloween. I so wish Dee and the kids could live in a home like this instead of our toxic three-flat. Yesterday, Tommy was complaining that *he* had menstrual cramps. He's clearly spending too much time with Ma lately.

I take in the neighborhood from the cheery area underneath the wide portico (technically, it's not called a porch), where terra-cotta pots brim with purple-and-yellow pansies next to white Adirondack chairs. In the corner, there's a big cushioned swing, the ideal spot to while away an afternoon, lost in one of the bodice rippers that I read on vacation.

The trees lining the street are truly magnificent. They create that desirable shady canopy in the summer, with little bits of sun dappling all the manicured lawns. Even on the hottest days, the giant oaks create a cool, green oasis and it's a pleasure to be outdoors. Homes on this block don't open up often, so I'm showing these new clients a pocket listing, meaning it's not yet live on the MLS. The listing broker owes me a favor, so we're getting in early.

Even though the market has slowed, I am sure this place will be gone by next week when it goes live on the MLS. My listing agent friend priced it right.

I'm planning to show a lot of fantastic places today, and it will be nice to bring my buyers to properties with modern kitchens and updated baths. I don't get to show listings in this price range nearly often enough because I'm so busy with Chase and Jase's castoffs and managing the office. (Do I sound bitter? I hope I don't sound bitter! I've just tolerated getting less and losing out for so long that my frustration is beginning to surface.)

Before I can ponder this further, I get what I assume is a text from Michael. It's a photo of a man's lap—I assume his—clad in bespoke pants. That he's not on the toilet speaks to his progress.

A luxury vehicle pulls into the pea gravel drive and a sixty-something couple steps out. Presumably, these are John and Joyce Vandergrift. "Hello, hello!" I call, waving. "Welcome to—"

"What's with all the birds?" Joyce asks. I must admit, I was expecting a more traditional greeting like "Good morning" or "Hi, I'm Joyce." Her permed hair bouffants into an impervious helmet, all black with a large white streak on the side. She has the pinched lips of someone who always complains the soup is too cold. (I note that it was her driving and wonder if this is an important detail.) She's wearing stretchy pants and a sweater that has so much faux fur on it, it appears to need a shave. But my first impressions could be misleading; I have to extend the benefit of the doubt. I scan the area in case I'm missing something, like an enormous sandhill crane having landed on the lawn. We're not that far from the Skokie Lagoons, so it's possible to run into some interesting wildlife here. I saw pelicans a few weeks ago when they were migrating! Actual pelicans! "You mean the birds . . . in the trees?" I clarify.

"They'd have to go," she says, nodding as though she's making a fine point.

"The trees?" I ask, confused and a little afraid. The trees make the neighborhood!

"No, the birds. I hate birds."

"Hates birds," John adds. I'm already getting the vibe that his wife takes the driver's seat in everything, so it will be her approval that I'll gauge today.

No matter what I consider a selling point, there will be someone who hates that feature or wants to change it. Magnificent fireplace? I've had clients board them over because of perceived drafts. Gunite pool with a waterfall feature? Fill it with dirt, stat. Tiffany chandelier in the entry hall? Replace it with a builder-grade boob light. So not liking the sweet songbirds that make this street so enchanting? It happens.

"The birds could easily be taken care of with an eco-friendly solution. I mean, I enjoy birdsong, but I understand why you might not care for the noise. An easy way to repel them is to simply hang a flag out front. Birds are—forgive the pun—super flighty . . ." Neither John nor Joyce smiles, even for a second, so I continue. "When the wind makes the flags flap, they get spooked. Hanging any sort of flag is an attractive, inexpensive way to scare them away from your property. There are smells they dislike too—right off the top of my head, I know they hate peppermint and garlic."

A client not liking birds is hardly the biggest obstacle I've come across as a Realtor. I had one guy who wanted to live on a street that didn't allow cars, because he was a day sleeper. Since those don't really exist on non-island-based urban properties, I instead found a place with a soundproofed room. The previous owner had used it as a recording studio.

I add, "There are also spike strips, spiral reflectors, garden statuary, netting, just a whole host of solutions. We can make sure birds won't be an issue."

"Why don't we just kill them? Bring in a guy and get rid of all of them in the neighborhood," Joyce suggests.

"You mean, *extermination*?" I ask. I must have misunderstood.

"They won't bother us if they're all dead," Joyce says. John mimes spraying them with an imaginary machine gun, you-dirty-rat style.

Um, that's a new one. "Okay, I'm not entirely sure if it's legal to wipe out the entire avian population, but I can certainly look into it for you." I make a note on my phone to figure out some sort of compromise that doesn't entail death or dismemberment. "Now, shall we step inside? I'd love to show you the place."

We step over the threshold into this handsome property, and I slip on the blue shoe-covering booties and ask them to do the same.

"I don't bend," says Joyce. There's not a hint of mirth in her face. My mind begins to race about the other things she may not care for—if bending is difficult, she may do better in a home without stairs, or, barring that, a first-floor primary. She may even want grab bars in the bathroom. I immediately go to plan B. "Sure, no problem, bending is overrated. Would you mind removing your shoes, then?"

"I would," she replies. Nary a grin nor glint in her eye.

Okay, plan C. "Here, then I'll bend for you," I volunteer, as I don't want to disrespect the homeowner's property by tracking in outside muck. After I get Joyce set up, John holds out a foot. I guess he doesn't bend either.

On the continuum of weirdness I've seen in my ten years as an agent, this barely even registers. First of all, everyone's fully clothed. I have far more naked stories in my repertoire than I care to recount. And the accidental (sometimes intentional) nudity stories never involve anyone you'd want to see sans pants. That's a hard—again, pun intended—truth.

We enter the living area, accented with wide windows and a stunning brick fireplace with a formal mantel. "If you'll look down . . ." I pause, waiting for Joyce to tell me she can't turn her head, but she remains quiet. "The flooring is original and freshly refinished. These hand-scraped planks were covered up for years, but the current owners just completed a yearlong rehab project, and you're the first to see the finished product! Isn't the flooring fabulous?"

I'll often ask questions even though I'm pretty sure I know the answers. Sometimes it helps a potential buyer to hear their responses.

Instead of confirming this absolute truth, Joyce asks, "What used to be here?" Chase worked with these homeowners a few years ago, back when they bought this place to flip. (Interesting that they didn't ask him to sell it for them.) Regardless, what a mess it initially was! Over the years, so many of the original details were painted or patched over, and the floor was covered in a hideous, unkempt, Cookie Monster–blue synthetic shag. My legs itch just thinking about it. I'm so glad to see the home returned to its former glory.

I tell Joyce, "The original floors had been covered with a very thick, old carpeting."

Joyce's eyes light up. "Nice! I love carpeting."

"Loves carpeting," John adds. I wonder if he's permitted any original thoughts.

"I hate hardwood," Joyce explains.

Almost as if on cue, John adds, "Hates hardwood."

Not really the answer I expected, but I pivot. Selling real estate is like a Choose Your Own Adventure book, only it's the clients who are opening the pages to new scenarios and I must react in kind. "Of course, I understand that bare floors aren't for everyone and carpeting is a fine way to add warmth and sound insulation. I'm sure it would be easy enough to lay carpet over the planks." It would be a *travesty*, but it wouldn't be *hard*. "A rug would also work."

Joyce says, "Oh, no, I hate rugs." We both look at John, anticipating his echo. But he says nothing, just blinks back at us from behind big glasses that make him look like an owl. "The hardwood would have to go. I wouldn't want to know it was under there, lurking."

"To be clear, you'd prefer to go to the expense to tear out all the original hardwood and put down new subflooring, rather than just carpeting over it because you don't want it *lurking*?"

"Wouldn't everyone?" she replies, dead serious.

I have no idea how to address this, so I suggest a change of venue. "Perhaps we should move on to the kitchen. Do either of you like to cook?" This place has a chef's kitchen, but that won't matter if they don't prepare their own meals.

"I do!" Joyce says. "And he loves to eat, so we're quite a match."

"Great! I bet you'll appreciate this stove." I point out the top-of-the-line gas Viking range.

"They'd need to take that with them. I only like electric," she says.

"Only likes electric," John adds.

Unkindly, I think, *For a woman who hates birds, it's surprising that she's married to a parrot.* But I grit my teeth and smile, saying, "I have so much more to show you!"

🦋

Joyce finds fault with every single thing about this home. She's even offended by the sellers' furnishings. I mean, the couch isn't staying; don't get mad at the whole house about it. As the sellers bought this place to rehab and flip, it's not even their stuff; it's just staging. I always urge my buyers to see past cosmetic concerns and concentrate on the big-dollar things.

I'm not surprised that Joyce has been complaining the whole tour, even after I offered to cut it short. This is a common ploy. For some reason, buyers often believe they have to act as though they don't like a place with their agents, as if it will somehow get them a better deal. Normally, I'd keep this thought to myself, but today feels different.

Midcomplaint, I say, "Joyce, let me stop you for a minute. I need you to understand that I am your *advocate*. I work for *you*. Please, be honest with me; it's the best way for me to help. Playing games helps no one. If all your complaints are an act or a ploy to get me to pressure the seller, I need you to level with me. We are a team here. I am on your side."

I feel almost breathless after I verbalize all of this. I've never been firm with a client like this before. I've always allowed them to run roughshod over me, but today feels different.

Whatever I said must have made some impact, because both of them are quiet while we view the rest of the home. When our tour comes to its (merciful) end, Joyce announces, "I've made a decision!"

"Well, that's fantastic!" I say. Sure, if she wants this home, she'll have to change every single thing she finds offensive, which includes but is not limited to the luxurious primary suite and the new triple-paned windows, but if she's happy, I'm happy. Heck, I'm already happy that I was able to assert myself.

"What decision have you made?"

She peers out the windows. "The trees would have to go too."

I'm beginning to suspect Jase and Chase didn't give me these buyers out of the kindness of their hearts.

❦

When I get home after a very long day with the Vandergrifts, I'm dismayed to find my parking space filled with pieces of drywall. I have no idea who's doing demo, but they're definitely not allowed to dump their debris in my space. It takes me twenty minutes of circling the block to find street parking.

My mother's door is wide open when I step into the vestibule, and I can now see the source of the drywall. My mom's unit is an unholy mess. All her things are piled in the center of the room, and she's torn one wall entirely down to the studs. We've pulled no permits, filed no plans; what is happening here?

"They had to come down," my mother says, materializing behind me. She's in overalls and her chin-length hair is held back with a bandana. She's a couple-decades-older version of me. The biggest difference is the gray streaks and crow's feet (and currently, the fine coating of drywall dust).

She managed to avoid COVID over the last few years, but the pandemic turned her attention-seeking behavior up to eleven.

I'd be more likely to buy her constant string of illnesses if she didn't have the strength to rip down and haul off walls by her damn self, like a stevedore working the docks. We've been trying to get her to a therapist, but according to her, only the Bennett side of the family needs psychological help. *Her* people are a paragon of mental health . . . save for her cousin Augie, who was featured on *My Strange Affliction* because he wanted to marry a bridge. Not a bride. A *bridge*. Specifically, the DuSable Bridge, more commonly known as the Michigan Avenue Bridge. And we don't talk about Bruno, her uncle Bruno, who was institutionalized for schizophrenia. Of course, there's my grandmother, who suffered from incapacitating depression. When I was a kid, she'd sit in a dark living room with her handbag on her lap for hours on end, waiting for the Lord to come claim her. But now that she is on Lexapro and has moved into a senior center, where she hustles all the other residents in her weekly poker game, I guess she doesn't count either.

"Why did the walls have to come down?" I ask. I feel weary and I'm dreading her answer. There wasn't a thing wrong with the drywall. I'd know. I take care of all the maintenance in the building.

"Mold."

Last month, Deandra discovered a tiny leak under her kitchen sink. It was literally a puddle and she caught it almost immediately. The plumber came, fixed it right up, and assured us there was no damage. In an abundance of caution, I called one of my colleagues who does mold remediation, and he did a thorough inspection. My friend is a bit of an odd duck; he lives for mold. Like, nothing makes him happier than finding spores. If he could, he would order remediation upon finding a day-old loaf of sourdough bread on the counter. But he assured us the plumber was correct and the water didn't cause additional damage. No mold. None. Nada.

I take a deep breath to calm myself.

"I wouldn't do that if I were you," she says, her hand perched on her cocked hip.

"You wouldn't breathe?" I ask.

"The air is filled with an aspergillus species. I had to take down all the drywall to get it out," she replies.

This is always a challenge. I want her to feel heard, but at the same time, I don't want to play into her psychodrama. "Do you know something that neither Jerry nor I know?" I ask, referring to my mold fanboy buddy.

My mother shrugs. "His tools aren't accurate. But I know." She thumps her chest, which releases a plume of drywall dust. "I know in here. I've been sneezing and my nose is runny. My eyes itch like the devil. Those are all symptoms of mold poisoning." They're also symptoms of hay fever, and our pollen counts have been off the charts in this warm weather. "And today, I started coughing."

"Is it possible that you started coughing *after* you started pulling down drywall without a mask?"

"No way."

I don't know what to do here. I want to scream and run away, but instead I text my sister.

Are you aware of what she's doing with the drywall?

She immediately texts me back.

Obvi why u think we went 2 movies

I can't blame her. I get why she pushes this stuff off on me. Her plate is already so full that who knows what would happen if she were solely responsible for dealing with our mother. I would like to be anywhere but here right now too. I wish we had a training session tonight; I could use it.

My mom sneezes, and I see a familiar glint in her eye, the one that more often than not requires me to spend the evening in the hospital ER waiting room.

You know what? I don't actually have to be here, even if we don't have a training session.

I quickly send out a group text:

I know it's dinner time, but does anyone want to meet up for coffee?

The responses fly in:

yaaasss queen

Of course, on my way

♥♥♥

I interpret the photo of an odd angle of Michael's chin as a yes as well.

I give my mom a quick hug and say, "Well, it looks like you have this all covered, so I'll leave you to it. See you later!" I don't look back as I leave, but I suspect her jaw is on the ground. And I'd be lying if I said it didn't feel good.

Chapter Fifteen

EMILY

I may have traded one obsession for another.

In the past few weeks, I've been thinking less about the old days. I no longer let every thought pull me back into Jeremy's world. I'm living more in the now. That's a positive. What's less positive is that I've become consumed with trying to figure out Zeus's deal. I mean, what kind of dark magic is he practicing—on us, nonetheless?

I'm seeing real, tangible changes in the group. For example, Michael figured out how to download Grindr, and he's been swiping or tapping or whatever the date-creating protocol is. Apparently, his longtime partner left him around the time his assistant retired, and he's been struggling on all counts ever since. I don't think Michael's done much of anything for himself in years. That said, he figured out Grindr all on his own. He says understanding technology is easier when there's a prize at the end.

B-Money has been doubling down on his music, so much so that he's dropped down to part time at the coffee shop. He hadn't informed his parents of this development as of last week, but working up the courage to follow his dreams should be commended.

Vishnu says he's writing a couple of pages every day, but what's more significant is that he paid Liv a compliment without turning purple. On paper, those two have so much in common, from feeling pushed around at their jobs to not wanting to disappoint their families. I suspect there could be something there.

As for Liv, she's demanding more from work, and she's not letting her family rule her life as much. Just last week, she came to our impromptu group karaoke night instead of letting herself get roped into her sister's drama. Granted, she overpaid B-Money's friend to babysit her hell-spawn niece and nephew when her sister had her crisis du jour, but she didn't take the task on herself, and that is progress.

Personally, I've never been a Deandra fan. The first time she visited Liv in Ann Arbor, it was crystal clear that Dee was incredibly jealous of the life Liv had carved out for herself on campus, but Liv kept making excuses for Dee's criticizing everything she did. Bullshit, in my opinion—Liv was a child of the same divorce and that didn't turn *her* into an opinionated, entitled asshat.

There is zero love lost between Deandra and me, but Liv supports her unconditionally, so I try to respect it even if I don't like it. My point is, for Liv to even challenge her sister is progress.

We're all progressing, so I don't know why I can't just appreciate that and not obsess over Zeus's origin story. It's almost like I'm only happy when I'm unhappy, but that defies logic. No one would revel in feeling miserable on purpose, denying themselves little pleasures and constantly flagellating themselves over survivor's guilt . . . right?

"'Sup, fam?" B-Money asks, sidling into the chair next to mine. His T-shirt reads *Supreme* and his expensive sneakers are beyond white. I don't know how he keeps from getting coffee on them at the shop. He and I have gotten tight. He's the only other person vaguely curious about how Fearless Inc. came to be.

I tell him, "I still haven't found anything about him. It's driving me to distraction. How do you just not exist online? Him having no digital footprint makes me so skeptical about what the whole 'Master your life' thing is really about."

"It's completely sus," he agrees.

"Did we accidentally join a cult? Are we about to be hit with an MLM pitch, like, if we want to be Fearless (Inc.), we're going to have to start selling supplements? None of this sits well with me." Then I look down at my biceps, which are visibly more toned. "But I've lost five pounds since we started boxing."

Michael glances over and nods. "Five down, ten to go."

I poise to confront him, but B-Money grabs the back of my shirt. "Not worth it, sis. Anyway, we gotta ignore him. I got my own problems."

"Why, what's happening?" I ask. He's not his usual larger-than-life self today.

He runs a palm over his twists, which now have little gold beads at the end. They glint under the fluorescent lighting. "My folks are all over me. They were not down with me cutting my hours at the café. They said I need to either start working for my dad or move out because I've been freeloading for too long. Facts."

"Would you want to be in your father's employ?" Vishnu asks. "I work for my father's radiology practice. Zero stars. Do not recommend."

B-Money says, "I'd have to start in the field doing exterminations, but I don't mind the idea of blue-collar work. That's not the problem. All the best MCs kept it real. You feel me? Biggie drove a UPS truck. Kendrick Lamar was a security guard. Kanye worked at the Gap."

Michael snorts. "Kanye worked at the Gap? That explains so much."

B-Money shoots him a poisonous look. "Nah, son. I'm allowed to mock Kanye, not you."

Michael pretends to wipe dust off his shoulder and returns to his app. "Whatever."

"But my big problem is a major bug phobia. Not down. Anyway, I've got a week to cure that or I'm out on the street, cut off."

"That's terrible!" Liv says. She and Vishnu are sitting together. Again, he's so not her type, and I would bet cash money he's never seen a real woman naked, but I could see *something* there. He's kind and asks for nothing; Liv could use more of that in her life.

"Yeah, and my dad won't let me live on my boat either," B-Money says. "Guess he's still salty I went to three universities."

"I also went to three universities!" Vishnu exclaims, delighted to have a commonality. He raises his hand to high-five B-Money, who is too empathetic to leave Vishnu hanging. The sound of their hands clapping together resonates through the warehouse.

"But you're a doctor. You got out with a BS and an MD. I'm just a guy with no degree who's scared of bugs and even more scared about being kicked out."

Out of nowhere, Zeus materializes. *How* does he do that? How is he able to approach with no sound whatsoever? See, it's stuff like this that makes me suspicious. Being able to silently advance seems like some kind of Special Forces training. Now, if he were an ex-SEAL or something, that might explain why he's so secretive, and also why he's left no sort of electronic trail. How do you not have Yelp reviews? Someone even Yelped the lobby of our condo building. It's a lobby! Sorry the elevators aren't fast enough for you, *Bob*.

I try to get some information when we chat during breaks, but he's like the sphinx—silent and mysterious. And somehow he also has so much charisma; it's like he compels me to keep prodding.

Zeus just stands in front of us like a statue until we're all rapt with attention. Again, this hints at some sort of special training. Normal people can't stay still like that. They twitch, they pulse, they burp, they breathe, they . . . *something*. But he can practically turn himself into a tree. Once he's sure all eyes are on him, he says, "This week, we tackle everyone's greatest fear. Who can tell me what that is?"

Liv's hand shoots straight in the air, just dying to please. "Saying no? Being impolite?" Liv guesses. "Oh, or not smiling when a man on the street tells you to smile?"

"Interesting guesses, but no," Zeus says. "Vishnu, what do you think?"

"Telling your parents you do not want to follow in their professional footsteps, because you cannot imagine anything more boring and soul sucking than sitting in a little room by yourself, staring into a bright light and interpreting the results of X-rays and ultrasounds and MRIs? Then sometimes, after squinting at strangers' insides all day, having to share the worst news a patient may ever hear?"

"That's a little specific, so no. Michael?"

Michael chews on this for a second. "Unnatural fabrics?"

"Not even remotely. Emily?"

I can't help myself. The words pour from my mouth before I can stop them, like wild horses bursting through a fence line. "Getting scammed by a mysterious guy who says he can make you fearless?"

Zeus inhales so powerfully, I'm afraid he's going to suck all the air out of the room. His exhale ruffles my hair. How does he make having an active respiratory system hot? How??

"The answer is performance anxiety. Statistically, what people fear most is getting up in front of a crowd. So, we're having a talent show next week and—"

I stand up, forming my hands in a T to make the timeout gesture. "Whoa, hold on. We need to change the syllabus."

Zeus stares at me long, and I feel a flash of heat zip from my head to my toes, ending up just below the waist. (Why? *No.* Why??) Finally, he says, "Because?"

"Because B-Money's about to be kicked out of his parents' house if he doesn't fix his entomophobia."

Michael huffs into a handkerchief. "Well, I never! I thought we were friends!"

Vishnu whispers to Michael, "It does not mean he hates the LGBTQIA+. It means he is afraid of bugs."

"Never mind, then," Michael says, but takes his first two fingers and points to his face and then at B-Money, then back at his face, like he's going to keep watch for homophobia, even though B-Money is super inclusive.

I explain, "Because B-Money is about to be kicked out of his parents' house if we don't help him fix his fear of bugs."

"So?"

"He'll be unhomed," I say, exasperated. I swear Zeus is trying to be obtuse.

"He can't live on his boat?" Zeus asks.

"Right?" B-Money says. "Wait, how did—"

Zeus claps his hands with a thunderous sound. His trademark, apparently. "Anyway, performance anxiety."

I make another timeout sign. "I'm sorry, you're just going to ignore what we need and do what you want?"

A rare, slow grin spreads across Zeus's face, and something primal inside me stirs when I see all those straight white teeth aimed in my direction. Oh, fuck me, there's a small dimple. The full wattage of his smile could light the Vegas strip. Even Vishnu makes a little gasp. Is this how my students feel when they see, I don't know, Tom Holland or Zendaya? "You're catching on, Professor. Addressing your performance anxiety is more important. Trust me, this is what he needs. It's what you all need. Are you in or are you out?"

He goes around the room, looking us each in the eye, and one by one, I can feel my friends bending to his will. They fall in line, readily agreeing to whatever Zeus has planned for us next.

I imagine this is what it felt like to be in the Russian court with Rasputin. Even I find myself saying, "In."

"On a scale of one to ten, how afraid are you of bugs?" I ask.

Liv and I are having lunch at the coffee shop because B-Money is working and we want to help him. I wonder if coming together as a group is part of Zeus's plan. It has to be, right? All of our exercises are done together. We've had no individual challenges. Vishnu offered to call in sick, but considering what a hard-ass his supervisor-father is, we told him we could handle it.

Michael is also in the café, although he wasn't invited. He just happens to work around the corner, so he's in and out all day long. He's currently ignoring us, poking at his laptop screen and grumbling under his breath.

B-Money answers, "Infinity? A googol? Which is the most?"

"Hmm," Liv replies. "What scares you the most, specifically? Is it the crawling, the flying, the burrowing?"

B-Money squirms, visibly uncomfortable at the mere thought. "All of the above."

"What about exposure therapy?" I ask. "Have you tried it?"

He nods. "Like twenty times. My dad even hired a lady to come to the house. She brought a cage full of butterflies. She tried to get me used to them first 'cause who doesn't think butterflies are dope? All those pretty wings? She pulled one out and showed me how gentle it was, and I was like, 'A'ight, not so bad,' then she pulled out another one. Problem was, she was old AF and her grip was shaky and she dropped the cage, and those fuckers swarmed me like in a remake of *The Birds* or some shit. That made it a million times worse." He swats at himself, like he's trying to get them off. "I've got nowhere to go! I can't live in my car! Where would I plug in my frozen daiquiri maker?"

From his corner, Michael snorts.

"Are you even trying to help?" I ask.

"Oh, was I not clear that I don't care?"

"Then why did you come?"

"I like the coffee. It's so watery!"

"Usually, I get real nervous about performing. But I'm so scared that I'm gonna fail when I go to work with my dad later this week that I'm not even sweating the talent show," B-Money tells us.

I'm relatively sure the show won't be a big deal, largely because it's taking place here in the shop. "If we're lucky, ten people will show up. If we're really lucky, Miles won't be one of them."

"You haven't dumped his boring ass yet?" B-Money asks.

"Not yet, but she will once she figures out the best way to let him down gently," Liv assures him, giving my hand a comforting tap.

Honestly, the deeper into this we get, the more I realize I haven't been fair to Miles. I've said as much to Liv, who surprised me by agreeing. He's never been anything except exactly what he presents, yet I blithely plowed forward, thinking I could turn a tabby into a tiger. That's not on him, that's on me.

I've spent our whole relationship comparing him to Jeremy, and measuring all the ways in which he falls short. But because I'm thinking about Jeremy less now, I'm finally seeing our deficiencies as a couple for what they are. We wouldn't have worked even if my heart had been in it. We don't mesh. We don't challenge each other. We don't bring out each other's best traits. I always wanted to be in a relationship where I'm 100 percent and he's 100 percent, but together we're 1,000 percent. Before that can happen, I have to get myself to that 100 percent. I think Fearless Inc. could get me there. Miles deserves better than I've given him, but I haven't got it in me to articulate all that, at least not yet. So for now, status quo.

I clear my throat, eager to change the subject. "Anyway, what should I do for my talent? I'm thinking of lecturing on the water table."

"Everyone loves a lecture," Michael says with a smirk. *Why is he even here?*

Liv says, "I was a majorette in high school. Would baton twirling be too weird?"

"Absolutely not," I start to say, just as Michael butts in with "Absolutely."

"What's Vishnu doing for his talent?" Liv asks. "Something with his writing?"

"He says he's gonna read one of his short stories," I say.

"Good for him!" she replies.

Michael starts aggressively poking his screen.

"Problem, my man?" B-Money asks.

"How do I fatten up a YouTuber?" Michael replies.

The three of us look at each other, each more confused than the last. "It's too thin, it needs to be fat," Michael clarifies, as though that explanation and his use of jazz hands will help.

As I'm attuned to figuring out my students' slang and bullshit, I field this one. "Do you mean, 'How do you make a video full screen?'"

"Yes."

"As miserable as you are, do you seriously expect us to help you?" I ask. I cross my arms and scowl at him. I'm getting tired of his attitude. Everyone else in the group is open and vulnerable, and he's just a wall of negativity and snarky remarks. B-Money follows suit with his body language, and grudgingly, Liv does the same, but still mouths an "I'm sorry" when she thinks we're not looking.

We all watch as Michael continues tapping fecklessly at his screen. He finally slams it shut, defeated. "Fine. Y'all win. I created an ad campaign for the new insectarium exhibit at the Lincoln Park Zoo. The director owes me a favor. I'll call her. Maybe she can help B-Money with his problem," Michael says.

B-Money absolutely lights up. "Michael, thanks, my man. That may keep me living indoors! I owe you one of my world-famous frozen daiquiris. How do you feel about mango?"

Michael shudders. "I feel sorry I mentioned anything."

"Friends, family, followers—welcome to the Fearless Inc. talent show!" says Zeus, addressing the sparse crowd. For some reason, he's dressed like a stand-up comic from the 1980s, wearing high-waisted acid wash jeans and an oversized leather coat. He looks ridiculous, but he's carrying it with such confidence that it works.

I'm at a table with Miles, who insisted on coming. Michael walks past us with his coffee and stops to admire Miles's handbag. "I love your satchel," he says.

"Thank you!" says Miles. And to me, he says, "I told you it's not a purse." Argh. I know our problems are my fault, not his, but damn, he doesn't make this any easier.

"Olivia Bennett is kicking off our performances tonight with a twirling routine. Everyone give it up for Liv!" Zeus says, clapping his way off stage, which is really just a small platform by the Brew and Chew corkboard.

Liv enters from stage right, dressed in a modest skirted leotard, baton in hand and a huge grin on her face. From the back of the room, Trevor from her office catcalls, "Take it off!" Her face falls, and I shoot him a *look*. He has the good sense to appear chastened.

The lights dim and Liv hits a switch on her baton, which glows with LED lights. She used to twirl a flaming baton—that was *the best* party trick in college—but she's afraid she's out of practice and doesn't want to burn down the Brew and Chew. Probably a good call. Regardless, her routine is impressive, with lots of spins and passes, and I cheer loudly with every catch and spin. By the time she finishes, she's all smiles again. Funny how a little burst of achievement can do that for you. I give her a standing ovation and I don't sit down until everyone follows suit. Knowing my eyes are on him, Trevor claps the loudest and longest.

After Liv, Michael gives a rather spirited talk about how to tell the difference between a silk tie and a silk-blend tie. Of course Miles is riveted. He's probably mentally shopping for matching ties with the Chairman as we sit here. I'm aggravated that Michael's talk is actually informative, especially when he mentions the environmental dangers of synthetic fibers. This is what he does: he pushes us all to the edge and then manages to redeem himself right when we're about to vote him off the island.

Vishnu reads a short story that borders on erotica. I mean, move over E. L. James. Though his presentation is halting and stiff, his words paint an indelible picture. Liv pulls at her neckline, flushed.

"Is it just me or was that . . . *whoo*," Liv says, fanning herself with a menu. She dabs at her neck with an ice cube from her water glass.

"That was a way hotter story than I anticipated," I agree. "He may well have hidden depths."

"My man is a freak, hard stop," B-Money says.

The loudest applause for Vishnu comes from his more confident doppelgänger, who we find out is Sanjay, a.k.a. Jay, Vishnu's brother. He and Liv catch each other's eye, and Jay raises his latte to her in a mock salute. I don't know if it was the story or Liv's increased confidence from her brilliant baton performance, but sparks are flying. I'm glad she decided not to invite her family, because I guarantee they'd have just demeaned her and made the night all about themselves.

I give my talk on the water table, which is met with exactly as much enthusiasm as I anticipated. For a minute, I thought I'd sing something. I pulled out my vintage acoustic guitar and tried one of the old Blues Traveler songs we used to sing around the campfire, but I was too out of practice. When I hit the chorus on "Run-Around," Miles came rushing in because he thought I'd stepped on Chairman Meow's tail. (It's possible I was never good, and we were all tripping too hard on shrooms to notice.)

After I finish my talk, I ask if there are any questions. Taylor, who's now in the summer session of my class, raises her hand. "Professor Doctor, do I get credit for being here?"

Feeling generous, I say, "Why not?" I don't want to see her again this fall.

B-Money closes out the show. He's planning to perform an original piece. He bursts onto the stage, full of swagger. Performance anxiety? Not him. He's got this. He sort of has to make a go of it—the insectarium was an unmitigated disaster. All his screaming frightened the children, causing a small stampede. He may well have created a new generation of entomophobes.

B-Money surveys the audience, waiting to speak until he's captured every single person's attention. "Gonna do something tonight inspired by my struggles. See, this week, I got kicked out of my house because I couldn't rise to the occasion and kill some bugs. I couldn't even be in a room with bugs behind Plexiglas. Oh, God, they were just so crawly and hairy and . . ." He trails off, wincing. But he composes himself and speaks like he's at the United Center and not on an ad hoc stage in the third-tier coffee shop where he slings espresso. "I tried, I failed, and I was offered no grace. This is about change. This is about making do. This is about having a dream. I've been keeping it real, sleeping in my car, because I know I have *it* inside me. And I'm 'bout to let it out, so go off."

We all cheer, and he has to wait a few beats for the applause to die down. He's got this. We're all in the palm of his hand. If he can be half as good as he is when he's just freestyling to himself while cleaning the espresso machine, this performance is going to be *lit*.

B-Money begins to rap about the story of how his life was totally flipped, entirely turned upside down, and . . . is . . . is he doing the theme song to *The Fresh Prince of Bel-Air*?

"I love this song!" Miles says. So, confirmed.

B-Money, what are you doing?

It dawns on him that in giving in to his performance anxiety, he's entirely plagiarized that old Will Smith song, and he freezes. He looks wildly around the stage for his easiest exit.

"Don't quit!" I yell.

"I believe in you!" Vishnu calls.

"You've got this!" Liv says.

Oh, yeah. He's about to run.

But before he reaches the exit, he stumbles over a bag of the shop's terrible coffee beans, secured with a length of rope, gets twisted up in the burlap, and slips on the spilled beans.

Vishnu flies out of his seat to help right his friend. Poor B-Money's eyes are wild and he's hyperventilating as Vishnu attempts to push the beans out of the way. He stares at the door, and I'm so afraid he's going to run out and never come back, that he's going to let this moment define him.

"Stay, stay, stay," I whisper, more of an incantation than an instruction. He needs this. We all need this.

"We love you, B-Money!" Liv shouts.

"We know you can do it," Vishnu assures him, patting B-Money's back.

Zeus watches the whole scene unfold. Shouldn't he be doing something? Or is *not* doing something the something he should be doing? Finally, he shrugs and says, "Life is a classroom," as though that were in any way helpful. WTF?

B-Money grabs the length of rope from the now-open bag of beans. He's thinking, processing. Most importantly, he's staying put.

"Don't hang yourself!" Michael calls. The entire room whips around, and no one is madder than Liv.

"What the *fuck*, Michael?" Liv hisses, and I feel such a surge of love at her anger and profanity that I spontaneously hug her.

Michael's confused. "What? I was being supportive."

B-Money holds the rope for an uncomfortable silence. Then he reapproaches the mic. "Yo, my bad. Guess my new rap isn't ready. Sorry 'bout that. But lemme show you something that's even more important. I'm talking about how to save your life on the high seas, deadass."

He launches into a knot-tying tutorial, and it's actually incredibly entertaining, as he mixes his knot tying with tales of adventures he's had on solo sails. He shows us bowlines and stopper knots, calmly explaining when you'd need them. By the time he finishes teaching us how to create a clove hitch knot, the audience is eating out of his hands. He takes a bow to thunderous applause and performs two knotty encores.

🦋

By the end of the night, it's just the five Fearless Inc. acolytes and Zeus sitting together. There's a certain irony that we're back where the police first interviewed us, but the vibe is entirely different. No more baked potatoes here! Miles was miffed when I told him to go home without me, but tonight's about us, not him.

"Who knew knots would be such a big hit?" B-Money muses.

"What a night!" Liv agrees, although I'm curious as to how much of her enthusiasm stems from Jay's insisting he take her out to dinner this week. Vishnu thought that was a capital idea, but I wonder if that's how he truly feels. Given that he's inhaled seven stale crullers in a row, I suspect he's eating his feelings right now.

"I guess I'm glad about the knots and all, but I'm still homeless," B-Money says.

"Homeless how?" Vishnu asks.

"As in, I don't have a place to live?"

"That is magnificent news!"

We're all trying to parse Vishnu's meaning when Michael says, "Aren't you all going to dogpile on him? Y'all would nail me to a cross if I said that."

Vishnu quickly explains, "Oh, sorry, I meant it's magnificent news because I have a spare bedroom. My Realtor insisted I would want a nursery."

"That's wonderful, Vishnu," says Liv. "Not about your bad real estate agent. So, B-Money can stay with you?"

"That depends . . . ," Vishnu says, pausing for a dramatic beat. "On if you bring your daiquiri machine!" B-Money drops all pretense of coolness and wraps Vishnu in a grateful hug. Vishnu needs company more than he needs rent money, so they agree that B-Money can stay for free as long as he'd like, especially if he keeps the daiquiris flowing.

Zeus rises from the table. "Mission accomplished."

"Um, no, not exactly. B-Money still can't rap in front of an audience and he's still afraid of bugs," I remind him.

"Tonight wasn't about performance anxiety or entomophobia. It was about addressing B-Money's fear of failure. He didn't quit when it got hard, he soldiered on," Zeus says.

B-Money offers a wry laugh. "Yeah, and it only cost me my pool house and my boat and—"

Zeus claps him on the back. "A win's a win. You're on the right track now. Sometimes the monsters are just trees. See you next week." And like that, he's gone. Poof. *How does he do that?*

B-Money pulls out an iPad and sits next to me. "Yo, Emily. Been meaning to show you this. Check it out." He presses play on a YouTube. "Have you seen the new Taylor Swift video?"

I let out a quick yelp of laughter. "Um, no, because I'm not twelve. Also, her song 'Lover'? It's basically just a remake of Mazzy Star's 'Fade Into You.'"

B-Money takes a deep breath, as though trying to compose himself. "I'mma let that disrespect slide, this time but don't you come for the queen again," B-Money says, in all seriousness. "But look here." He expands the video—also known as fattening up the YouTuber—and points to a hulking, familiar figure in the front row of what looks like a live performance, dancing alone in a sea of Gen Z. "Is that who I think it is? What is up with his mystical white boy shit? And how did he know about my boat?"

I squint at the screen. Yes. The face, the biceps, the profile. It's him. It is definitely Zeus, and dancing is definitely not his strong suit.

Who is this guy and what is he hiding?

Chapter Sixteen

Liv

The waiter tops off my champagne glass and clears my dessert plate. Jay and I clink our glasses and I take a sip, enjoying how the tiny bubbles tickle my nose. I feel ensconced in a warm, golden glow, and all is right with the world. Everything about this date has been perfect so far, and I can't get over what a good guy Jay is. He's a radiologist, a job he absolutely loves. He's tight with his family, he's a World War II buff, and we listen to all the same true crime podcasts, so our conversation hasn't lagged for even a second. Emily asked me to text her a play-by-play, but I've been so in the moment that I totally forgot.

Jay's not doing that distant thing where I feel obligated to chase him. If he says he'll text, he'll text. He calls to ask about my day, and we talk about our goals and dreams for hours. He puts thought into everything. For example, this may be the most creative date I've ever been on. On our first night out together, I mentioned how much I love dogs. As tonight is our third date—and we all know what that means— he's put together something so thoughtful, he's completely knocked my socks off. (Ostensibly, the rest will come off later, and I am giddy at the prospect!)

Instead of going out to dinner, Jay arranged for us to have a sunset meal here, at the Montrose Dog Beach. Is this a picnic? Oh, no. This is an elegant meal, complete with a waiter. When we walked up, I couldn't believe this elaborate setup was for us—I thought we were just taking a nice beachfront stroll before going to a restaurant.

It's a perfect early summer night, not too hot or humid. We're at a table on the sand, with white linens and crystal glassware and tons of pink peonies (one of my faves!), but the twist is, we're doing it in the midst of all these darling dogs romping and frolicking in the water. He even brought dog treats, so whenever the pups come up to us, we have something to give them. So far, I've pet four square-headed pit bulls; three woolly Goldendoodles; five Labs in a variety of colors, every one of them soaking wet and desperate to get at the food on our plates; a wire-coat retriever; and three wiener dogs. A large Newfoundland drooled on my bare feet, and a funny little Frenchie tried to climb on my lap. I'm in heaven!

I was already predisposed to like Jay, as I have such positive feelings about Vishnu. There's got to be some transference there. Plus, they're brothers, so they share family traits—they're both smart and funny and sweet, with warm brown eyes and swoopy black hair. But somehow these same features hit different on Jay. He's brimming with confidence. I guess the difference between average and smoking hot is self-assurance, and Jay has it in spades.

"What do you say we wrap this up and head down to my place?" he asks, cupping my cheek and making me absolutely weak kneed. If the way he kisses me is any indication, tonight will be something special. "You don't have another early morning, do you?"

"I do not." The past two times we've been out, I've had to end the date before the good stuff because the Vandergrifts have been so demanding of my time. Lately, they've wanted to hit the ground running by 6:30 a.m. Let me tell you this: no homeowner wants their house shown that early, so I've had to find properties that aren't currently occupied. Why so early? Who knows. Maybe they're secretly farmers.

I think Jay was disappointed when I begged off by 9:00 p.m. last time we were out, but that won't happen tonight. I have my whole morning free because I fibbed and said I was having a colonoscopy. Apparently, Joyce and John are big supporters of preventive medicine, so this was an acceptable excuse. Perhaps a more acceptable excuse would have been for me to tell them, *It is completely absurd and unreasonable to see homes at 6:30 in the morning, so we're going to wait until 9:00 a.m. like everyone else,* except I'm not quite up to saying it like that yet, but I have been practicing in the mirror. I managed to push back a little, and we're only doing it twice a week, so it feels like progress.

"Oh, wait," I say, and I can see the disappointment flash across his fine features. He must think I'm trying to avoid alone time with him, and that is so not the case.

"Not the nightmare buyers again," he says. He's been so patient, listening to me vent about their demands and brusque demeanor. They put the "mean" in "demeaning," but I imagine they suffered something in their life that made them this way, so I try to shake it off. It's hard when they say, "What are you, stupid?" when I suggest something they don't like, but I guess putting up with their attitudes and ableist language is the cost of doing business. Lately, when they try to insult me, I'll take the insult and twist it, like, "Am I stupid? Yes! I'm stupid in love with real estate!" It's not entirely sensical, but it has at least tempered their aggression.

I tell him, "No, not this time. All I was going to say is, you're all the way down in the South Loop. My place is half the distance away in Rogers Park." I rise and brush the sand off my skirt. "Shall we?"

He takes my hand. "We shall."

I'm still recovering from date night two days later. I told Emily I'd save the full story for when I saw her in person because I've had my hands so full of the Vandergrifts that I've barely had a second to process anything else.

Like today, I've been fielding texts from them since before sunrise. Technically, I didn't respond until 7:00 a.m., because for the first time in my professional life, I put my alerts on mute. These two text me all day, every day, in the limited moments I'm not driving them around the greater Chicago area. When we're in the car, they insist on sitting in the back seat, as though I'm their chauffeur and not a professional Realtor. Given the way Joyce backseat drives, I'm surprised they want to ride with me at all. When I did ask if they'd prefer to meet me at a property, Joyce said, "Why should I waste my gas when we have yours?" I keep telling myself there is a finite number of properties in their desired area, so this can't last forever.

I hope.

The more places we see, the more they want to see. It's a never-ending cycle. Chase and Jase did not "gift" them out of any sort of kindness or gratitude, I'm sure of this now. The Vandergrifts' only saving grace is that they're prequalified for a huge mortgage; I'm sure, because I collected their paperwork myself. If I'm miraculously able to show them something they like, at least I'm confident they can buy it. They are without a doubt the most difficult clients I've ever met, and I once worked with a D-list reality star who wouldn't allow me to look her in the eyes when I spoke. I had to fix my gaze at her obviously fake diamond earrings whenever I had anything to say.

After the Vandergrifts and I toured our thirty-seventh house yesterday (I wish this were an exaggeration), they insisted on seeing a generic bungalow that met absolutely none of their parameters. But they liked it as we passed by, so I immediately called the listing agent for the lockbox code, and we viewed the property right then.

There was nothing special about the house. It was literally just a small bungalow, and not particularly well priced, which is why it was languishing on the market. (You must price well to get offers! You must!) Each room was an aggressively neutral box with no flow and little natural light. The square footage they wanted wasn't there, it wasn't in a neighborhood they desired, and the home needed significant work, like a new roof and replacement windows, even though Joyce and John insisted on turnkey. But oddly, they liked it. They even kicked me out of the house while they discussed it. "Get out. We're talking," Joyce said. If they were trying to hurt my feelings, mission accomplished.

The good news: they liked that boring bungalow so much, we went back there again yesterday afternoon, and a third time first thing this morning. Naturally, they wouldn't share their reasons for liking it with me, so whatever attracted them is still a big question mark and gives me no actionable information.

If a prospective buyer takes a third look, it's almost always the sign of an impending offer, so I was super relieved because it felt like the end was near. Getting a written offer doesn't mean the deal will close—a million things can go wrong between the offer and escrow stages. Trust me. I've seen it all, like when the oh-so-important starlet couldn't secure financing (lesson learned and the irony was delicious). But it's a positive sign.

When Joyce and John joined me on the stoop this morning after they kicked me out again ("Piss off, girlie" was her choice phrasing today), I was right—they had decided to make an offer. Hallelujah! I'd still have to deal with negotiations and inspections, but the idea of not being with them from dawn (literally) till dusk made me want to break out the Veuve. I was already plotting my stop at Binny's to buy something bubbly, but then the Vandergrifts decided to *Vandergrift*.

I should have known.

We were discussing offer specifics and they were actually listening to my strategy, which considered all the factors—time on the market, per-square-foot comps, being aggressive enough for it to be a good deal but not so aggressive that it insulted the sellers, etc.—when a neighbor came outside. Their bungalow across the way was fixed up so beautifully. The lawn was uniformly cut in parallel lines (how do they do that?), and symmetrically placed tiger lilies bordered the walkway. Pretty flowers spilled from containers down each step up to the covered porch. Clearly, that owner was house proud, and that's exactly what you want in neighbors when you buy on a street without an HOA. I don't love HOAs because they can be draconian, but like Mussolini, they keep the metaphorical trains running on time in the neighborhood. Because there's no regulation on this street, an owner could easily park a rusty Chevrolet on blocks and allow weeds to grow rampant, and no one could do anything about the eyesore. But this lady? This lady was best-case scenario. She was helping me sell and she didn't even know it.

The lady spotted us and waved, and I waved back, giving her a bright smile. She was dressed in cargo shorts and had come out to swap her flags. She first saluted the American flag before pulling it down and folding it properly into a triangle. Then she unfurled a bright rainbow flag to take its place. "Happy Pride Month," she called to us, waving.

"And to you as well!" I said. This lovely neighbor would be a blessing. "Looks like your neighbor is really friendly!" I said.

I have never witnessed two people turn on a property more quickly. The way those two hustled me into the car reminded me of Zeus's training exercise. You'd have thought we were fleeing a crime scene. Long story short, now the Vandergrifts are furious at *me* for *their* liking a home in Andersonville, one of Chicago's largest gay and lesbian–friendly communities, as though diversity isn't something to celebrate.

So, I'm deep in thought when I hear, "Mind if I take the seat next to you?"

Wait, do I know that voice? I glance up and see a delighted Miles accompanying a visibly irked Emily.

"Just sit down, Miles."

"Hi, Miles, have you decided to join our group?" I ask. I haven't had a chance to run in the morning with Emily for the past few days and download, but she's clearly pissed. Her nostrils are flared and her jaw clenched. This group is *her* thing. All Miles has done is cast doubts about the training.

"I've decided I'm ready to kick some booty too!" he says. Emily squeezes her eyes shut and pinches the bridge of her nose in a "God, give me strength" way.

Zeus materializes out of the darkness and we all gasp. I wonder how he does that. Zeus fixes his attention on Miles. "I see we have a new recruit tonight. Welcome to Fearless Inc. Are you ready to master every aspect of your life?"

Miles seems delighted to have attracted Zeus's attention. "Not to blow my own horn, but I'm already the master of a few things."

Under her breath, Emily says, "No. Stop talking."

Miles begins to tick off his accomplishments. "I'm a master recumbent cyclist, a master vegetarian chef, and I'm a whiz at gluten-free muffins, so you could say I'm a master baker—"

B-Money snickers and Emily looks pained. He shrugs. "Sorry, that shit was funny."

Miles turns to chat with Michael while Zeus works out our pairing for the next exercise.

I whisper to Emily, "I thought you wanted to spend less time with Miles, not more."

"He invited himself. He says he needs a boost of confidence for 'something important.'"

"Oh, no, is he going to put a ring on it?"

Emily dispassionately examines her left hand. "He can't if I cut it off first. Anyway, enough of him. You're killing me with all the secrecy! I'm dying to hear! How'd date number three go? Did you make it official?"

I feel a pang in my chest. "Sunday night was fantastic . . . until we got to my place and my mom needed me to take her to the ER."

Emily blinks slowly at me. "Please tell me you're lying."

I shake my head.

She looks as disappointed as I feel. "What was it this time?"

Only my mother could run across a mouse in the basement and immediately think she's caught the bubonic plague. I shrug. "Does it matter?"

Emily gives me a hug and I let my head rest on her shoulder. "I'm so sorry. You want to tell me what happened, kiddo?"

"The three of us sat in the ER for hours because she's a 'super-utilizer' and the staff knows not to prioritize her anymore. I'm glad my morning was clear because we didn't get out of there until 4:00 a.m."

"Shit. Where was your useless sister?"

"We knew it was going to be a late night and she had an early shift," I explain. "That's what she said, at least. Her car was still there at 11:00 a.m. when I left for the office, so it's possible she wasn't being honest. It wouldn't be the first time. But her life is just so rough. She still has a dead-end job, an ex who doesn't hold up his end of the bargain, and two difficult tweens. She deserves someone to offer her a bit of grace."

Emily studies my face. "Liv, be honest with me. Do you really believe she deserves as much grace as you've given her? Do you owe her so much that she can just fuck up everything you're building because she made bad choices?" Emily has never warmed to my sister, not ever, and I'm finally starting to see why.

I consider her question, really and truly ponder it. "I'm starting to think I don't."

Before we can say anything else, before I can describe how disconnected Jay has been for the past two days, and how badly I feel about it all, Zeus addresses the group again. "This week, you'll work in teams to address your fears of rejection. Tomorrow, you'll head to the university quad to collect signatures for this petition." Then he unrolls a banner that reads, *Support Cosmetic Testing on Animals*, featuring a monkey in false lashes and an alpaca wearing lipstick. We let out a collective gasp.

"No one would support this cause!" Emily exclaims.

"This is awful!" Vishnu cries.

"Is this legal?" says Miles.

"Deadass. Cringe," B-Money says.

"I don't care for the outdoors," Michael says.

Zeus looks smug. "Probably going to face some rejection, then, huh?"

Everyone is grousing about the assignment except for me. If it means a couple of hours away from the Vandergrifts, sign me up.

Chapter Seventeen

EMILY

Zeus has sent us into the community for a challenge. Today we're on familiar ground. We've set up shop overlooking Deering Meadow, one of my favorite spots. Deering is a wide expanse of green in the middle of campus. Tons of students are hanging out, sunning themselves, studying, playing Frisbee; it's a real gathering spot, a place to see and be seen. (Naturally, Zeus has parked himself in a lawn chair in the middle of it all, observing from a distance.) Anyone here for summer school or a university tour is likely to pass by us and our three sets of card tables.

Given our task, I hope I don't run into anyone I know. My idea was to wear a wig so I wouldn't be recognized. Fortunately, Miles had the foresight to brief our department chair that he and I were participating in a sociological experiment that he'd likely publish, so I'm not concerned about professional blowback. I guess that's better than a disguise.

Liv and I are paired, and our banner features a fluffy lop-eared rabbit in neon eyeshadow and cat-eye liner. B-Money and Vishnu's table has a fully contoured pig who looks oddly attractive. Neither Miles nor Michael can figure out how to hang their banner with its pink-ombré poodle, so it's still folded on their table. Zeus must have known I wasn't behind Miles's joining, so he put Michael and Miles on a team, and they're getting along like a house on fire. They're so busy talking at each other, I can't imagine they're hearing what the other has to say.

This will be unpleasant, but the best way past is through, so I dive in. A clueless first-year student with a pronounced Adam's apple passes by and I stop him. "Sign a petition to—ugh—support cosmetic testing on animals?" I can ask people to sign, but I don't have to like it.

Instead of arguing with me, or asking me to spew some bullshit about why this is a good (awful) idea, to my dismay, I see the kid grasp the clipboard with his orange-stained fingertips. For all the nice things I think about a lot of Gen Z, there are always outliers. Cheetos fingers here is one of them. People like him ruin it for everyone.

"Can I borrow your pen?" he asks.

"Wait, you're really signing this?" I am equal parts incredulous and furious. "You're just going to sign this ridiculous fake petition, just like that? No questions? Where's your curiosity? Where's your engagement? Where's your outrage? When I was your age, I was busy organizing a campus march against using plastic straws in the dining hall—what are *you* doing with your one wild and precious life? How are *you* making the world better? Do you just indiscriminately do what people say?"

The kid tries to talk, but it takes a second for him to find his voice, and then it comes out hoarse and afraid. "Um . . . yes?"

"You know, people on the street used to call me a worthless hippie for prodding them to give a fuck about the environment, but you're willing to harm animals just because you're eighteen and don't know shit from shit?"

Now he looks like he wants to throw up. "Yes? No? I don't know?"

I rip the clipboard from his hands. "Get to class!"

In the distance, I see Zeus peering at me over his sunglasses. Argh.

Liv gently takes the clipboard from me. "That was a terrific effort, Emily, but maybe we should change our approach? Remember how well Cans for Cans worked? Perhaps get their signature *without* making them cry? I know you have big feelings, but remember, others do, too," she suggests, using her "teaching unruly kindergarteners/gentle parenting" voice that she normally only applies at work or with her family. "If Zeus wants us to do this, he has a reason, and we should engage wholeheartedly."

"Okay, fine. Maybe you're right. But how about you try." I scan the area, looking for a potential sucker. "Look over there, I see a fortysomething man coming our way. He has finance-professor vibes. I bet he'll sign because animal testing would benefit some awful company in his portfolio. Give it a whirl."

I don't know if I'm supposed to be rooting for us to fail or succeed, but if Liv wants us to do it square, I'll give it an honest effort. She approaches him like a flight attendant welcoming a VIP to first class; the only thing missing is a hot towel. "Hi there. My name is Liv. It's so great to meet you! Quick favor, if I'm not asking too much—would you please consider supporting our cause, cosmetic testing on animals?" Liv speaks with the confidence of an accomplished sales professional while looking like a game show hostess.

He snatches the clipboard away from her. "I'll support anything you'd like."

Sometimes I forget that pretty-girl privilege is *real*.

A marching band member passes in front of Michael and Miles's table wearing part of his uniform and carrying his instrument in a big black case. Michael barks, "Hey, Tuba, sign this," and the kid complies.

Why is this so easy? Why is no one engaging with us? Are people so wrapped up in their own little worlds that they're willing to endorse anything, as long as it's no challenge to their intellect? I already hate this exercise so much. What is it that we're supposed to be learning? That most people suck and don't care about anything that doesn't directly impact them? I didn't need today for proof; I discovered that long ago.

No one will help me and I'm out of time and money. I've done every-thing I can to confirm what happened with Jeremy. I mean, I know. I heard the shot. But I don't know, not empirically, and I'm a scientist. I need that proof. I've spent days trying to get answers, desperately seeking justice or accountability, and I've uncovered nothing but dead ends and apathy.

The attitude is, it's a big country, things happen. It's maddening. So many shrugged shoulders.

The bureaucracy here in Brazil is like nothing I've ever experienced, not to mention the corruption. Apparently, I don't have the financial means to convince anyone to care. I've also been to the Australian Consulate-General in São Paulo—Jeremy was one of their citizens. They should be outraged, but mostly they're just confused. They keep saying they have no record of his visa. I've talked to journalists, but no one will tackle this story. I've haunted the Polícia Federal, and they have no answers, no leads. Nothing I'm doing is working. I can't even get more than basic information out of Planet BlueLove, but I don't blame them. They'd give me more if they had it. In this line of work, it's better if we don't ask a ton of questions.

I've been trying to locate Jeremy's family in Melbourne, but thousands of people there have the surname Jones. It's like finding a needle in a haystack, and the Wi-Fi here isn't as reliable as it should be. I feel like I'm failing at making sure his life had meaning. I want to go to Australia; I'm sure I'll have more luck in person.

I can't eat, I can't sleep, and I have so little fuel in my tank that I'm starting to hallucinate. Yesterday—on my way back from the embassy, again—I could have sworn I saw him through the window of a gourmet restaurant, sipping a caipirinha with a group of well-groomed Brazilian men in suits. I tried to push past the condescending maître d'. Such was my state of agitation, he first assumed I was unhoused and wouldn't let me enter. Once I got inside, the table was empty. Obviously, my mind wasn't right. But for one moment, I was so sure.

I am spinning out down here and I don't know what to do. The consensus is that I need to go back to the US and regroup, but I want to go to Australia. Only Liv has supported me. She even paid for another week in the hotel, despite the fact that I said no. She's still waiting tables part time as she builds her real estate career. She's offered more, but I can't take it, and I will 100 percent pay her back the minute I can.

Even my normally supportive family has had enough. They're so worried about me that they're demanding I come home. My dad says there's a ticket with my name on it at the American Airlines counter. He's so anxious for me to get out, he's offered to pay for graduate school. He thinks I should become a professor . . . exactly the life I swore I'd never have.

If only I could get someone on my side, everything would be different.

Liv has always had my back, so if this exercise is important to her now, I have to prioritize it. "Let me try again," I say. She raises an eyebrow, skeptical. "I'll be nicer, pinky swear." We lock fingers and she visibly relaxes. Our pinky swears are as solid as a notarized contract. I haven't violated one in the fifteen-plus years we've been friends, and neither has she.

Finally, she hands me the clipboard, and I easily get signatures from three prospective students from Delaware. They're not old enough to sign anything legally, but since it's all a farce, it doesn't matter. Plus, it made Liv happy. I feel like she needs a win.

B-Money is having equally good luck getting signatures. I observe as he approaches a goth student in head-to-toe black, the male version of Wednesday Addams, complete with lace-up platform boots. He's carrying a parasol to shade his unnaturally white skin. "You down with signing a petition to support testing on animals?" B-Money asks. There's no way this kid will sign—he has to be antiestablishment.

Shockingly, the student is totally into the idea. "Your performance art is slay."

After two hours of this, our clipboards are depressingly full of autographs. The only person who's not gotten any signatures is Vishnu, and the poor guy is beating himself up about it. He crumbles every time he tries to approach anyone. If he had one iota of his brother's charisma, a single ounce of Jay's confidence, he'd be the one going out with Liv, I know it.

Despite similar features and build, it's like Jay and Vishnu aren't even from the same planet, let alone the same parents. Jay's assertive and smooth and completely charming. Given how opposite Dee and Liv are, the brothers' differences make sense. You can have the same of everything—nature and nurture—and still turn out entirely different.

We're all trying to pump Vishnu up since neither Liv nor I want to leave him before he gets a single signature. (Miles and Michael took off half an hour ago. The signatures were super easy for them because everyone recognized Miles from TikTok and people lined up to talk to him.) I spot the perfect target and grab Vishnu.

"That girl, right there? The one filming herself while she walks? That's my student, Taylor. You met her at the talent show. Ask her," I instruct, giving him a gentle shove.

Ever so politely, Vishnu approaches her. "Hello, Ms. Taylor, excuse me, I'm Vishnu. May I have a moment?"

She says, "I don't know?" but she still stops to hear him out.

Vishnu tries to compose himself. "Thank you so much. Would you please consider endorsing this petition for animal testing in the cosmetic industry?"

"Do you mean against animal testing?" Taylor asks. She looks at the banner and goes from zero to pissed before returning her attention to her live stream, speaking more to the camera than to Vishnu. "Because I know you did not ask me to hurt baby animals when there are so many ah-may-zing cruelty-free brands?"

"I'm so sorry," he stammers, "I just—"

"Do you even know how medical stuff works?" Her voice gets louder with every word. She's starting to attract a crowd. I imagine the hearts from her live stream are pouring across her screen right now.

"I mean, I am a radiologist, so—"

"You think because you're, like, a radio-ologer, it's okay to blind puppies and kitties? Spoiler alert, they don't have seeing-eye dogs for dogs!" She addresses both the crowd and the audience on her phone as Vishnu attempts to melt himself into the sidewalk. "This guy? He wants to experiment on your pets? When the FDA doesn't even require animal testing as a methodology? Is your name Dr. Vishnu *Mengele* or something?"

I have to admit, *That kid is starting to grow on me.*

❧

"Did you see? The crowd literally threw a tomato at poor Vishnu," I say. "I didn't know that happened outside of cartoons. I have no idea why everyone turned on *him* specifically, as we were all out there. But he runs like the wind, I'll give him that. He should come to the track with Liv and me."

Zeus and I are chatting during a break. I wouldn't say that I come up with excuses to converse with him every session, but I also wouldn't say that I don't. Last week, he, B-Money, and I spent so long talking about the Bears' preseason (this is our year, I'm sure of it!), Michael and Miles left and Liv and Vishnu fell asleep.

However, I find the best way to interface one-on-one with him is to complain about his methodology, which is annoying because he's unflappable and my ire seems to amuse him. I say, "So my question is, why? How is getting Vishnu pelted with old produce going to move the needle? In what ways is this training improving us?"

That I feel like our sessions are working sort of makes me angry. It makes no logical sense. We're participating in bizarre activities, and we keep coming out the other end stronger, for no discernable reason. And every time I ask Zeus about his protocol, he gives me deliberately random answers. He's a mystery, wrapped in an enigma, who should be on the cover of *GQ*.

"Emily," he says. He places a strong hand on my shoulder. His palm is warm without being too hot, and I try to ignore the frisson of electricity that it sparks. "I'm going to paraphrase a bit of wisdom from one of my favorite thinkers. So often people make a choice—that choice is to obsess over the negative things people say about you or obsess over the positive. The problem with either of these approaches is that they both point to *you* being obsessed with *yourself*. Giving up that obsession is the key to happiness."

"Is that Aristotle?" I ask. I appreciate Aristotle. Along with being one of the greatest Sophists in recorded history, he delivered his philosophy in a scientific context. His quote vibes with Aristotle's thoughts on virtue, which can be best described as all things in moderation, including how we see ourselves in the world. Or maybe this is more Kant or Hume. I've got it! I snap my fingers. "John Locke?"

"No, it's Taylor Swift." I laugh before I realize he's not joking. Still, surely he's kidding. Grown men do not quote pop stars; they just don't. But then I remember that YouTube video. Before I can grill him, he says, "Emily, this is difficult because you're learning to be a sheepdog instead of the wolf you once were or the sheep you are now."

"I am *not* a sheep," I say, even though I can think of a thousand times I've gone along to get along in the past ten years. What else would you call it when I finally boarded that flight to come home to the US rather than go to Australia? Rather than making the more difficult choice to find Jeremy's people.

Zeus fixes his topaz gaze on mine, and I have to remind myself to breathe. Is this what it's like to be around an alpha man again? I mean, we're having this intense conversation in a room with my boyfriend of more than three years, and I've almost entirely forgotten Miles's existence. The worst part is, Miles is oblivious. He's knee deep in a conversation with Michael about amino acid–based hair conditioner. Ironically, it's produced by a company that conducts animal testing.

Zeus says, "Let me explain it in the terms of Dave Grossman's parable. It's something he came up with to describe how law officers should view their role. Law enforcement is most effective when officers consider themselves to be sheepdogs that protect the flock."

"But we're not police officers. Wait, were *you* a cop? Are you one now?" I ask. Zeus had to have been either law enforcement or some sort of soldier. He gives off such military vibes. Hold on . . . what if he works for a black ops agency? Like a shadowy conspiracy? Although why would an entity like that be interested in any of us? I'm not even secretive about what's on my final exam. What important information are any of us hiding? Michael doesn't password-protect his phone. Liv sells condos. B-Money makes coffee. Vishnu is an amateur romance writer. We're not exactly huge intelligence assets.

Zeus ignores my question. "Sheepdogs keep the sheep safe from danger outside the fence. The sheep? They resent the sheepdogs because those dogs are scary—they look too much like wolves. They growl and bite and have sharp teeth and strong jaws. You know who else hates the sheepdogs? The wolves. Because the sheepdogs are doing their jobs, the wolves go hungry. But every day, the sheepdogs perform their duties, putting their lives on the line to protect those who resent them, and with zero thanks."

I consider his words, trying to extract their essence and apply them to our group. What I realize is . . . "That makes no sense."

Zeus is steadfast about this philosophy. "Of course it does. If you train the weakest sheep to become ad hoc sheepdogs, those wolves will never see it coming. You guys are powerful and capable. Collectively, you're a secret weapon, and you should never lose sight of that. Anyway, this will coalesce more after this next challenge." He claps his hands and everyone jumps. "Gather round, we need to discuss what you're doing tomorrow."

I am 95 percent convinced whatever we're going to do next is ridiculous and that he is a complete fraud.

But I am absolutely living for the 5 percent that actually believes in him.

Chapter Eighteen

Liv

"You're really buying this? You truly believe that these challenges are helping us become our best selves?" Emily grills me. It's our third time in a week behind the card tables on campus. I had to finagle to get away from the Vandergrifts, so I compromised by starting extra early with them today.

I understand Emily's reticence. The paces that Zeus has put us through over the past week have been . . . trying. That goes without saying. I was worried about how our doing this was going to impact Emily's job. This is so not kosher. Miles actually stepped in to save the day, as he's somehow tied this into a research project that *Scientific American* has expressed interest in publishing, so the university has given us free rein. (Of course, instead of this making Emily relieved, she's just annoyed.)

We thought the animal testing was hard but had no idea what waited for us—lobbying against the campus smoking ban. We handed out cigarettes! Actual cancer-causing cigarettes! I had to stop Michael from letting children have them! Only giving away firearms on the quad would have made many of the passersby angrier. That Zeus may have been laughing at us from a bench behind a newspaper did not help appease Emily.

What's ironic is that so many of the people who were furious with us for promoting smoking lectured us with vapes in hand. Of course, Emily had to engage with them. Equally dismaying were all the people excited to take free cigarettes. One girl asked Emily if smoking would help her lose weight. Emily was all, "I imagine you'll drop a few pounds during the chemo." And then the girl took a handful, almost a whole pack! The more I learn about humanity, the more convinced I am that most people will accept anything if it's free, regardless of how offensive, reckless, or dangerous.

Today, though? Today might just finish Emily off. She is positively fuming because we're *lobbying to end women's suffrage*. I assumed that students would be savvier, that they would understand we were asking them to endorse a petition to revoke a woman's right to vote. But the wording on our materials is deceptive, and most people are so distracted by their phones, they're only half paying attention. "Suffrage" is a tricky word, kind of like "apartheid." The definition is so important, but also easy to confuse for the opposite meaning. I'm sure that is exactly why Zeus chose the topic.

The petitions aren't the hardest part, though, because a lot of people also conflate suffrage and suffering, so they figure it's about reversing the Supreme Court decision on Roe v. Wade and happily grab a clipboard. Argh. But that's not the worst part. That honor goes to giving signees their free gift—a BPA-full (not BPA-free) plastic water bottle with a graphic logo that reads, *No Votes for Fat Chicks*. It's a lot to swallow while maintaining a good attitude.

Before I can answer Emily's question about whether these challenges are actually helping us, a frat rat clad in flip-flops and a basketball tank sidles up. He signs the petition without any convincing. Emily is livid, with spots of color high on her cheeks. "You realize this is to end women's suffrage, right? As in deny women the right to vote?"

"Amen, I'm with ya. Let's repeal the Nineteenth Amendment, baby!" crows the frat rat as he pumps his fist in the air.

"Thank you so much for trying to set back the women's movement one hundred years," Emily hisses. I can see her calculating whether she wants to risk a seventh arrest or whether it's worth ruining her chances for tenure. It must not be, because she backs down, but begrudgingly.

The guy stands there with a cheese-eating grin on his face. "Well? Don't I get my water bottle?"

Lightning fast, Emily hurls the bottle at him, and it nails him in the breadbasket. For someone who hasn't played the sport in years, her pitching arm is still quite something. The bottle is light, so it does no damage, fortunately for Emily's current relationship with freedom. The frat guy appraises us while stuffing a crumbly brown wad of dip between his lip and gum. "You just proved my point. That's exactly why you don't deserve the right to vote." As he saunters off, I notice he's using the water bottle as a tobacco spittoon. Gross.

Emily points to Zeus and his newspaper. "*He* has gone too far. Every time I think our challenges can't get worse, they do. We're not out here being rejected; we're out here getting mad."

Every time Zeus assigns us something, Emily comes more alive in her opposition, possibly because he's watching us. The only feeling Emily loves more than righteous indignation is fighting the powers that be, and Zeus has delivered both in spades. This challenge couldn't be more perfect for her. She won't admit it, but he's forcing her to find the purpose she lost long ago, exactly as he promised in our initial session. She's practically reborn. I love every part of Emily, but I missed this take-no-prisoners side of Action Emily. She's been hiding behind messy buns and apathy and Miles for far too long.

"Right, and I'm sure that's the point," I say. "This task isn't about facing our fear of rejection. It can't be. So far, every assignment has been some sort of misdirection. What if the real goal is for us to get fired up enough to, say, quit the brokerage or dump Miles? You can't take this task literally. No sane person would have us out here promoting smoking, animal cruelty, or reversing the right to vote."

I'm not sure she's ready to see the genius of his plan, but my words have nudged her needle out of the red. She seems to collect herself. "What if . . . what if it's about us exercising our free will? What if he wants to see that we'll buck the rules? Like we're conquering a fear of nonconformity? Like we think this is bullshit, so we pack it up early?" Emily suggests, hopeful that I'll agree.

Who knows? That might be exactly his plan. I nod with encouragement.

I look around to see how the guys are faring. Miles and Michael abandoned their table after giving out their water bottles. They left, saying something about having watery iced coffees at the café. B-Money and Vishnu are in the thick of it, still in possession of most of their inventory. I spot a crowd of pretty girls in sorority letters, led by Emily's student. They're advancing on Vishnu, who looks like he's ready to cower under his card table. It's clear *they* understand what the word "suffrage" means.

"I agree, let's wrap it up," I say. I'm supposed to see Jay later, so I like the idea of ending this a bit early. We've had such an amazing time over the past few weeks, but I'm worried I'm losing his interest. A couple nights ago, I was set to cook him dinner, but my stove broke. I've wanted that thing to crap out for years, but not on what was supposed to be a special night. DoorDash delivery wasn't the evening I'd planned. And this time, he'd had to dip out early because of some work emergency. I feel like I need to get it right tonight, or else.

We notice the crowd around Vishnu growing louder and more aggressive. Emily says, "I should intervene. These kids know me and they'll listen to me. Do you mind packing up the table? Then we can take it all to the car together."

"Of course!"

As Emily heads down the path, I notice something small, round, and airborne on a collision course with Vishnu. He ducks down as the object explodes with a red splat on the card table he's now using as a shield.

Where does everyone keep finding these tomatoes on campus?

❦

This is the second emergency session Zeus has called this week. I suspect we're building up to something. The first time, I had to let down Jay again. He didn't even sound mad, just . . . resigned. At least it wasn't my fault this time. Sparring will feel good; I have some frustration to release.

To prepare, I'm stretching by the boxing ring; Vishnu and B-Money join me. "I meant to ask last time—did any of the tomatoes hit you?" I ask Vishnu.

"No, no, no problem! I was fine," he assures me.

"You were picking tomato seeds out of your ear, my man," B-Money says.

"Maybe just a few. Definitely not enough to make a whole marinara sauce. Anyway, Liv, how fortuitous it is that you hit it off with my brother. Jay talks about you every day at work. Which does not bother me in the least," he says.

"He has to be so frustrated," I say. I bend over to loosen up my hamstrings. "Between work and home, I feel like I'm getting sucked away with too many unnecessary obligations."

"All that sucking in so many directions must be painful," he says. He's also flipped upside down to maintain eye contact.

B-Money slaps Vishnu on the small of his back. "What?" Vishnu says, righting himself. "I'm having a conversation."

"You were having an aneurysm, bro. I'm saving you from yourself," B-Money says.

I love seeing how their friendship is growing. They're such an unlikely pair.

"Anyway, at least I didn't have to let him down tonight. He was the one who had to cancel for a work thing. You guys must be so busy too," I say. I was relieved when he had to bail.

Vishnu appears puzzled. "But he doesn't work—" Before he can complete his thought, Zeus materializes from the darkness and we all gasp.

"You should wear a bell," Emily grouses.

"First order of business," Zeus says. "I want to say that Vishnu received the fewest signatures on all the petitions. Vishnu, can you come over here?"

"I am terribly sorry," Vishnu says as he makes his way to Zeus. "I will try harder to—"

"That means you're the winner!"

"What? How does that make *him* the winner?" Emily demands. Even though she found every exercise repugnant, she hustled hard enough to leave everyone else in the dust. She even got twice the signatures I did and I sell professionally. I think there's something very familiar about clipboards for her. Maybe they feel like coming home.

"He had the most rejections, which means he had to face his fear of rejection most often," Zeus explains.

"What'd my man win?" B-Money asks.

"Our admiration and respect," Zeus replies.

"Well, thank you very much. I never win anything!" Vishnu says, beaming with pride.

"You also receive this." Zeus hands Vishnu a straw basket lined with a gingham napkin. It's full of ripe tomatoes. "How much better will these tomatoes taste when they're not being whipped at your head?"

"Quite a bit, I suppose," he replies. What a lovely man he is. He genuinely seems grateful for everything.

"There's a card too."

Vishnu opens the card and then squeals with delight. He does a happy little jig before announcing, "There's a gift card! A $250 gift card to the Olive Garden! I hope everyone will please join me for a delicious dinner!"

We all cheer, even Michael, jazzed to see Vishnu so pleased. See? Our tasks are never quite what they seem. I'm glad to see Vishnu get a win; he deserves it.

"It's not going to be tonight, though," Zeus says. "We'll be working late because I won't be here next week."

"But we have less than two weeks left!" Emily exclaims.

Zeus shrugs. "I have an urgent matter."

"What sort of urgent matter?" she persists.

"You're doing spy stuff, right? Pretty sure my man is James Bond. Who are you working for, the CIA? MI6? Better not be the GRU, hacking elections and shit," B-Money says.

"This is exactly what I've been saying all along!" Emily exclaims. She and B-Money put their heads together and begin to whisper. B-Money and Emily are convinced that there's some higher purpose to Fearless Inc. and that all is not what it seems. They are bound and determined to find out.

Zeus ignores them. He picks up a manila folder adorned with some kind of anime-looking strawberry logo. Cute! He briefly reads the contents and then says, "The task is to address your fear of saying no. Because saying no leads to confrontation. And you're all terrified of confrontation."

I don't know that that's entirely true. Emily's not afraid of confrontation. It used to be her raison d'être. Then I spot her glowering at Miles, and I realize that breaking up with him would be a form of confrontation and she's been dancing around it for months. So I guess Zeus isn't wrong. Most of us nod. Guilty as charged.

Michael says, "I'm not afraid to say no. I say no all day long. It's literally my job."

"Great," Zeus says. "You're in charge."

"Are you kidding?" Emily fumes.

"Say what?" asks B-Money.

"Congratulations?" says Vishnu.

"Congratulations," declares Miles.

Zeus stares me down. "Liv? What do you think?"

"I think you have a plan and we should trust it?" I say.

Zeus looks deeply disappointed. He crosses his arms over his chest, hugging the folder. "None of you said no to Michael leading the group, not one of you. You all failed the first part of this assignment." He nods toward a preening Michael. "Except for you, brother."

Zeus then vanishes into the din and returns with a small object. He tosses it to Michael. Michael inspects it and then blows hard on the silver whistle, saying, "Look at me, I'm the captain now."

"I'll have a bottle of Chianti," I say. I'm late meeting the group at the Olive Garden. Joyce and John wanted to check out how a place on Old Glenview Road looked in the twilight. I took them at their word, but really, they wanted to see if any "unsavory" elements were on the street at night. The only thing unsavory was Joyce's sartorial choice. Four different plaids in one ensemble are three too many. We ran into Dr. Farooqi, the oral surgeon who removed my wisdom teeth, and now the Old Glenview listing is out because of "the ethnic element." I'm disgusted. How does anyone expect to find a place when they despise everyone who's even a tiny bit different from them? Since when did hate become a reasonable strategy by which to conduct one's life? Or real estate search?

"Wait, do you mean a glass?" the waiter asks.

"I do not." While I wait for my wine to arrive, I help myself to an already open bottle on the table, tossing it back like a shot rather than a full-bodied cabernet.

Emily looks up from her phone, mouthing, "WTF?" but I just shake my head. I don't have it in me to explain.

"Welcome to our group dinner! And hello, Liv, how was your day?" Vishnu asks. He seems so proud to be hosting us. As much as I like Jay, there's something so childlike and guileless about Vishnu that Jay's missing. I don't know why someone nice hasn't swooped him up, except it would probably terrify him.

I drink another shot/glass. "Fan-freaking-tastic. My incredibly demanding clients are racist, sexist, misogynist, and ableist." The last one surprised me. Who knew that they'd take issue with a home accommodated for the injured Iraq war veteran who lived there? That hero lost a leg to an IED *while fighting for America*. How can you have an issue with that? *How?*

"That's a lot of 'ists.' At least they are not homophobic?" Vishnu offers.

I take another chug, thinking about the rainbow flag incident earlier in the month. "Nope, they were that first. I accidentally left that out."

From across the table, B-Money shouts something, then he and Emily hoot and high-five. "We did it!" Emily cheers, holding up her phone like it's the golden ticket.

"Did what?" Vishnu asks.

"Found Zeus's Instagram!" B-Money clarifies.

"How?" I ask. "Emily's been cyberstalking him for weeks and nothing." I shoot a look in Miles's direction and clap a hand over my mouth. I should not have said that out loud. Fortunately, he and Michael are too busy debating over the appetizer list.

"I cracked the code. See, Emily tried every iteration of all things Zeus, but she couldn't find anything. Then I remembered how he told us he has two great loves. We started plugging in every exotic bird type and Swiftian song lyric and finally hit on it!" B-Money and Emily are absolutely elated.

"What is his username?" I ask.

Sheepishly, B-Money says, "Zeus_loves_birds_and_Tay."

"That's some fancy sleuthing, kids," Michael snorts. "Okay, I'm ordering for the table. Everyone like fried calamari?"

"Ugh, no, too rubbery," Emily says.

"I don't mess with tentacles," B-Money says.

"I am allergic to mollusks," Vishnu says.

"Do they have a face? I don't eat anything with a face," Miles says.

"Fifty-three homes. How can anyone hate fifty-three homes? It's statistically impossible," I say, then drain my glass again. The waiter brings my bottle, and I snatch it out of his hands before he can place it on the table.

"Um, Livvy? Do you want to cut that with some water? Maybe a Diet Coke?" Emily asks. "Remember that night at Lambda Chi when you didn't realize the punch had rum in it?"

We had to throw out our metal waste can after that night, and to this day, I can't look at rum. I assure her, "I'm good."

"Okay, then," the waiter says. "May I start you with some appetizers? Everyone loves our spinach-artichoke dip and our toasted ravioli." We look at each other and nod—they all sound good. "We also have a special tonight. It's deep-fried squash blossoms." More nods of approval. "I forgot, there's a cheese plate."

Fuck cheese plates, I think, at which point everyone stops what they're doing and looks at me with widened eyes. Uh oh, I think I said that out loud.

Michael says, "Six orders of calamari, please." We all grumble and Michael blows his whistle. "Y'all just failed the second test."

"Does Jay like me or does Jay *like me* like me?" I ask Vishnu. I'm having a wee bit of trouble seeing him through my haze of tasty wine. Vishnu's face looks funny. I poke at it because his head is like cotton candy or a piñata or an emoji. So bulbous. So big and kind. His eyes are little slits and his lips are like Polish sausages. "Why do you have hot dog lips?"

Vishnu tells me, "I know that he is fond of you, and who would not be? You are a fine lady and beautiful on the inside, where it is most important. But I believe my brother is a man who might not yet be serious, so please do not pin hopes on him, I beg you."

I feel like Vishnu is trying to tell me something, but I don't know what. "I'm always serious," I say. "Is your face usually this round?"

Michael blows the whistle. "That's for your allergic reaction."

"You insisted I taste your clam linguini!" Vishnu says.

"You didn't say no," Michael counters.

"I did say no! Many times. Mollusk allergy."

"Did you say it fifty-three freaking times?" I ask.

"Who's driving Liv home?" Emily asks. "I'm happy to do it, but she's in the opposite direction from me."

"I thought we had plans," Miles protests.

"You really think I'm going to leave my best friend this drunk in a chain restaurant?" Emily replies. She seems expaster . . . exparest . . . extrapo . . . mad.

"I don't need your ride. Jay is picking me up. He told me to call when I was done and maybe he would be free. I've been calling and callllllllling but he's not answering."

B-Money clucks his tongue and exchanges a look with Emily. "Guuuurl . . ."

"He must not be free," I say. I look at my phone. "There's a lot of texts but nothing from my boyfriend."

"Is Jay your boyfriend now?" Vishnu asks.

"He is in my head," I reply, and I begin to hiccup. "I believe I was overserved. Someone should speak to the maamager . . . manger . . . mandible . . . person in charge."

"I would be happy to drive you home, Liv," Vishnu offers.

Michael blows his whistle and starts barking instructions. He points to Vishnu. "You, take your fat head to the ER." To Emily and Miles, "You go home with your boyfriend and have a conversation."

To B-Money, "You, well, you don't have to go home but you can't stay here."

Our waiter says, "Why can't he stay here? We're open for another hour."

Michael blasts his whistle again and points to me. "You. Let's go."

"I assumed you had better taste," Michael says, surveying my apartment. He runs a finger over an armoire, checking for dust, and turns my knickknacks over in his hands. "The couch and rug are nice, artwork's decent, but those kitchen cabinets? That countertop? Jack and Chrissy want the Ropers to upgrade, stat. Blech."

"I'm sorry, I don't know who your friends are, but Ma won't let me change things. She says it's gotta stay the way it was when Daddy left in case he ever comes back," I explain.

My balance is not balancing. Were my floors always so tilted? I feel like I'd recall them being tilted. Oh no . . . I think my floors have slanted, like a villain's lair in the old Batman show. Now I'm so sad. Am I the bad guy now? My slanty floors point to yes. I start to tear up and sniffle, so I reach into Michael's jacket for his pocket square and blow my nose. Because I am polite. Then I hand it back to him.

"Yuck. Don't get your sad country western lyrics all over me, honey," he says, rejecting the square. For good measure, he blasts his whistle, and I clamp my hands over my ears.

So loud! So sharp! "I am not a fan of your whoostle."

"Confront me, then. Tell me to stop."

I consider the best way to do this. "Sir, if it's not too much to ask, would you mind hooting your whoostle a teeny lil bit less?"

He blasts his whoostle again. "Fail. Try again. Demand, not ask."

Before I can rephrase my request, Dee comes busting in. "You have to take Ma to the ER!"

"Now what?" I ask.

"Polio."

"Marco?" I ask.

"No," she says. *"Polio."*

"Marco?"

Michael blasts his whoostle and that helps me understand what she's saying. "Oh, polio. The horses who play golf. Sounds legit to me. And you can't go because . . . is it because the horses can't swim?"

"Can't have my kids catching polio."

I think I am too drinky to argue.

"Polio?" Michael says, seeming appalled. "Is it 1934 again?"

"'Sa long story. Can you drive us?"

He laughs. "You certainly can't."

"Ma!" I shout. "We're coming!"

Michael takes one last look at my apartment. "Have you ever considered moving out?" he asks.

"Fifty-three times every day." I reach for his whoostle and blow into it. He quickly swats it out of my hands.

"Stop it. That's annoying."

I grab his face with my hands and look deep into his eyes. "Teach me your ways."

Chapter Nineteen

EMILY

"Emily, I've been trying to talk to you for a while now, but it feels like you've been avoiding me," Miles says. "Might we have a confab?"

"Just say 'chat,' Miles," I tell him, not even looking up from my iPad, where I've been studying photos on Zeus's Instagram. As always, Chairman Meow is on my shoulder. I tab through Zeus's grid, and there are literally hundreds of shots of him in the same exact poses in different locations. He's partial to pursed lips and a peace sign. While his feed is somewhat disconcerting in its uniformity, I can guarantee it's far more interesting than whatever Miles has to say next.

"I feel like you've been pulling away from me," he says.

I'm glad he's picked up on that, as it's exactly what's been happening. I give him a "Hmm" in response. I'm tired and full of dinner and I'm trying to unravel a particularly knotted thread with Zeus. Now is not the time to talk about us, and I'm hoping my body language conveys this. I do want to do this—and I need to do this—but not right now.

"I even joined your group as a way of getting closer to you. I wanted to see what was so important to you that you had no time for Memily." This is his longtime portmanteau for us, and I refuse to acknowledge it. I would kill it with fire if I could. "This experience has opened my eyes, and now I have the testicular fortitude to do what should have been done a long time ago."

Before I can suggest "Just say 'balls,' Miles," I glance up to see him standing in front of me. I don't like the look on his face—it's too sincere, too serious. I can feel the rigatoni and five-cheese marinara begin to roil in my stomach, along with far too many breadsticks. Why do they have to be unlimited? Why? Nothing that good should be unlimited. But I hate waste! As a matter of fact, I hate the Olive Garden . . . in theory. I recently read a study about the waste accumulated from their unlimited portions of salad and bread. In practice, I—hold on, why is he kneeling?

Oh, shit, he's *kneeling*.

He is on *one knee*. No. *No*. Meow flies off my shoulder and runs toward the bathroom. Even he doesn't want this. Why is this happening? Haven't I done everything to dissuade him from wanting a future with me? Except for saying it outright, and I swear it's coming soon. He begins fumbling in his pocket, and I want to run, but I can't because all the gluten is weighing me down like a boat anchor.

"This has been a long time coming, and we both know it."

Do we, Miles? Do we both know it? I feel like we do not. With his right hand, he gently takes my left, and for a moment, I profoundly regret not chopping it off while I had the chance. We could have gone to one of those new axe-throwing bars my students talk about; I could've made it seem like an accident. What does liability insurance look like in those places? First, we pump the patrons full of booze. Then we give them full-size axes to hurl and say, "Good luck." This can't be a wise business model.

He nudges open my clenched fist, and I feel the weight of something cold and metallic dropping into it. I squeeze my eyes shut because I can't even look. It's heavy. Why is it so heavy? How big is this awful blood diamond that it's so heavy?

"Damn it, Emily, you're making this more difficult than it should be."

I'm so surprised by his sharp tone that my eyes snap open. When I look down at the future pending in my hand, I see . . . my house key. My house key?

"You're not the person I thought you were, Emily. I can't do this anymore. Obviously, we'll keep it professional at work, and also in the group, but I deserve more than this. Memily is no longer going to happen, but I will make it my job to ensure that we can remain friends."

And just like that, I am racked with sobs. To spare his feelings, I do not tell him that they are tears of joy.

"Lemme get this straight, my man dumped you. He took in all of this"—B-Money swipes his hand in a circular direction in front of me—"and said, 'Nah, I'mma do better.'"

Even if the group has been unsuccessful on every level—and I'm not saying it has—it has at least succeeded in opening up my (almost nonexistent) social circle. I've made new friends that I didn't know I needed and now can't imagine being without. I love waking up to whatever dog or cat meme Vishnu has sent us to start the day. I love how the only opinions Michael shares are unfiltered. I never pictured myself becoming confidants with the too-cool-for-school kid from the lousy coffee shop, yet here we are. I'm now as vested in his life and success as I am in Liv's. Did not see that coming.

"Aw, thanks. That is exactly what happened," I tell him. I cannot stop smiling. I haven't been this happy since . . . before. The joy in my heart brings me back to that day that Jeremy told me what we had was real. To always remember that. And I do. I remember the pure joy I felt.

B-Money snaps me out of my reverie. "How relieved were you that he didn't propose?"

I laugh. "What's the highest number? Infinity? A googol? That much."

What's weird is that Miles seemed just as relieved as me, once we recognized that we aren't a match. We ended up talking for a couple of hours afterward and it was all so easy. I actually think we can be friends. I bet I'd even like that, strange as it may sound. He earned my respect by doing what I could not bring myself to do, by verbalizing that he wasn't getting what he needed. He literally took control of the situation; I didn't know he had it in him. We worked out visitation rights for Chairman Meow; I would genuinely hate for Miles to lose his true love. I let him keep the key for any cat emergencies. Besides, it's not like he's ever coming in without knocking first, anyway.

What's interesting is, he admits he also joined the group to gain confidence, specifically, confidence to tell me my tenure is in real jeopardy. The chancellor doubts my commitment, which makes sense, as *I'm* not entirely confident in my commitment. Miles gave me the heads-up that she'll be monitoring my class before the summer session ends and that I should be prepared. He's been texting me advice on how I should handle this, which I now find less annoying and more touching. But the more I think of it, the more I wonder if teaching is the best use of my passion or talent, so I don't see the point of worrying.

"Enough about Miles," I tell B-Money. He's going to be fine. He actually showed me some of the DMs he gets on his Instagram, and I can't believe how many women are into him. Like, cute, normal women. He gets propositioned left and right, and they can't all be Russian bots. There's too many! I suspect he won't be alone for long.

Regardless, at the moment, we have bigger fish to fry.

"Let's crack this mystery." I pull up Zeus's grid on my iPad so we can get a closer look. "What do you make of all the selfies in the same pose?"

"Do you watch *Survivor*?" he asks.

"The show where people are dropped in a jungle?"

"That's the one."

"Maybe once or twice. I kind of lived it, though. Does that count?"

"In this case, nah. And I do not even want to imagine the kind of bugs you encountered there." He's right; he doesn't.

"So, what about the show?" I ask.

"Okay, people find these hidden immunity idols, right? The idols protect them from being voted out of the game. Sometimes these idols only have power if a person on the other team has one too. So they have to identify themselves to let the person on the other team know they've got it. But they can't just say, *Yo, I got the left half,* and also, the teams are separated, so they can't get together and talk."

"This doesn't sound like my experience in the jungle at all."

He frowns at me. "Are you always such a buzzkill?"

"Actually, a lot less so now than I was before we started," I admit.

"Big yikes. Anyway, the people with the idols, they have to say a phrase to identify themselves when the groups come together before a challenge. They gotta say something nonsensical like *They say a stitch in time saves nine, but I only count eight.* They sound like the heat has gotten to them, and everyone's all, 'Bruh, what?' But the one person who knows what it's supposed to mean is alerted, and they can make a plan from there."

I don't get it. "Bruh, what?"

B-Money shakes his head and it makes the little gold beads click against each other. "These selfies. I am saying they are some straight-up spy shit. They could be secret codes, because his face is the exact same in each shot, but the backdrop is different."

"Code for what? For 'I only have one look'?"

"Let's zoom in on this one. First, there's the caption, '*Feeling cute, might delete later?*' That's code! That's code for a meetup time. Then, check it out—do you see that street sign way in the back? He is giving someone a location. This is a where and a when."

I love that B-Money is into this too, but I sort of hate that he's figured out more than I have. "But how would we possibly know where that is?"

"Reverse image search, girl. Lemme just . . ." He taps at his phone and less than thirty seconds later, brings up a map. "He was here." He points to a place in the industrial park beyond O'Hare.

"Whoa. I've never seen that before. Do you have some special software or app for that?"

He looks at me like I'm completely clueless. "It's Google. And it's not *the* Google. Just Google."

"Are you calling me old?" I ask.

"I'm not *not* calling you old," he replies. He's not *not* right. "I'm just saying maybe you should stick with LinkedIn."

I know this is supposed to be an insult, but I do use LinkedIn to find out what my former teammates are up to. None of them are out in the field anymore. A lot of them hold jobs that aren't even related to environmental causes. We all used to be so passionate. I should reconnect. I bet some of them might be able to relate to what I'm going through. You know what? If I've learned anything from Fearless Inc., it's that no person is an island. I need to open myself up, let people in, and I bet I could help some of them with what I'm learning. I am definitely going to be better about trying to connect and reconnect.

I ask him, "So, what do we do now?"

"We wait for him to post again."

Okay, okay, I probably care about my job a little more than I let myself believe, although it's hard to tell when I'm stuck teaching the non-science students. But I *do* care, meaning I have to work on my lesson plan. Of course, I find the water table riveting, so we should cover that for the next few classes.

Creating a new lesson plan would be easier if I weren't consumed with refreshing Instagram every fourteen seconds.

Something is up, though. I mean, how did Zeus know so much about us? Like, how did he know about B-Money's boat? That's super specific. How was he able to scoop us up after the kidnapping exercise? What is the likelihood that five people who so desperately needed a change were in the same place at the same time? Was that planned too? Were the woman with the stroller and the foiled robber plants of some sort, all part of some master plan? Are we being recruited for something? If so, what?

I could see my skills or Vishnu's medical training used in some grand caper, but where do Liv and Michael and B-Money fit in? Does the CIA need Realtors and Luddite ad men and MCs? I don't want to sell short what they do, but how do those skills gel with espionage? *Is* this espionage? What's to be gained by turning us into would-be heroes, when we've clearly been anti-heroes for so long?

Or did we just join a gym with a new spin—creating a mind-body-spirit connection with a false derring-do narrative? Like, is this some ultrafunctional fitness fad everyone's going to follow instead of SoulCycle or Barry's Bootcamp? Is it strange that I'll be so disappointed if it is?

I'm afraid I won't be able to get anything done until we figure out where Zeus has gone; it feels like it's the key to whatever this is. I mean, *I* can't just disappear from class right before finals. We only have one week left—how does it make sense that Michael's in charge for what should be the most important week? Something is afoot, I just know it.

What if *this* is a mission? What if we're supposed to be looking for him? Is that what he wants? My mind is racing, and I just can't concentrate on making the normally fascinating turbidity of groundwater interesting.

I start poking at my phone, refresh, refresh, refresh, refreshing. Nothing new from Zeus, but I do have a LinkedIn notification. I have always ignored these. When I was with BlueLove, all I wanted to do was tell everyone where I was and what I was doing. I don't feel that same thrill now, even though I'm proud to be at a top-tier university. Bottom line, *teaching* instead of *doing* feels like giving up. Look at me. I'm the establishment now. I have a mortgage. I have a 401(k). I have *underwear.* I was an iconoclast and now I'm someone who DVRs *Below Deck.* I should be shaming yacht owners for conspicuous consumption, not tuning in to find out if Gary is going to hook up with Daisy again.

And what if I don't get tenure? I'm not in love with this job, but that doesn't mean I'm desperate to lose it. I worked so hard to get here. Not being given tenure is pretty much the university's way of saying "Thanks for trying, but no thanks," and my time as an assistant prof will wind to a close. Then what? Maybe I should spend some time on LinkedIn. I should cover my bases, see who's out there and what other opportunities exist. Maybe the private sector isn't so bad? The few BlueLovers I keep up with ended up there, and they seem happy enough.

The only LinkedIn notifications I get are for people who are already connected to people I know, so maybe the algorithm is onto something. I did say I wanted to reconnect with people, maybe broaden my professional horizons, share a little hard-fought wisdom, so I decide I may as well peruse the site while I wait for something new to populate on Zeus's feed.

I click on the LinkedIn profile from the suggestion email, and even though this person has connections with some of my old BlueLove colleagues, I can immediately tell he is no one I'd want to associate with. This guy from Tennessee has been working as a "special project manager" for food and beverage companies for years, which, no thanks. Absolutely not. I know exactly what that nebulous job title means, and it's nothing I support. I mean, Big Food and Beverage is just so gross in their practices. I just read in the *Washington Post* that they are paying registered dietitian influencers to hawk unhealthy eating because weight loss drugs are cutting into their profits.

So much of the trouble we're in environmentally comes at the behest of Big Food, and there are a lot of oily lobbyists working hard to maintain the status quo, like this guy and his "special projects." They're willing to do whatever it takes to use the environment to better corporate profits, despite the fact that the industry is responsible for 36 percent of all global emissions (let alone the damage they're doing to public health).

Don't even get me started on the inequity between the greenhouse gas emissions from raising livestock versus the calories it produces. There's so much more protein bang for the buck when you go plant based. One of the reasons I was in Brazil was the global demand for soybeans, which was leading to deforestation since the overwhelming percentage was used to feed—

Suddenly something catches my eye and throws the emergency brake on my internal rant.

Wait.

What the fuck?

What the fuck?

This guy's profile photo looks *exactly* like Jeremy.

Chapter Twenty

Liv

"Did I fall asleep?" I sit up quickly and pay immediate consequences. My equilibrium is way off. The room is spinning, and I have to cling to the narrow bench I'm draped across to make it stop. Thank you, Olive Garden's finest midpriced red.

"No," Michael says. He hands me a bottle of water. "You passed out. Big difference." For all his bluster, I notice that he used his suit coat to blanket me while I slept. The jacket has the same comforting citrus-and-spice smell as my dad.

We're in the waiting room at the ER. It was packed last night when we got here. People do careless things when the weather gets warm. As a veteran, thanks to my mom, I possess all kinds of ER info. For example, you'd think cuts on the head would be expedited due to all the blood, but they can often be the most superficial wounds. I hate that I'm here enough to understand how the hospital triages cases. I hate everything about this place, from the magazines I've already read to the flat-screen in the corner with its endless loop of game shows. I hate the Spanish moss that surrounds the plants. I hate the way the nurses' shoes lightly squeak against the linoleum. I hate the shitty coffee and how there are never Oreos in the vending machine. I hate how many nights and weekends I've sacrificed to this waiting room. Mom's never once been admitted during one of these runs. Not once. I feel such impotent rage that if I allowed myself to scream, I'd never stop.

The waiting room has largely cleared out, winnowed down to a couple of people. The only ones left here are the cute red-haired boy with his hand stuck in a vase and a middle-aged man with a barbecue fork protruding from his shoulder. Ouch.

Vishnu approaches us, and his head looks a lot less round now. He must have been treated. "Vishnu! Are you better?" I ask. I know we ran into him here last night because his head was swollen to the size of a BOSU ball, but I don't recall why. Last night is rather hazy.

"Oh, yes, thank you, good as new." He takes a seat next to us. "Shall I wait with you? Michael told me what happened with your mother while you were asleep."

"Passed out," Michael corrects him.

"Or would it be more helpful if I were to pick up some breakfast . . . or perhaps a toothbrush?"

I'm just mortified. "This is not who I am," I explain.

"I know that, Liv. You're allowed to have a bad day. We all have them. Being human is what makes us . . ." Vishnu trails off, looking for the right word.

"Human?" Michael suggests.

"Exactly," Vishnu replies.

We sit in companionable silence, broken only when Michael asks the vase kid's mother, "Did you tell him to release whatever he's holding in there?"

The mother is furious at his suggestion. "Are you kidding? How would I not have said that first, before spending the entire night in the emergency room? Are you implying that I'm a bad mother?"

Michael neatly crosses one leg over the other, still impeccably polished and unwrinkled. I don't know how he does it. "No, honey, I'm implying that your child might be a dullard."

Uh oh. The mother draws a breath like she's getting ready to yell, and I can't say that I blame her. But before she can get a word out, the kid sheepishly withdraws his arm from the vase. "Look, Ma, no hand . . . in vase!"

After an awkward silence, the mother hustles the child out in such haste that they leave the vase behind.

"I wasn't wrong," Michael says, picking a bit of lint off his trousers.

The guy with the shoulder wound peers expectantly toward Michael, who says, "I've got nothing for you, Forky."

"So, have you seen Jay yet?" Vishnu asks. "He should just be getting here for the early shift. He starts at 6:00 a.m. today."

"No, he told me he was working an overnight—that's why he couldn't answer my calls," I say.

A strange look flashes across Vishnu's face. "I must be mistaken, so sorry. If you'd like to say hello, go down one flight of stairs, and then left, then left, and a third left."

"You are an absolute peach," I tell him. I kiss him on the cheek, and for good measure, I kiss Michael's cheek too. That they both allow me to do this despite whatever died in my mouth feels like tremendous progress.

After I've fixed my hair and repaired my raccoon eyes in the bathroom, I realize I've completely forgotten where the lab is. A helpful young nurse directs me to radiology once I get downstairs. I suspect I'm still a little bit drunk. When I get to the office, I spot Jay through the open door. That cute nurse lingers with me a second, looking from Jay to me before leaving.

Jay is staring at his phone. He doesn't notice me in the doorway. I bet he just had his first chance to text me back. I check my phone, but there's nothing yet.

"Knock, knock," I say.

Jay practically throws his phone face down on his desk. "I didn't think I'd see you *here*. What's going on? Are you checking up on me?" he says. He's smiling, but that familiar grin doesn't seem to have reached his eyes. Something is missing. And if he worked an all-nighter, why is his thick, dark hair still damp with comb tracks, like he's just out of the shower? You know what? I'm not going to ask questions I don't want answered.

"My mom's in the ER again."

"Now what? Yellow fever? Ebola? Is her prostate acting up again?" His tone doesn't have its usual teasing quality, and I'm so ashamed.

I can't even look at him. "She thinks it's polio."

His level of disgust cuts me to the bone. "You can't let them run you around like this. You have to take a stand."

He's not telling me anything I haven't told myself a million times. "I know."

"Did you even try to object? Reason with her? Maybe just flat out say no?"

"I wanted to." I have gotten better at this, I know I have. I mean, I let her deal with the drywall on her own. And I haven't let myself get roped into babysitting in weeks.

From the look on his face, I know what's coming, because I've seen it and heard it before, again and again. "Liv, I like you, but between your family, your clients, and your class, there's no time for us. You say yes to everyone but yourself."

His words hit me like a dead weight. They are devastating. Why am I perpetually trapped in this Groundhog Day loop? I thought I was making some progress. Am I just making the same mistakes over and over again? "I'm so sorry. I would—"

He points to a screen. I can't be sure, but it looks like an outline of a My Little Pony stuck in a pelvis. "Listen, I can't do this with you right now. I've gotta go see a man about a horse. Literally. But I wish you well, I really do. If you ever learn to say no, you have my number." He gently whisks me out into the hall and closes the door behind me.

Standing here alone—again—I'm reminded of a Karl Marx quote I learned in college: "History repeats itself, first as tragedy, second as farce."

I have to figure out how to break this farcical cycle.

❦

Michael drops Ma and me off at home. She doesn't even thank me for sacrificing my entire night in the ER. Weary, I climb the stairs, then chug a glass of water, swallow a couple of ibuprofen, and collapse face-first into my couch.

I wake a few hours later when I hear someone pounding at my front door. The seeds of hangover I felt earlier have fully taken root. I drag myself to answer. It's Michael. He's daisy fresh and nattily dressed. He pushes past into the apartment.

"You. Toothbrush. Now."

I'm so confused. "Why are you here?"

"For some tough love. I'm here to help you because you clearly refuse to help yourself. You can't live like this."

"That's not true—" He cuts me off with a whistle (why do I want to call it a *whoostle?*) blast.

He guides me over to my favorite gold-leaf antique mirror. It's from a cute vintage shop in Winnetka. "Look at yourself in this God-awful mirror. What do you see, other than someone who desperately needs an interior designer?" He takes my chin in his hands and makes me look when I demur. "Look. I mean it. Look at yourself and see what everyone else sees."

What I see is a mess, wrapped in the doormat that everyone steps on, cloaked in the inability to prioritize myself.

"Now, I need you to say, 'You is kind, you is smart, you is important.'"

That's not what I expected to hear. "You want me to quote *The Help?*"

"Yes. It has 'help' right in the title. Because I am your help. Say it," he instructs.

I feel silly, but I do it anyway. "You are kind, you are smart, you are important."

"Excellent. To make sure you don't forget, I'll be with you all day. Whatever shame spiral or cycle of sadness you're in? It ends here."

I offer up a quick prayer to God or Zeus or whoever inspired Michael to help me out of a lifetime of yeses and I'm sorrys.

I always assumed Emily would be the one to coax me out of my bad habits, but she's too gentle with me, and she's mired in her own shortcomings. Deandra has no compunction about being unkind, and likely she could have helped inspire me to make different choices. But it occurs to me it's not to her benefit for me to change. My being stuck makes her life easier.

I wish I wasn't actively trying not to vomit on the day someone's decided to help me change my life, but perhaps that's the cost of doing business. Still, I hate the idea of being a burden. I search for excuses. "But . . . don't you have to go to work?" I ask.

He shrugs. "My company, my rules." I am so overcome with gratitude that I wrap him in a hug. He immediately makes a face.

"You. Shower. Now."

We make it in time for my noon staff meeting. It took some spackling with my heaviest foundation and an extralong shower, but I manage to look like a close approximation of myself. The plan is that Michael will shadow me today, pointing out when I allow people to take advantage of me. He doesn't think I realize how often it happens, so he'll be with me to document the process. When I asked Michael how I was supposed to explain his presence in the office he said, "You don't owe anyone jack shit."

I begin the meeting and breeze through the usual housekeeping pieces. When it comes time to assign the open houses, I can feel that lump of dread forming in my stomach. "We need someone to run the Wilson condo open house. Who can help?"

Apparently speaking for the group, Trevor says, "You're, like, so good at selling condos. We feel like it should be you."

Michael, who has been sitting unobtrusively in the corner, examining his manicure, blasts his whistle. Everyone jumps, including me. I thought he was going to document instances like a quiet observer, not a pissed-off hockey referee.

"No, I need someone else to manage it." Okay, it felt good to say that. "I can't. I have back-to-back showings that day on more valuable properties. Who can please step up? Trevor, do you have other showings this weekend?"

Trevor is the most notorious about getting out of open house duty. He looks around at his buddies for support. "It's less of a *can't*, and more of a *don't want to*."

Michael blows the whistle again and Trevor looks rattled. Everyone does. The more the whistle throws off the team, the more empowered I feel. "Who's this dude, anyway?" Patrick asks. "Cool suit, though."

"My new real estate coach. It's a Tom Ferry thing. Now, Trevor, I'm not asking. I'm *telling* you I need your help," I say. I try one of the power poses Michael showed me earlier, feet hip-distance apart, hands firmly on hips, chin lifted, spine straight.

"And I am telling *you*, I don't want to," he says, mimicking my pose from his seated position. He laughs and throws a couple of peace signs at Darren and Party Marty. Those two also laugh, but more out of discomfort than mirth. They both glance over their shoulders at Michael, trying to size him up. Michael blinks back at them, with serial-killer cool, before slowly, deliberately raising that whistle to his lips. This time, the blast is longer and sharper and louder. Then he gives me the briefest of nods, like he's paved the way and now it's time for me to get behind the wheel.

This is it.

This is my time to claim my power.

This is my chance to take a stand. You know what? I don't need to leave this brokerage. Heck, I helped build this brokerage; my sales are one of the reasons it's on the map and my management is why it remains there. Why would I walk away and try to start over? I need to make this place work for me instead of me working for it. I need to ask for what I deserve. I always knew I didn't have to take it, but now I *know* know.

Things are about to change around here.

"Trevor, you'll do it or you're fired."

Oh my gosh, did those words just come out of my mouth? Everyone is stunned, including me. Mostly me. The room goes dead silent, and the team is poised, ready to renounce their allegiance to whoever backs off first.

Spoiler alert: it's not going to be me.

"Fine, whatever, I'll be there," he concedes. Victory! "But you don't have to be such a—"

Before Michael can even react, I form my thumb and index finger into a V and whistle so powerfully there are probably cabs stopping out front right now.

Trevor is completely cowed. "Standard cheese plate okay?"

Chapter Twenty-One

(Action) Emily

Not only is Jeremy apparently alive and well, he's currently working *for* a multinational food and beverage consortium. And he's not from Melbourne. He's not even *Australian*. Where did he get the accent? Did he just watch a bunch of old Mel Gibson movies to get into character?

How is this real?

And what bizarre twist of fate got me to click on that profile? Of the hundreds of notifications I get every year, why was I so lucky to have decided that was the one I'd click in the hopes of forwarding my professional development? If I saw this same thing happen on a TV show, I'd be pissed, like it was almost too convenient.

To say I feel like a fool is the understatement of the century.

Now that I have all the pieces in front of me, it's maddeningly easy to piece it all together, and I feel like the biggest patsy. He was a plant. Jeremy was a plant. He infiltrated our group. I'd heard of this happening in other volunteer organizations. College friends in activist political groups told me they always had to be vigilant because people would pretend to be these enthusiastic volunteers, dressing and acting the part, all while feeding information back to law enforcement or opposing entities.

Jeremy has to be the reason it often felt like someone was one step ahead of us, why the arrests increased after he came on board and events went off the rails more frequently. But I never thought anyone would spy on us for profit, sabotage our plans, all to benefit some faceless corporation's shareholders.

How does any person with a soul decide, *Fuck the rain forest; what really matters is this quarter's earnings report?*

All the pieces are coming together. The Australian consulate didn't have information on him because *he didn't exist.* That's why I couldn't find any Melbourne family. Because *he didn't exist.* The police weren't helpful, because they were likely paid not to be inquisitive. Not that it matters. Because *he didn't exist.*

BlueLove didn't have additional information on him, because he was a total fabrication. There was never an actual gunshot, because he was working *with* the guys posing as guerillas. That's why my escape was almost too seamless. Did they go back to the campfire and laugh at me as I ran for my life through the jungle that night, bereft over my loss? Was I just a big joke? An obstacle to neutralize?

Mission accomplished.

I have been stuck in time for ten years, mourning the ghost of someone who spent every moment we were together lying to my face, ripping out my heart, and sending me off to a new life I didn't want.

My fury is profound and I have all this energy coursing through me, but I don't know what to do with it. I'm awake most of the night, going down the rabbit hole of who Jeremy, wait, "Norman" is. His name is fucking *Norman.* How did I not see through him? What signs did I miss or ignore? Did he ever try to tell me? Maybe I was just so in love that I chose not to see? Suddenly I'm reliving some memories that were more deeply buried.

"This was a mistake."

I can't help it—I laugh at him. "Didn't feel like a mistake to me. Either time."

There's an intensity that comes along with the job, and hookups are frequent and no strings attached. At the end of the day, when you're amped on adrenaline and endorphins, you need to channel that passion into something. The energy of our group breeds a kind of closeness, the kind that develops at summer camp, with couples constantly aligning and realigning, regardless of history.

Jeremy has just joined our merry band here in Tennessee, where we're protesting (possibly sabotaging) the expansion of a pipeline. I was attracted to him from the beginning, but he did this weird hard-to-get thing, and I have to admit, it made me more determined to win him over. It's like he actively tried to avoid entanglement.

Whatever his initial reticence was, he eventually got past it. (I am just that charming.) Last night was incredible. We separated from the group, setting up camp on a high bluff, where the only witness was the majesty of the starry night sky.

"Listen, shit happens. I'm not looking for anything serious. So unless you're secretly married or something, this is no big deal," I assure him.

"I don't want to break your heart," he says, and he sounds so sincere that I laugh again.

"That tells me you think very highly of yourself," I reply, then I climb back in the sleeping bag and show him exactly what a mistake this isn't.

Special Projects.

That's what he calls his time sabotaging our work at BlueLove on his profile. The single most significant event in my life wasn't caused by a bullet, but rather a bullet *point* on a two-page résumé. His end date on the special project is two weeks after the day I thought he'd been killed. Isn't it so professional that he gave them adequate notice? Good for him, what a pro.

Again, thanks so much for the "suggested contact," LinkedIn.

What would I have done if I'd actually heard from him after the fact? Why didn't he reach out and apologize? Would I have forgiven him after my initial shock? No, that doesn't sound like me. I may well have caused him grievous bodily harm. He was probably terrified that I might find out.

What do I do now?

What's my next step?

How do I move forward, now that I know everything I believed in was a lie?

I want to pull up to the split-level ranch I've tracked him to in Nashville (Jeremy! A ranch house! Nashville, not the outback!) and scream at him, pummel him until my fists bleed, sack him like I'm legendary Bear Richard Dent. But how would that be satisfying? What would that change? Jeremy's not real. He was never real. The love of my life was just a contractor, an actor playing a role, trying to get close enough to stop me from doing what I knew was right.

If there's one shred of grace here, it's that I'm in a different place because of Fearless Inc. If I'd found out sooner, I don't know how I would have reacted. I hesitate to imagine. But Fearless has reminded me of who I am and who I can be. Regardless of Jeremy's motives and subterfuge, *I* was real and *I* was true. I loved who I was and the good I accomplished. He can't take that from me. It's mine. My history is mine. I earned it.

All I can do is let him know that I found him out, let him live with the guilt of betraying me. Of being Judas for thirty pieces of silver. I wonder if he even feels guilty?

I do the most civil thing I can imagine. I message him on LinkedIn with a single question: *How did this happen on my watch?*

That's it. That's my whole being extrapolated into a single question, and the answer won't make one whit of difference.

Almost immediately, my phone pings with a notification. I hold my breath as I read it. Of course, it's not Jeremy/Norman. It's too quick. It's from Miles:

Here's the heads-up and you didn't hear it from me. The chancellor is monitoring your class today. Good luck. I am

rooting for you. Show them how much you deserve to be here,
I know you can. Miles.

My first inclination is to respond "Don't sign your texts, Miles," but I realize that he's the one who's always been on my team. Miles is the one who's been there. He's been the one coordinating his outfits with my cat, not Jeremy. And I never gave him a chance, not fully, because of a fucking ghost.

❦

Yes.

This is exactly what I need.

To find out the last ten years of my life have been a lie, followed immediately by trying to teach a pack of uninterested Gen Zers why it's important that the world doesn't burn, all while my future career hangs in the balance. No pressure there.

I gaze out at the sea of young faces, as well as the chancellor's. She's tucked discreetly at the back of the hall, as though I wouldn't notice her. My water table lecture is going nowhere fast, and not a single person in the room is engaged.

Fuck it.

Fuck it all.

I drop my notes. "Do you guys understand what it means when I say that CO_2 levels are rising?" I ask. "You hear it, but do you understand it?"

Taylor raises her hand. Of course she does. "That the levels of CO_2 are rising?"

I can hear the aggravation in my own voice. "You just restated the question, Taylor. So yes, but no. What it means is, the collective global temperature is going up. Do you have any idea why people like me are trying to limit global warming to less than two degrees Celsius by 2100?

Do you? Do you get why this specific language is written into the Paris Climate Agreement?"

No one says anything. "What are two degrees, right? What harm can two degrees do? Well, let me tell you something. Two degrees is a big deal. It's a big fucking deal."

Did I just say "big fucking deal" in front of the chancellor? Uh oh. Yet I can't pump the brakes. I've unleashed something and now it's rolling downhill, snowballing.

"When the temperature jumps from one-point-five degrees to two, that increases everything we don't want by a third. Okay? All the stuff that makes us miserable? One-third more. That means heat waves? They'd be a third longer. Huge storms? They'd be a third more intense. Flooding? One-third more. The sea level? It'd be that much higher and, spoiler alert, those coral reefs you think are so pretty to snorkel past on vacation are going to degrade and die, and so will the aquatic life that depends on them. We have only 44 percent of our coral reefs left. We've already blown through 56 percent. Fifty-six percent. More than half. Poof. Forever."

The room is dead silent, but for the first time, I may actually have everyone's attention. Not a single person is looking at their phone.

"What isn't explicitly clear about that degree jump is that it can mean as much as a ten-degree difference in certain climates. Do you know what happens next? Crops that are already growing at their heat threshold *will not persevere*. Breadbasket crops like soy and corn *will not persevere*. Dead. Gone. Sayonara. And don't even start me on the pests and the bacteria that will thrive under more extreme heat, because you do not want to know more about *that* shit show. It's already happening—look at how malaria's popped up again in Florida."

I pace back and forth and every eye is on me.

"Understand this: your life as you know it will not be the same. The grain that makes the beer that you swill at parties? *Will not persevere.* Road trips? Spring breaks? Cavendish bananas in your smoothies? Or how about staples like coffee and chocolate and avocadoes? No more brunch. Clean, pure water when you turn on the tap? Over. It's all going to be game over."

At this point, I'm fairly sure I'm shouting. Can't stop, won't stop.

"If this feels like life or death, *that's because it is.* There's an analogy about what happens when you microwave a bag of popcorn. During that first minute? You don't see anything happening, even though it is. The heat has gotten inside the kernel, and the steam is roiling beneath the surface, creating a chemical change. But you don't see, hear, or smell it, so it doesn't seem real. That's why society at large has ignored climate change for so long—it wasn't immediately evident. Right now, this change doesn't seem real to so many of you, because if it did, you would preserve every resource you encounter. You get a beautiful day here in February and you're all celebrating like it's a gift or an anomaly rather than the direct result of greenhouse gases. You laugh when I talk about the possibility of a coastline in Las Vegas. It isn't funny. Every uninformed decision you make pushes us closer to the brink, every piece of fast fashion you buy, every aluminum can you toss in the trash, because you think to yourself, *It's one tiny thing, what's the difference?* The difference is we are on the second minute of the crisis right now, okay? Those kernels are about to blow, and once they do, *we cannot go back.* The corn can never go back into the hull. This is where end-stage capitalism has gotten us."

A student raises his hand and I gesture for him to speak. "Ma'am, I'm from Texas. Are you telling me that it's possible that it's gonna get hotter there in the summer? It can't. Our ranch won't survive."

They're starting to get it.

"It can get hotter and it *will* get hotter if we don't make changes. All those wildfires that we're seeing? Those aren't *accidents.* They are a *by-product* of how we live. This is what happens. We are seeing the end result of not caring enough to protect this planet. All those animals we loved seeing at the zoo when we were kids? We're going to lose them as the warming sea melts the glaciers from underneath. We've already lost five hundred species in the past hundred years. Tasmanian tigers?

Gone. Japanese sea lions? Gone. West African black rhinos? Gone. In a hundred years from now, we're not going to see krill or blue whales or ringed seals, because their habitats are being destroyed. Game over."

A girl wearing a pretty smocked blouse that showcases the whale tattoo on her forearm pulls a Kleenex out of her backpack and dabs at her eyes. Oh shit, I made her cry. Making students cry cannot reflect well on me, but they need to hear this. I'm going down swinging—chancellor, eat your heart out.

"We're going to see more drought. Do you understand me? Our storms will be more severe. Those cheesy blockbuster environmental disaster movies are going to be documentaries in a hundred years. Do you hate inequity? Well, buckle up, buttercups, because it's only going to get worse. The poor are going to get poorer and they're going to be displaced. The wealthy—the ones who are making money off all the chaos—they're going to get wealthier."

Everything I haven't said in the ten years since I left the rain forest is spilling out.

"Here's what I don't get: Why aren't all of you rioting in the streets, yelling, 'Not on my watch!'? You are our last, best hope! Our future depends on you! Yet so many of you are blithely wading into a shit-storm wearing your Shein sundresses, playing your *Animal Crossing*, and making your TikToks, and you have no concept of what's to come. I am sick to death of people not taking action. Sick. To. Death. I hope you come out of here today with your eyes open. Every cause you support is important, but none of them will matter if we don't have a habitable planet anymore. This is it—this should be your apex priority. I hope you spend the rest of the day furious with me for bursting your little bubble. And I hope that spurs you to do *something*. Because you are capable and the only thing stopping you is you."

I look into the lecture hall and see the chancellor's face, her mouth open in a perfect O. Dozens of phones are out now, recording me and my rant.

So . . . that's it.

I have probably cratered my career at this university. I can't imagine the chancellor will look fondly on my casual use of profanity, or all the yelling, or any bad PR that comes of the video content. I will absolutely not earn bonus points for making a couple of students cry. Yet, for the first time, I feel like I'm getting through to these kids, and that is what's most important, so I press on.

Consequences be damned; I am making a difference, so I keep on.

At the end of class, a few dozen kids linger by the front table. They seem reticent to leave, and many of them have questions about doing more. I did it—I got them to hear me. Finally.

This may well be everything I ever wanted.

I worked with BlueLove because I hoped to change the planet, but I realize now I was just one person. What if my real purpose is inspiring the hundreds of kids I teach every quarter to go out and do the same? What if that's why so many encouraged me to go into teaching? I could make my reach exponential.

If I'm not fired first.

I wish I'd realized sooner that I have been exactly where I should be, that there's not something better on the horizon.

Taylor approaches me and says, "Professor Doctor, I want to volunteer for Planet BlueLove?"

I'm so thrown that I must clarify. "Is that a question?"

She looks at me like I'm the fool here. "No."

Chapter Twenty-Two

Liv

I'm back at the Craftsman home of my dreams, but this time I'm show-ing it to the cutest couple. Annika, the wife, is pregnant and positively glowing. Her husband, Arturo, is solicitous of her every move, holding her arm through each doorway, and rushing ahead to make sure all the rugs are flat so she doesn't trip. I love their interactions so much it makes my heart smile.

I want what they have, and I'm starting to believe that I deserve it. Maybe Jay wasn't it. But I'm grateful to have met him because he showed me point-blank that my desire to please other people is in direct opposition to pleasing myself. I can't keep putting everyone ahead of me. I could not have learned a more valuable lesson.

Everything feels different today, brighter and sunnier, partially because yesterday's hangover is finally gone, but mostly because I finally asserted myself at work. The twins were actually in for once. I strolled into their office without an invitation and said to them, "If you want to keep me, everything here needs to change."

Chase literally dropped his cruller into his lap. (It was amazing.)

I explained exactly what has to happen in terms of commission splits if they want to keep their top agent. It's nothing I haven't hinted at before, nothing that they didn't know I wanted. The difference was this time, I didn't ask, I demanded.

What shocked me was that they really listened instead of shining me on like when they stuck me with the Vandergrifts. They were far more amenable than anticipated, and they're coming up with a new contract for me right now. Things are going to be different going forward, and if they aren't, I always have the option to strike out on my own. They finally understand I mean business.

Bless Fearless Inc., Michael, and his whistle for helping me realize what was always inside of me.

"I can see why you've been raving about this place. This is the perfect first home, but I'm worried we'd outgrow it too quickly," Annika tells me, running a hand over her swollen belly. "We haven't told anyone yet, but it's twins."

"Oh my gosh, congratulations!" I say. "My sister has twins too. You must be so excited."

"Also terrified. Mostly terrified," Arturo adds.

Annika taps him lightly on the arm. "No, sir. You only get to be terrified when you push two watermelons through a keyhole. Scared? Anxious? Nervous? Fine. Not terrified."

He tells me, "We spent the first weeks thinking about what it was going to be like having a new baby, and now, we're getting two for the price of one. There has to be a word for something that's so magical and also so scary."

"Yes, it's called parenthood," Annika says.

I want to make sure they're set up for success before the babies come. I mentally scan all the listings about to hit the market and hit on one that might be right for them. My colleague Jackie is about to list it. "I know of a home that's going live later in the week. It's in an established neighborhood right off the Metra line, so it's walkable to downtown Wilmette and also provides easy access to Chicago. There are lots of young kids, lots of parents your age. It's three bedrooms, but it also has an in-law suite in the basement with a separate entrance, full kitchen, and full bath. That space could be used when your folks come to visit, and it's also zoned for rental if you want extra income."

"Sold!" Arturo says.

"Maybe we should see it first." Annika laughs.

"That's probably a better idea," I say. Every relationship needs the dreamer and the realist, and I'm charmed at how these two complement each other.

We make plans to view the property later in the week, and then I watch as Arturo gingerly guides Annika down the stairs. "I am not a carton of eggs, Arturo. I won't break," she tells him, but he keeps guard over her anyway. I love it.

I've already seen this place a dozen times, but I take myself on a little tour again. My life would be so lovely if I lived here. I'd have a glass of wine on the porch and wave to the neighbors. I'd grow my own tomatoes in the backyard. I'd cook hearty pots of soup on that beautiful stove. If this were mine, I'd opt for simple window treatments, light-weight and airy so the sheers would flap in the breeze on a spring day. In the winter, I'd keep fragrant cherrywood in the covered nook by the kitchen door and make a roaring fire every time it snowed. Structurally, I wouldn't change a thing, not a single switch plate or tile. The current owners' refresh is impeccable, with sage walls accented with original wainscotting and crown molding restored to its original luster. This place would be ideal for me now, and I could finish off the basement or attic if I ever needed more space to accommodate a growing family.

Before I can delve too deeply into my daydream, there's a knock at the door. The Vandergrifts are meeting me here so we can see houses fifty-four through infinity. I sort of wish Michael and his magical whistle were with me, but I am in a better headspace to handle them today.

"Hello!" I say, swinging the door open. "I just need to grab my bag and we can go."

Joyce pushes her way inside. "Wait, what's this place?"

"This is a 1920s Craftsman-style home, which is an outgrowth of the earlier Arts and Crafts architectural movement. When I tried to show it to you weeks ago, you said you didn't want to see any old homes. I believe you called old homes the 'R-word'"—I refuse to utter the actual term—"so I took it off our list." I do not mention that when I said "It's a Craftsman," Joyce replied that she hated this style and John confirmed and they wouldn't even let me drive past.

"Then that's on you, because I like this," Joyce says. Today's outfit entails contrasting zebra stripes, feather cuffs, and lots of rhinestones. I'm glad I'm not hungover, because the print would give me the spins.

"Likes it," John confirms.

I take them through the house, but I don't point out each lovingly restored or professionally upgraded piece. The two of them deconstruct every perfect detail, telling each other what they'd want to fix, from the charming hexagon tile and clawfoot tub in the primary suite to the handsome fireplace mantel. Essentially, they'd want to change everything that gives the home its character and personality.

Normally, this wouldn't bother me. It would be their right as new owners to make changes. But in this case, I also represent the sellers, and I know how attached they are to this place. All offers being equal, they'd go with whoever appreciated all their work as is. I imagine they'd be as appalled as I am, hearing how the Vandergrifts want to tear out the original stained glass to install those terrible blacked-out windows you see mucking up "modern farmhouses" in subdivisions. It's disheartening.

Joyce is extra imperious today. Given yesterday's events, I had to cancel on them, and she's not inclined to forgive my all-night family emergency. "Your behavior was unprofessional," she says as she opens the homeowners' fridge, helping herself to a LimonCello LaCroix. "I don't care if your mother was in the emergency room, we brought you on to do a job and we expect you to do it."

She opens the can and takes a big sip, then pulls a face and spits it back into the can. "Ugh, is this lemon? No."

"Hates lemon," John tells me, as though I hadn't heard her say that 0.2 seconds ago. She discards the cold, dripping can on the magnificent mantelpiece, like water rings aren't a thing, then opens the fridge again, looking for something better. She settles on a Diet Coke, promptly cracking it open, then rifling through a glass-front cabinet for a glass.

"This isn't an open house and I didn't provide any of the beverages. Those belong to the homeowner. We can swing through Starbucks or McDonald's if you'd like me to buy you something different to drink," I volunteer.

"No, this is fine. Now get out. We need to talk," Joyce tells me while essentially shoving me out the front door.

Standing on the porch, I remind myself that things are different now, that I am different now. I can't keep doing the same thing over and over and expecting different results.

Today, I choose a different path.

I'm stuck outside with my thoughts for a solid half hour while they debate, my mind racing with possibilities. Finally, Joyce lets me back in and announces they've come to a decision.

"Tell them we're going to offer this much," Joyce says. She slides a folded piece of paper across the counter. I do a double take once I see the number. Joyce and John seem to have mistaken my selling them a "home with a garage" with a "garage sale." Negotiations don't work this way. Pricing doesn't work this way.

"Did you forget to add a zero?" I ask. There's no way this could be their offer. This is what you'd pay for a new car, not a lovely house in the better suburbs.

"Nope, that's the offer. And they're going to need to tear out the awful buffet and the shelving if they want a deal," Joyce explains.

"Okay . . . ," I say, trying to maintain my cool. What a colossal waste of my time this has been. I'm used to buyers and sellers jerking me around—it's the nature of the business. But this is next level. "I am legally obligated to bring this offer to my seller. I suspect a counteroffer will not be forthcoming, because this number is more in line with a van down by the river than an impeccable Craftsman in a desirable neighborhood."

"Oh, we don't want that," John says. He points to Joyce. "Hates rivers."

🍃

"Tell me again what happened next," Emily says. She rests her chin in her palms, all dreamy, like a teenage girl watching a K-pop video. She's in remarkably good spirits for the blow she's taken about Jeremy.

I'm so angry for her. I can't believe what he did. I should probably focus my ire on how he sabotaged BlueLove's operations and the consequences for the planet, but I can't stop thinking about my best friend. He stole most of her twenties and her early thirties, and for what? A paycheck? How do you do that to another person? How do you use them like that?

His "death" put out her fire for the longest time, and I'm just furious with him. I met him only a handful of times, but I'm glad I can finally stop holding my peace and admit that I disliked him. I thought he was shady. He never did anything wrong (well, at least not that I knew), was never disrespectful, from what I witnessed. I could never put my finger on what was wrong, but I knew something was off. No one is that perfect for someone else. He may as well have come directly out of central casting.

Ironically, I don't get that feeling about Zeus, and he is kind of, well, perfect. Maybe because Emily argues with him a lot. *A lot.*

If true crime podcasts have taught me anything, it's to trust your gut. My gut always said Emily should *run*. Jeremy (a.k.a. Norman) never fought with her, not once. That's unnatural. When they came to Chicago for a visit together, it was as though he was studying her, watching for what she would do and then reacting in kind. It was almost like he was following a script, or performing an incredibly complicated piece of improv. That's what confidence men do, per the podcasts. They shadow you. They give you what you want and need until you let them in, trusting them completely. (Usually, it's guys who want to groom the victim's children, but the concept feels the same.)

While I'm not the best at spotting when someone's playing me romantically, my radar for others is top notch. Spend enough time by yourself in an unlocked open house and you develop a sixth sense. That man made the hair on the back of my neck stand up for no good reason, or so I thought. He checked all the boxes on paper, but there was an ephemeral nature about him, like you couldn't latch on to anything real.

As a lifelong Bears fan, Emily claims she's used to bouncing back from disappointment, but I hope she isn't pushing away her grief. To me, the situation seems pretty different from garden-variety football loss.

We discussed as much as Emily would share, as sometimes it takes her longer to process and I wasn't going to push. I said to her, "Looking back, I wonder if it wasn't that you were so in love with him."

"What do you mean?" she asked.

"What if what you were really in love with is how you took bigger leaps because of him, how you tried to swing harder and jump higher?" After meeting Jeremy, she was bolder, more in your face, braver. Maybe she didn't love *him* so much as the Emily she saw reflected back by him? With Jeremy, she was Action Emily to the nth degree.

When Deandra and I were in our early teens, we saw some random Rose Byrne movie. I don't recall the title, but I never forgot the line "Love makes you do crazy things." It's kind of true. Who actually knows how to map the human heart? Who knows what makes us love others? Who knows what makes us love ourselves, really?

At some point, Emily and I will talk in-depth about this. We're not nearly done with the topic, we've only brushed the surface. Most of our conversation was me asking her questions that I'm not sure she's ready to answer. At some point, we'll go deep. We'll pore over each detail and parse his every word over bottle after bottle of wine. We'll cry. We'll create a playlist that reminds her of those days, full of Coldplay and OneRepublic and Sara Bareilles. We'll have dance breaks. We'll construct a timeline, maybe connect it with red string like Claire Danes's character did in *Homeland*. We'll dissect it all like a lab specimen.

But it won't be now. That's not how Emily operates. She needs time and distance before she fully digests anything; I think it's the scientist in her. I recall when her grandmother passed away in the fall of our first year at school. Even though they were close, talked every day, she was fine for a long time, just stoic, proceeding with life, making plans. I couldn't believe how strong she was. But every February 2, her grandma's birthday, after that, Emily would completely break down, and I would spend the day listening to her recount what a great woman she'd been. Emily compartmentalizes, always has. So, if she chooses to be happy now, I'll support it until she's ready to be unhappy, and then I'll be there too.

That's what besties do.

"Yes, I would like to hear your triumph again as well," Vishnu adds, bringing me back. I'd all but forgotten I was telling a story about work.

"Obviously, I brought the offer to my sellers; I had to. They weren't even mad. They were just incredulous. My sellers didn't counter—exactly as I predicted—and they went so far as to forbid those two from even setting foot on the property again. A wise choice, in my opinion."

"Is your next showing with these people going to feel awkward?" B-Money asks.

"Not going to be an issue," I say. "Because I *fired them as clients!*" They were furious, accused *me* of wasting *their* time. I laugh to myself, considering all the paces they're going to put Trevor through. I'm not often one to say I'm going to get a bowl of popcorn and sit back and watch, but I totally am.

"Tell them the best part," Michael says. He is trying (and failing) not to act like a proud father. If he wants the credit, it's all his. He gave me the push (the whoostle?) I needed.

"The best part is, I fired my sellers too," I say.

"I don't get it," Miles says. "Why would you do that?"

"To prevent a conflict of interest," I say. "I can't represent them because I'm buying the house."

"For yourself?" Vishnu says, seeking clarification.

"Yep."

The group erupts in cheers and hugs and shouting. Vishnu jumps up and down so much, all the change spills out of his pocket. I can't imagine anyone being happier for me than these people, and it fills me with love. Three months ago, we were strangers in a coffee shop, brought together by our collective fear. Today, we're a family. Speaking of, I haven't told my family yet. They're going to flip out, and probably not in this happy, celebratory way. They're also going to have to get over it; it's time for me to leave the nest—permanently.

Our celebration goes on for so long that none of us even register the young guy anxiously waiting in the corner. He's holding a large flat box and wearing an apron and paper hat. "Um, hi? Is there a Mr. Zeus here?"

"Not yet. He likes to make a dramatic entrance," Emily says. "Why, do you need something from him?"

"Just for him to sign for this cake," he replies.

"Oh, one of us can do that," I say.

Michael signs the slip of paper and then reluctantly hands over a generous tip after Emily says, "Toss the salad, fancy pants," and gives him the stink eye.

The lid is clear, revealing a white sheet cake adorned with sugar roses and other little decorations. There's a poorly sketched mortar board and three lines hastily scrawled in red icing. It reads:

Congrads grads!

Congrads on your new home, Liv!

Congrads on your tenure, Emily!

"Hey!" Michael exclaims, scrambling after the kid. "You spelled 'congrats' wrong! I want a partial refund on my tip!"

"Wait a damn minute. Did you get *tenure*, Emily? I thought you crashed and burned?" I say. She told me all about her last lecture on our run, and it sounded an awful lot like her *last* lecture. But we were far too wrapped up in the Jeremy–not Jeremy saga to get into a ton of detail.

Miles fields this. "The chancellor was so impressed with Emily's zeal that the committee overwhelmingly voted in her favor. They want her passion permanently. Possibly with less profanity. That more than a dozen students want to change their major to environmental science now didn't hurt either."

Emily is elated. "I wanted to surprise you. Who knew that losing my shit was the key to unlocking my future? I feel like I've turned a major corner," she says.

She pulls Miles in for a hug. This is far more affection than she showed him when they were dating. It's odd but doesn't feel wrong. I can actually see them becoming great friends. She gives him a noogie. (She gives him a *noogie*? What is happening today??) "And this guy? He saved my derriere by giving me that heads-up."

Miles rolls his eyes. "Just say 'ass,' Emily."

"Emily, you are a rock star!" I say. It takes us a few minutes to quiet down and return to our seats. We're eager for our final class to begin, yet no one wants our time here to end.

"I'm impressed that Zeus was able to get those lines on the cake, when it only became official a few hours ago. Did you speak with him this afternoon, Emily?" Miles asks.

"No. I haven't talked to him since our last class, before Michael took over," she says.

That's strange. Then it occurs to me. "Wait, I didn't tell him about my offer either," I say. "How did he know?"

B-Money is flummoxed. "I still don't know how he knew about my boat."

"You guys . . . ," Emily says, looking around the warehouse. "Where is Zeus?"

Chapter Twenty-Three

EMILY

"This has to be a test. I bet this cake is some sort of Easter egg and he wants us to use it to find him," I say.

"Like, we gotta do this to graduate?" B-Money asks. "Like the hostage simulation? We have to pull together as a team?"

"Exactly. What does this cake tell us?" I ask.

We stare down at the big white slab of pastry covered in sugary roses and misspellings. Michael sticks a finger in the icing and rubs it between his fingers. "The frosting is grainy. That tells me he was too cheap to spring for real buttercream."

"Not helpful, Michael," B-Money says.

"Well, what if the clue is baked inside?" Michael suggests. Seconds later, we're tearing apart the cake, squeezing handfuls to see if anything points to where Zeus might be.

"Little help here, Michael?" B-Money says.

"No, I do not touch community cake," he replies.

"Isn't it magnificent the way he just says no," Liv observes. "He's just, *No, that does not sound like something I want to do,* and then he doesn't do it! He doesn't care about peer pressure. He doesn't care that others are depending on him. He just surveys and figures out what's best for him. That is his superpower."

"Yes, his saying no is a true delight," Vishnu says. "His most positive attribute."

"Whoa, did you just dunk on Michael, bruh?" B-Money asks, full of awe and admiration. "Was that sarcasm?"

"It was!" Vishnu confirms. B-Money goes to slap him on the back, but realizes his hands are full of frosting and cake crumbles.

After we've inspected every (white chocolate raspberry) crumb, we acknowledge the cake was not only a dead end, but actually quite appetizing for a grocery store cake. But we're not lost.

"Liv, can you grab the dry-erase board? Let's write down what we know," I say. I can feel Action Emily has awakened, ready to solve the puzzle, save the day. You can't take this away from me, *Norman*. I feel like there's going to be a road trip to Nashville this fall. This isn't yet settled. He did respond to me on LinkedIn, right before his profile disappeared. The only thing he wrote: *I'm sorry. We were real.*

Not enough, *Norman*. Not nearly enough. But I'm going to file away this anger and hurt because right now, I'm concentrating on my future, not my past, and finding Zeus seems to be the key.

"What do we know about him for sure?" I ask. "Let's make a list."

"He's a Swiftie," B-Money says.

"Okay," I say. "What else?"

Vishnu's hand shoots into the air. "He loves birds!"

"Loves birds," Liv echoes. I write this on the board.

"Also odd and I don't understand it. Did he ever mention any specific types of birds? If he loves seagulls, maybe he's at the lakefront. If he loves robins, he might be in a park. Think, everyone, think." I write these options on the board.

"He said something about *exotic* birds once," Miles volunteers.

"Now, that is good information," I say. I write it down. "Nicely done, Miles."

"Exotic? So he might be in a strip club," Michael says. I don't write this down.

B-Money begins to poke around the rest of the warehouse. "What if he left us a clue in his office?"

"Is that too obvious?" I ask.

"How would I know? I've never played detective before," he replies.

"Let's take a beat and think this through," Liv says. "Do we ever see him using a phone or tablet?"

"He must have one because we get texts from him," I reply. "Plus, he posts selfies."

"I never get texts from him," Michael says.

"That tracks," says B-Money.

"What if he's old school enough to want to write things down on paper? All that time he spent watching us on the quad, he never pulled out a phone. Maybe he doesn't want to leave an electronic trail?" Liv suggests.

"Are you suggesting that he has a calendar or a day planner? Maybe back in his office?" I say. "Let's check it out."

We try his office door, but it's locked. "Do we break in?" Vishnu asks.

"We haven't had a lot of luck busting down doors before," B-Money says.

"Emily, do you have any hairpins in your bun?" Miles asks. "I can pick this lock."

"No, you can't. I would have known," I say.

"It never came up in conversation. I learned when I was an Eagle Scout," he replies. Seeing my shocked expression, he adds, "I contain multitudes." Interesting. I take down my hair and shake it out. I can hear Michael muttering something about a dramatic before-and-after. I ignore him.

Liv's phone buzzes and she snorts when she looks at her texts. "What's up?" I ask.

"My mom says she broke her hip," Liv replies.

"My God, the timing that woman has. Do you have to go?" I ask.

Liv silences her phone and looks me squarely in the eye. "I do not."

While it takes him a few minutes, Miles is able to pop the lock on the doorknob, and everyone celebrates. *How did I not know this about him?*

Zeus's office is nothing like I expected. There's a nice chesterfield sofa in the corner and lots of healthy plants. His desk is a fine old antique and his shelves are filled with books by philosophers. It looks more like a high-priced psychologist's than the back office in a boxing gym. The only nods to his *Zeusness* are a photo of him with a large toucan on his shoulder (I never noticed his weird tattoo before—it looks like an electric strawberry) and a signed photo of Ms. Swift herself hugging him.

B-Money snatches it up. "'Zeus, my brother, thanks for always having my six. XO, Tay.'"

"What does that mean?" I ask.

"Wait, I know this from a podcast—it's a military thing. It means to guard someone's back," Liv says.

"He was guarding Taylor's back?" I ask. "Taylor *Swift*?"

"Looks like I'm not the only one who contains multitudes," Miles says.

The whole time we've been talking, Vishnu has been rifling through Zeus's desk. "I found a planner! And today's date says graduation! He was supposed to be here! He sent a cake!"

"What if my man's actually in trouble?" B-Money says.

"Would he have sent a cake if he were in trouble?" Miles adds.

"Has his Insta been updated since yesterday?" I ask. "He's pretty prolific. If he's not posting selfies, I think we should be worried."

Liv's fingers fly across her phone. "There's nothing!"

We completely toss his office, looking for something, anything, while Michael doodles on a pad of paper. "That isn't helpful," I say.

"Rosemont Park—Scott and Granville. Eight p.m."

"What are you talking about?" B-Money asks.

Michael holds up a pad that's been shaded with the side of a pencil. "This is the address that was written on the last sheet of paper he pulled off. This is our clue."

I am gobsmacked. "How on earth did you know how to do that?" I ask.

He shrugs. "It's easy. I'm old and I understand paper."

❧

We're all crammed into Liv's Audi. She and I are in the front, with Michael, Miles, and B-Money in the back. Vishnu sits crisscross applesauce in the hatch. We had to move some Open House signs to make room for him.

Liv being Liv, she breaks no speed records, but fortunately, we found the clue quickly enough to arrive while Zeus is still here. At least his car is; I recognize the FRLESS1 plate. There's a small symbol in the back window that I hadn't previously noticed. It's the same electric strawberry as his tattoo. I wonder what that means?

"I've seen that symbol before, but I don't recall where. It's cute, though, right?" Liv says.

"Is that important?" Vishnu asks. We all shrug.

Is it wrong to say how alive I feel right now? I can feel my blood coursing through every one of my veins. Action Emily is back, baby!

"What's our next move, coach?" B-Money asks. "Do we run up there, or . . ."

I'm not actually sure. Before I can make a plan, Vishnu cries, "He's there! He's in the car. Look at his caption on Instagram, '*Feeling cute, might be deleted later.*'"

Every one of my senses goes into high-alert mode. "'Might be deleted?' That's not what he says. He always writes 'delete,' not 'deleted.' That sounds like a cry for help. I . . . I think he might be in danger. Here's what we do." Then I lay out my plan.

B-Money and I are going to sneak over to the car for a better view, and Liv's going to stay in the driver's seat, in case she needs to swoop us up. Vishnu and Miles are going to watch his Instagram for more clues. Michael is going to . . . something. None of us know. But he got us here, so I have to give him credit for being so useful.

B-Money and I stalk across the street and crouch behind a minivan. We see a small box truck pull up behind him, and Zeus rolls down the passenger window, where a shadowy figure takes a fat stack of bills from him. I can't see the guy's face, but he has the same electric strawberry tattoo on the back of his hand.

"What the hell, Zeus?" I whisper.

"Straight from South America," the person says.

We can hear Zeus say, "Put it in the back," and the hatch flies open. The shadowy figure struggles under the weight of a large, wrapped parcel and places it gently into the back. He's so careful with his movements that I have to wonder how fragile the parcel is. Is it fragile like fine art or fragile like a bomb?

Zeus, what are you doing?? What is he doing? Is he moving drugs? Weapons? And for what purpose? How do we tie into this?

I signal B-Money that we should run back to Liv's car. As quickly and quietly as we can, we make our way to the Audi. "What's happening?" Liv asks as soon as we're secure.

"He just conducted some kind of transaction," I say. "He bought something big from South America."

"That does not sound good," Miles says. "Wait, what if he's not in danger? What if he *is* the danger?"

"Thank you, Professor Obvious," Vishnu says, swatting Miles on the back of the head.

"You're welcome, Dr. Smartypants," Miles replies, swatting him back. They fecklessly slap at each other until B-Money breaks it up. I feel weirdly proud of how easily Miles has integrated into the group. The other guys don't slap just *anyone*. He's one of us now.

"I know we might be risking life and limb and all, but can we take a second to appreciate how my man here has come out of his shell?" B-Money asks, grabbing Vishnu's cheek and planting a big smack on it.

"Yeah, we'll congratulate you on the other side," I say.

"Can we get another cake?" Vishnu asks.

"The cake thing is weird, though. Did he arrange it ahead of time?" Miles asks. "People in imminent danger don't send cakes. Then again, those who are the cause of imminent danger might absolutely send a cake. Like a calling card a Bond villain would send."

Damn it, he's right! I say, "Guys, I don't think he's in danger. I think Miles is on to something: he might *be* the danger. Liv, look! He's on the move! I'll stay on his six!"

Liv clicks her blinker and everyone in the car groans. "Now is not the time to be signaling!" Vishnu yells from the hatch.

"I've never done a car chase before!" Liv says, not offering her standard apology. We ease down the frontage roads around O'Hare as we tail him and end up at some kind of cargo warehouse. Zeus finds an empty space and parks, then he grabs the giant parcel, lifting it like it's nothing.

"He really uses his core," Miles observes.

"Okay, now what?" Liv asks.

Good question. We don't know what we could be walking in on. And I'm still not past how he knew so much stuff about us. That is some spy-level intel.

What is his game?

What is he doing?

Wait, what if he's involved with a cartel? What if it's human trafficking? Does this have anything to do with my time in Brazil? Is there something larger at play here? The Primeiro Comando da Capital is a massive and terrifying criminal organization down there, and they do their trafficking through cargo ships. And we *are* out here by cargo warehouses. Could this be a coincidence or something more? I did hear him speaking Portuguese one day on the gym's phone—does that mean something? My Portuguese is rusty, and it wasn't great to begin with, but it feels like there's a connection.

My mind races as I try to assess the possible dangers if we follow him. "I wish we had some sort of protection," I say.

"Don't worry, I'm packing," B-Money says. He asks Vishnu to hand him the giant gym bag he pulled from his car before leaving the Fearless facility.

"You have *guns*?" I ask, and I feel a spike of fear travel the length of my body. This just got a little too real.

"Pfft, I don't fuck with guns. I got something better."

We creep along in the darkness, just B-Money and me. We made everyone else stay back at the car. If something's going down, we want them to be safe. My adrenaline is pumping like mad, although I'm having trouble seeing clearly. The catcher's mask keeps slipping down since my head is smaller than B-Money's.

His "protection" entailed a bag full of sporting goods. I'm carrying a baseball bat and wearing the catcher's mask and protective vest, and he's in a life preserver, holding a lacrosse stick. If an intramural game were to break out, we'd be all set. Still, it's better than nothing.

We wasted precious time in the car trying to google "Brazilian criminal organizations" to see if they had any ties to Zeus's tattoo, and we thoroughly freaked ourselves out when we saw a member of the Comando Vermelho with the same ink. Then we also found that same logo on a frozen yogurt shop in Fort Lauderdale, so we're not sure what to think.

We're basically armed with nothing but our wits, and if anything goes down, I can't imagine B-Money's ability to rhyme any word is going to help much.

"If for some reason this is just an exercise, we're gonna get extra credit," B-Money says.

"Extra credit for stalking our instructor?" I ask.

"When you say it like that, it sounds kinda silly," he replies.

We steal down a darkened hallway. Ahead, there's a glow, and we hear the hum of voices in the distance. We're almost there . . . wherever there is.

"I'm scared."

"We can always turn back," I say.

"What if this is the test?" he asks.

I pause to consider. "Then we're going to pass with flying colors."

We fist-bump and continue creeping down the hall to an open doorway. The noise level elevates. What I see around the corner stops me cold, and I inadvertently drop my bat. The sound reverberates as it bounces on the cold, hard floor.

"Motherfucker," B-Money says under his breath. Neither one of us can believe our eyes.

We're in the doorway of a massive room, filled with people show-casing . . . *exotic birds in cages.* There are dozens of bird enthusiasts parading around in colorful feathered costumes, and there's an enormous banner that reads, *Welcome to BirdCon O'Hare.*

A vendor approaches us. "Can I interest you in a souvenir beak?"

We both just gape in response. Of all the situations I thought we might stumble into . . . I never anticipated this one.

"No?" the vendor asks. "No beaks? Maybe later, then."

"What in the fresh hell is this?" B-Money asks.

That's when Zeus, for some reason dressed like Johnny Depp in one of his pirate films, spots us and bounds over. "Hey! You made it! That's amazing, thank you. Didn't think it would be your jam, but it means a lot to me you showed up. Did the cake get there? I didn't have a chance to cancel it."

"Wait, did we pass? Was this our test?" I ask. I'm completely confused, as is B-Money.

"I don't know what you mean," Zeus says. "I postponed graduation until tomorrow. Didn't you get the message?"

"What are you talking about? What message?" I demand. I am so damn tired of men not being straight with me.

"I texted Michael and asked him to run things this evening and push the certificate ceremony to tomorrow night. I wasn't planning on coming here, especially after being out last week with my army buddies, but then Tater Tot arrived and I had to dip," Zeus says.

"Is this what an aneurysm feels like?" B-Money says, grasping his head. "Pretty sure I'm having one."

"Talk me through this," I say. "You texted Michael and said, 'Please be in charge tonight. I have to go to a bird show.' So, this wasn't a test or an exercise and at no point were you in any sort of danger?"

"Tater Tot is still getting used to me, so there's a possibility of some biting. You might want to watch your fingertips, and maybe don't take off the catcher's mask, because they can go for your eyes, nose, and lips. But otherwise, no. I'm sure it's fine. Here, come meet him." With boyish enthusiasm, Zeus leads us over to an enormous cage, where a brilliant green parrot glowers at us from behind his bars. "Emily, B-Money, meet Tater Tot. I read about her online and when I learned what she could do, I thought, *You belong with me.*"

"You belong with me," the parrot . . . parrots.

What is happening?

"She wasn't supposed to arrive yet, but she cleared customs early."

"Safe and sound," says Tater Tot.

I'm trying to wrap my mind around this situation. "Hold up. You're saying you put Michael, better known as Joseph Stalin, in charge. You let Mussolini run the show. You told Hitler, 'Welcome to Poland!' for a bird?"

"Bad blood. We got bad blood," squawks Tater Tot.

Zeus seems profoundly offended. "Please, this isn't any bird. This is a lilac-crowned *Amazona finschi.*"

"You're telling me we just spent the night *thinking you were dead* or that you were embroiled in some sort of international conspiracy all because Michael is a technophobe who can't read texts, and you bought a bird who spits out Taylor Swift song titles?" I shout.

"Shh, you'll scare the Tot," Zeus replies, trying to get me to lower my voice as he protectively cradles the bird's cage.

"We thought tonight was life or death, but it was all about a bird who speaks in pop lyrics?" My fury knows no bounds. "I am about to scream my fucking head off if you don't answer every single one of my questions right now."

"And mine," B-Money adds. He smacks the lacrosse stick menacingly across his palm.

Zeus shrugs. "I don't usually do that until the certificate ceremony, but since you guys found me—tracking is something you wouldn't learn until the next level—I guess I can finally let you in on my methodology."

"Now," I demand. "You'll do it now."

Zeus begins. "Emily, your job and your passion revolve around resources. We're burning through our resources and that's the problem you're trying to warn everyone about. But you know what resource is, unfortunately, renewable? Fear. Fear is self-perpetuating, and it's the biggest problem we face as a society. Fear is why we hide behind our cameras instead of acting when we see something bad going on. Fear is why so many are sheep instead of sheepdogs. The wolves thrive on fear. They cultivate it. Fear is why we don't know our neighbors. Fear is what closes us off from outsiders. Fear keeps us stuck, keeps us crouched behind the couch in the dark. Fear keeps us isolated and alone. And the pandemic? That took our collective fear to an entirely new level."

"Okay, but that explains nothing about what this group is or why it exists," I say.

"Patience is not one of your virtues, Emily. We should work on that. Next term. Anyway, I was afraid during the pandemic too. My boxing gym shut down. I had no streams of revenue, so I had to start driving for Uber," he explains.

"*That's* why you were able to pick us up that night," B-Money says.

"Yeah, I never deleted the app, because that challenge is something I do with every class," he says. "I thought I was going to lose my gym and my livelihood and that scared me. After the army, I spent my life building that place. My gym gave me my purpose. I felt like my duty was to help people get stronger. Suddenly I didn't have my purpose anymore and that threw me. You know anything about how that feels, Emily?"

Of course I do. I give a subtle nod and Zeus goes on. "I don't like being afraid, so instead I figured out how to make fear work in my favor. To channel it and turn it into a positive. While everything was closed down, I got certified online as a life coach."

"'A life coach'?" I practically spit out the words. "We've spent this whole time listening to a *life coach*? You have a doctorate in *bullshit*."

Zeus takes a long pause to look me intensely in the eyes, and my knees only buckle a teeny bit. "My bullshit is why your life has improved. My coaching has helped you get stronger, physically and mentally," he says.

"But—" I protest.

"No," he interrupts. "I'm not wrong. During the pandemic, I started to put it all together. I figured out how to help people channel the fear and sudden disconnection they felt into helping themselves. That's why I'm not forthcoming in the intro sessions. You've gotta find the answers inside yourself; they've been there all along. But the only way to get there is to make connections. You can't help yourself more than by helping your friends and neighbors."

"Like Dorothy in *The Wizard of Oz*," B-Money says.

"Exactly."

I'm trying to process but I still have so many questions. "Did you recruit us specifically? I don't understand how you put us all together."

Zeus opens the cage and sets Tater Tot on his shoulder, feeding him an apple slice. The bird gobbles it down and nudges the side of Zeus's face, asking for more. "You were loitering in a lousy coffee shop. You weren't there for the atmosphere. You definitely weren't there for the shitty cold brew. You were there because you wanted to connect. You wanted to be around other people and you wanted to see them, and for them to see you. You wanted to reach out and you didn't know how. Honestly, I get most of my business from lingerers in third-tier cafés. If people have their shit together and their life's going right, they don't hang out at the Brew and Chew. People with full, rich lives don't camp for three hours in a bad coffee shop; they go to one that's good. Brew and Chew is where people go when they're lost and they want to latch on to something."

Damn it. I hate to admit that he's not wrong. Liv and I were there because we both felt stuck. And the robbery pulled us out of it. That brings up another question. "How did you know we'd be robbed?"

"I didn't. But it's Chicago, so . . . something happening was inevitable."

"Shut the fuck up about Chicago," B-Money says, pointing his lacrosse stick at Zeus.

"Exactly," I add. But something is still nagging at me. "How do you know so many intimate details about our lives? We didn't tell you those things."

His laugh infuriates me. "Of course you did. You put your whole life out there on social media for everyone to see. When you post, you're fishing for connections. You want to be noticed and appreciated for who you are, what you think, and how you feel. You want membership in a larger community. So that's what I do. I see you and then I help you see yourself. You guys assuming I'm mystical or a spy is easier than taking a good, hard look at yourself, to see your own fear, to see your own need. You'll stare directly into the sun but never in a mirror, right? But once you get over being afraid of who you are, the world will be your oyster."

"I don't fuck with mollusks," B-Money says, but his fight is gone. He believes Zeus, as do I.

"Metaphorically," he replies.

"And what is the deal with Taylor Swift?" I ask.

"I work security when she's in town. I've gotten to know her. Good kid. Great pipes. Talented songwriter. Nice family. Someone did a survey recently. Did you know more than half the US population considers themselves Taylor Swift fans? When was the last time this country came to a consensus on anything? She brings people together, and I support that. She's all about connections. Now, let's commemorate this occasion. Everyone get in close. I want to take a selfie."

Because we don't know what else to do, we crowd into the frame and smile. I can't help but notice how nice it feels to be pulled in close to Zeus.

"Say *Speak Now*," Zeus instructs. He takes the shot and the flash scares Tater Tot, who nips B-Money on the ear.

"Ow!" he cries. "Why does this bird gotta be so mean?"

The ride back to Zeus's warehouse is quiet. I suspect some of us (mostly me) are disappointed that there's no greater mystery at play, that we weren't being recruited for something larger.

"He's not a secret agent," I whisper to myself. "He's an aviphile."

Michael is mad that we're teasing him for failing to read his texts. But I'm glad he didn't. We're all grateful for the experience. No matter what happens next, we're connected. We're bonded. We see each other and we are seen. For better or for worse, we're a family. And we're stronger and smarter and more empowered for it.

"He's an aviphile!? Thank God there weren't any children there," Michael huffs.

Well, maybe not Michael.

Chapter Twenty-Four

Liv

"Happy housewarming!"

I'm greeted by Vishnu and B-Money, both of whom come bearing gifts. Vish is holding a giant Boston fern, which will look amazing on my new front porch. And B-Money is carrying something that looks like . . . a frozen daiquiri machine? Fun!

"I can't wait to see the craft room!" Vishnu exclaims. We recently discovered our mutual love of doing arts and crafts while listening to murder podcasts, so we have a date next week to do both. Not sure if it's a date or a *date*, but I'm inclined toward the latter and I imagine he is too. We shall see. He did recently admit to me that his brother is a complete player, so I'm really glad to have dodged that bullet, even though it hurt at the time.

"Is this a shoes-on or -off house?" B-Money asks before stepping off the entry rug.

"Whatever you prefer," I say.

Vishnu says, "Look at these beautiful floors! They are newly refinished. Remove your shoes right now."

"But it's gonna ruin my drip!" B-Money grouses.

Vishnu swats him on the back of the head with his free hand. "Remove them right now!"

Begrudgingly, B-Money slips off his sneakers and places them next to the pile of shoes by the front door. Behind B-Money's back, Vishnu winks at me. So maybe it will be a *date* date after all. I feel a delightful twist of anticipation in my stomach.

Emily approaches the still-open door and hands me a gift basket of wine, cheeses, and crackers, my favorite! "Sorry, there's no plastic around it, but you know, I couldn't."

She kicks off her sneakers and heads to the kitchen for a drink. She's already been here, so she knows her way around. You never know how good a friend is until they help you move. The guys follow her. "If you want to go back to the great room, Miles, his date, and Zeus are already here, playing with Romeo and Juliet. Bit of a love story going on there between Zeus and the dogs. Anyway, I'll do the tour once everyone arrives," I say.

The tour of my house. *My* house. I closed on it a week ago and moved in the next day. My very next stop was the shelter. Romeo and Juliet are senior dogs, but they deserve to spend the rest of their lives being loved and cherished, so that's exactly what I'm going to do.

The bedrooms are still a mess, but the public spaces are practically set. I keep walking through it and marveling at how peaceful and serene it is. I'm so happy! I never knew how much I loved the word "mine."

Michael arrives next. He's brought me a silver whistle enclosed in a wooden shadow box. "You've earned this," he says. Then he looks around. "Or you will have, as soon as you call a decorator."

"Thank you, this means a lot to me," I say. And it does. I place it in the center of the mantel.

"How much longer will your mom be in traction?" he asks.

"Until the hip sets, probably another week," I say.

"Guess that was the wrong time to take a stand," Michael says.

"No," I assure him. "It was the perfect time."

Ironically, the experience of actually being injured was so jarring that my mother hasn't had a single other symptom in the last month. I'm not optimistic enough to think that her hypochondria has gone away, but in moving to my own place, I've stopped enabling her, and that's the first step. That they're making her talk to a counselor at the rehab facility is another. At some point, Dee will start speaking to me again, most likely when I tell her I scored Taylor Swift tickets through Zeus's connections. I know we need to discuss boundaries so I'm not sucked into old habits, but I feel more hopeful than ever.

Even though my mom and sister protested, I'm in the middle of some much-needed cosmetic fixes to my old place. And when that's done, I'll either sell it for them or rent it out at market price. I suspect when things feel less tight financially, they'll both be in a better headspace.

Everyone's gathered on the couches, set up with drinks. "To Liv," Vishnu says as I enter, and we all raise our glasses.

"To Fearless Inc.," B-Money says, and we toast again.

"To the Eras Tour!" Zeus says.

Miles's date, Rachel, is his female double. She found him through Instagram. Apparently, she has five Devon rexes and she thinks he hung the moon. He holds up his glass. "She's my favorite recording artist!"

"Me too!" Rachel exclaims.

"I'm willing to admit that I don't hate *Midnights*," Emily says, grudgingly holding up her glass.

In the last month or so, Emily has morphed back into an approximation of her old self, wearing her long hair loose and piling on woven bracelets with tie-dye tanks and jean shorts. She looks more like one of her students now than a tenured faculty member. I make note of how closely she and Zeus are sitting. Interesting.

"How's the writing going?" Zeus asks.

"So very well!" Vishnu says. "My synopsis is finalized and I have written more than ten thousand words."

"That's amazing," I say.

"Are you going to quit your job?" Michael asks.

"Well, no," Vishnu says. "That would be a terrible idea. I must eat and pay my mortgage. Maybe someday I will quit. If I finish my book and get an agent and we sell it. And, of course, if I am able to make a living as a writer. But now, I have many things in my life to look forward to and I am no longer unhappy or afraid."

"What's everyone else been up to?" B-Money asks. We haven't seen each other as much in the past month as we've all been so busy. I'm sure we'll get together more regularly once we start the fall course. "I'm doing another open mic at Subterranean next week. Trying out my newest material. So amped about how last week went, I'm letting that momentum carry me." We all congratulate him. That performance gave us a sneak peek at the potential he's unlocking, and I feel like a proud mama bear.

"Well, I have huge news," Michael says.

"What's that?" I ask.

"I hired a new assistant! He does everything for me. He even carries my phone! I feel like our long national nightmare is over," he says. "I never have to touch another computer again."

If he wants to pretend he's still a technophobe, I'm not going to tell how he went online all by himself and sent flowers to my mom in the rehab facility last week. It will be our little secret.

"What has been happening with you, Emily?" Vishnu asks. Look at him, leading conversations. You cannot tell me Fearless Inc. didn't work. You just can't.

"Well, I was thinking of taking a road trip before the fall quarter begins," Emily says.

"Where to?" he asks.

"The Great Smoky Mountains. I haven't been camping in ages and there's great hiking there. It'll be fun and you're all invited," she says. I wonder if her plan doesn't include some revenge, as she'll be just a few hours away from Nashville. She'll tell me if she wants to.

"Do you mean sleeping outdoors?" B-Money asks.

"In tents, but yes," she says.

"Pasadena," he says.

"I am working that day," Vishnu says.

"I haven't given you the dates," Emily replies.

"No, I am quite sure my calendar is full," he says, as the rest of us offer up excuses too. I've been camping with Emily and I am never doing it again. Her idea of fun is an eight-mile hike with incline the entire way. No, thank you.

"I'm happy to go alone," she says.

"I didn't say no," Zeus says. "One stipulation, though."

"What's that?" she asks.

"I pick the playlist for the car."

Emily lets out a laugh. "Not on my watch."

Our gathering extends all evening. My capellini pomodoro (minus the chicken for Emily and Miles) is a tremendous hit. It's amazing the ingredients you can pick up when you don't let the LuluMoms stand in your way. I feel like we're all at new stages of our lives, stages that will be more satisfying, fruitful, and connected. I couldn't be prouder of how far we've come.

As everyone begins to drift toward the door, B-Money asks Emily, "Are you at all bummed that our man's not James Bond; he's just James *Bird*?"

"Not one bit," she says. "I've had enough espionage and subterfuge to last a lifetime."

"Hey, it's gotten too dark for you to ride your bike home. Do you need a ride?" B-Money asks.

"No," she says. "I'm just going to put it in the back of Zeus's Suburban."

Wait, they're leaving *together*? Before I can say anything, Emily makes a slashing motion across her neck. Message received. I'll just scream inside my heart then. Woo!!

"Hey, before everyone goes, let's get a class picture for Insta," Zeus suggests.

Rachel poses us around my fireplace and the dogs gather at our feet. "Scooch closer, everyone. Closer!"

We throw our arms around each other, delighted with the odd little family unit we've formed.

"Everyone, say 'cheese,'" Rachel instructs.

"No," says Zeus. "Say 'fearless.'"

Epilogue

A uniformed four-star general presses a button to summon the elevator. He holds a file under his arm, labeled Top Secret. *He's taken down, deep, deep under a Colorado mountaintop. His ears pop as he descends, but he's used to the feeling. It comes with the job.*

The elevator opens into a bunker where life-and-death decisions are made in a split second. The walls are composed of massive computer monitors, each displaying a different feed from the world's hot spots: Afghanistan, Syria, Taiwan, North Korea, Venezuela, Iraq, etc.

Somber and sober, the Joint Chiefs and heads of state sit at the oversized conference table in the center of the room. The general sets down the folder. It has an electric strawberry logo on its cover.

He says, "Ladies, gentlemen, we have a problem. If I can direct your attention to the monitors . . ."

A technician pulls up Zeus's Instagram account, blown up across all screens. He tabs through the identical selfies.

He says, "As you can see, he relayed his data regularly. Everything was unfolding according to plan, until . . ."

He gets to the photo of Zeus, Emily, Liv, B-Money, Vishnu, Michael, and Miles posing in front of a fireplace.

Everyone in the room gasps.

The general says, "May God have mercy on us all."

ACKNOWLEDGMENTS

First, to my long-time readers, thank you for letting me tell stories that aren't about my own life. The thing is, when you embark on a career of self-improvement memoirs, no one tells you that if you do it long enough, you eventually fix all the stuff that doesn't work. My life is currently boring in so many delightful ways, and I credit all of you for this process. (Extra love goes out to our Substack family!) And if you're a new reader, thank you and welcome! I'm way less messy than I used to be.

I conceived of this book long before the advent of COVID, so it never occurred to me that people could be so weighed down by their fears. (Apparently, not everyone has the inclination to treat everything as a confrontation and take it head-on, so that was new to me.) While I have perpetually been suspicious of everyone and everything—please see first paragraph—I was never really afraid of anything until the pandemic. Living through 2020 and beyond gave me so much compassion and insight into those who need more of a jump start, and that was top of mind as I reshaped these characters. I love them so much that I wish they were real, and I hope you do too.

This book came from a TV series I developed in classes at Second City, so I want to thank Dale Chapman, Brandon (whose voice I will always hear when I think of B-Money), Nick, Mak, and Jil. You are some of the most talented people I know, and you deserve so much success. Nick, I'm still waiting for the *Zoo Crew*. Make it happen.

I am so grateful to the team at Little A, particularly my editor, Laura Van der Veer, and associate publisher, Carmen Johnson. Thank you for your continued support and for pushing me to do my best. You are the very best team. Also, many thanks to Laura Chasen, my developmental editor—thank you for understanding what I meant so say, even when I didn't. I'd also like to thank Nicole Burns-Ascue, in production, and my copyeditors. I am so much more diligent, because it's my goal to make these teams not want to assassinate me. Your thoughtfulness and attention to detail make all the difference. And for publicity, art, marketing, and sales—it takes a talented village.

I have a phenomenal team behind me at Folio Literary, so I want to extend my warmest thanks to Steve Troha and Erin Niumata, as well as the rest of the team. It's a pleasure to be part of this Holy Trinity. I am profoundly grateful for your diligence, dedication, and good cheer.

For my friends at The Alpine Club . . . thank you for making our summers memorable again. I'm still not writing about you (yet). I love being an honorary Marcucci, and I'm so grateful for how you swept us into the fold, making us feel like we've been a part of it forever.

Thank you to the staff at the Vet Specialty Clinic and at the Animal Hospital of West Lake Forest. Your care of my senior pets has given me so much peace of mind over the years.

For my ghostwriting clients, y'all know who are and why I'm grateful. You rock, every one of you, and I can't believe what I get to learn under the guise of "work."

Obviously, I want to shout out the world's most supportive Zoom crew, including Joanna, Gina, Karyn, Lisa, and Alyson. How lucky I am to have sisters like you. Special thanks to Karyn Bosnak, who will be writing her own damn books again because the world demands them. (See, Karyn? I'm manifesting this by putting it in print. You have no choice.) Gina, thank you for the wedding of my dreams, even though it was technically yours. I don't buy eleven dresses for just anyone. Alyson, you are a "Ray" of light, always and forever. Lisa, you are the best and most enthusiastic cheerleader even when I try to tell you "aboot" the six

Canadian provinces, including Toronto, Vancouver, and Ottawa. And for Joanna, you are my rock, who's been there ever since I took over our dorm room in August of 1985. How lucky were we to find each other?

As always, thanks to Fletch for being Fletch. I've thanked you in, like, twenty different books, so I don't have a lot of new ground to cover here. Also, you don't read my books because you largely live them. But if you actually run across this passage, then I promise to start using the password keeper and stop putting paper towels in the recycling bin. Do let me know. XO.

ABOUT THE AUTHOR

Photo © 2016 Jolene Siana

Jen Lancaster is the *New York Times* bestselling author of the novels *Housemoms, Here I Go Again,* and *The Gatekeepers,* and the nonfiction works *Welcome to the United States of Anxiety; Bitter Is the New Black; The Tao of Martha; Such a Pretty Fat; Bright Lights, Big Ass; Stories I'd Tell in Bars; Jeneration X; My Fair Lazy; Pretty in Plaid;* and *I Regret Nothing,* which was named an Amazon Best Book of the Year. Regularly a finalist in the Goodreads Choice Awards, Jen has sold well over a million books documenting her attempts to shape up, grow up, and have it all—sometimes with disastrous results. She's also appeared on the *Today* show, *Oprah, CBS This Morning,* Fox News, NPR's *All Things Considered,* and *The Joy Behar Show,* among others. She lives in the Chicago suburbs with her husband and many ill-behaved pets. Visit her website at www.jenlancaster.com.